Greyscape

I0649737

Bryant Wiley

For Jeff and Leslie
You didn't have to, but you did,
and I get it...
Thanks.

CONTENTS

WHEN I WAS 7 (A TRUE INTRODUCTION)

I was making my usual rounds on social media, when I was reminded of an incident that occurred when I was a young boy living in Queens, NY. Admittedly, my childhood was not the greatest. There were fun times, sure, but most of the days were spent trying to wade through a vast ocean of complex emotion and situations far too advanced for a young, developing mind to grasp. What follows is a detailed account of something I thought had been long forgotten. Alas, years of attempting to bury this deep within my psyche have failed. I am left to believe the only true way to purge myself of this burden is to share the story openly, in its entirety.

Grocery shopping is a mundane necessity. It's the ritual by which most of us obtain the food used to sustain ourselves and families over extended periods of time. It is essential. It must be done. However, try explaining necessity to a hyperactive, imaginative, and gullible seven-year-old.

We—my brother David, and I—were too young to stay at home on our own. David was older, but only by one year. Back then everyone thought we were twins, and so to further the distinction between us we would make sure to specify our births were fourteen months apart. Every other week, our elderly foster parents packed us into the car and we were escorted away from our home, where there were toys, and television, and outside, and friends to occupy the time, to the quiet town of Valley Stream, Long Island. There, a fairly large grocery store sat, just off the freeway. Forgive me for not including the name of the store, I am not certain whether the place still exists or not and wouldn't want to besmirch the name of such a fine grocer by including the name in my recounting of a specific horror. Though I suspect anyone who reads this, that lived in the area back in the late eighties knows exactly what store I am speaking of. The one whose sign proudly boasted the name "*Rhymes With Cows*."

On one of our first trips to the store, my brother and I discovered there was a section near the exit where children could hang out and not be bothered with the tedious chore of food shopping. This was no playground though. The space consisted of three arcade cabinets, a bench, and a small candy shop. We didn't have money. In fact, more times than not, all we could afford to do was stand in front of the arcade machines and watch the same demo screens cycle over and over, as the words "*Insert Coins*" flashed constantly. Sometimes other kids would show up and play a game. I would watch in excitement, while deep down hoping the person would walk off, not realizing they had more than one life, and I could swoop in and take over like some video gaming prodigy.

Still, there were occasions when the two of us did show up with some change in our pockets. These moments would always prove to be lessons in decisiveness, as we would have to choose how to spend both the time there, and the money we had. Choosing video games was always a risk. You can't tell a child they are not the greatest at any game, especially back then when games were so much less complex. But, when the spiky-backed turtles and lobster-fly looking things changed color and started moving faster on the original Mario Bros. game, and you've already used up the "POW" brick, reality sets in as fast as a bullet. So does the fact that all of your quarters are gone. The other option was to spend the money in the candy store because boredom is hungry work.

On the day of which I am writing about, I had coins jingling in my pocket begging for me to use them. When we made our way to the dismal little play area, there were some bigger, older kids on the arcades, and they didn't look like they were going anywhere any time soon. Some grand cosmic design had opted to make the previously mentioned difficult decision for us. We walked into the candy store. My brother, having more money than me, carefully selected a pack of coconut crunch donuts and cherry Now N Laters, as though he was curating pieces of art to be displayed at some fancy ball. I was much more impulsive and reckless. The shiny and colorful packages stimulated and overloaded my senses, calling to me from the rows of metal shelves, "Buy me," they said, "no, me," "No, you'll absolutely love me, I'm cream filled."

Of all the possibilities surrounding me, none caught my attention more than what I'd spotted on the shelf below the counter at the register. The package gleamed white, with giant block-style red letters. A cartoonish illustration of a baseball player beneath. Big League Chew. I had to have it. At seventy-five cents, I would need to spend all my change, but the choice was an exceptionally economic one. A pack of gum that big was sure to last me pretty much the rest of my life. Tunnel vision set in, and all I could see was the gum. I moved toward it, slow and careful, so as not to scare my soon-to-be prize away. Within a few moments, it was in my hands. This was destiny. The papery, foil package belonged with me, like my grasp was designed to heft its weight from the very beginning. With effort, I pulled one hand away to dig the coins out of my pocket, paid the clerk, and floated out of the store.

I hadn't noticed my brother was waiting for me until he said, "What you get?"

I held up my prize, sticking my chest out in a proud display, "Big League Chew," my voice was thunderous and registered at least two octaves lower than my normal high pitched, pre-pubescent timbre.

"Oh snap, that's fresh," the words were muffled, as he attempted to speak around a mouth full of donut. "Yo," crumbs flew from his mouth in all directions as David attempted to rein in the excitement of his idea, "I dare you to eat all of it. The whole pack in one shot."

At seven, there are things which never register in the mind of a child, due to not yet having the capacity to understand. Such as, say, the inner workings of a computer, or the complicated ideologies of political parties, or the fact one could simply choose to not take on a dare. Eager to impress my older sibling, I tore open the pouch and exposed the chewy treat to the outside world.

"Man, you're gonna blow the biggest bubble anyone's ever seen," the donut was gone, and now every word David spoke was clear.

Be it one year, or ten, gullible little brothers tend to see the difference in age as a measure of wisdom. My big brother told me I would blow a giant bubble, I believed him. And so, I began packing the shredded gum into my mouth. About a quarter of the way through, I'd already run out of room. My mouth was only as big as a seven-year-old's could be. I chewed on what I had, hoping to pack the confection down and make more space. When that failed, I shoved the wad into my cheek and began to shovel more inside, more, more, and more still. Until at last, I reached into an empty pouch.

My face swelled with the huge blob of gum I was trying to contain. I was unable to close my mouth. Spit ran freely from the corners of my lips to my chin, where syrup-like drops fell and spattered the worn tiles below. The wad pressed against my tongue with such force the strained muscle was pinned to the bottom of my mouth and could not move. The sugar, in all its refined sweetness, burned in the back of my throat. I made a desperate attempt to close my mouth, biting down with all the force I could muster. The gum fought back, however, turning the act of chewing into an impossible feat. I started to close my mouth little by little, and the gum, taking on a maniacal life of its own, decided to try a different tack. The closer my jaw came to full closure, the further back the mass moved, eventually reaching a point where gum ended up blocking my air supply. I had gum in my throat, my nose, even my tear ducts were being pressured by the big pink blob.

Spitting it out crossed my mind for only the briefest moment. I pushed the thought away. Terrible idea. I'd spent seventy-five cents to get the item. Three whole quarters. Almost an entire dollar. That kind of money was not readily available to me. I resolved to keep the sugared assassin in my mouth at least until the flavor was gone, but almost certainly longer.

The gum seemed to have some measure of control over the situation, allowing me to draw in short breaths at random intervals. Even when I did though, the air was corrupted by the vile, powdered sugary sweetness coating the inside of my face.

I continued my attempt to chew, but my jaw grew tired and ached with the effort. A soreness I'd never known clamped down hard on my mandible and I knew I'd would never be able to move my mouth again.

As the time slipped away, one thing became clear. This is how I was going to die. Soon my jaw would freeze completely and refuse to move, then the gum would stop allowing air to be breathed in over it. In that moment, I realized the world around me had gone still. My brother stood only a few feet away, frozen. An expression of bliss on his face, with a donut stuck halfway into it. The older kids on the arcade machines were still as well. The world had screeched to a halt, while I fought for my continued existence.

Warm, shimmering golden light surrounded me. For a second, if seconds still existed, I forgot all about the sweet mass of pink slowly killing me.

"Fret not, my child. For I am come to save thee," the voice came from somewhere above me. In an instant, a being of pure white light descended to the ground before me.

Though there was much about the world around me I did not understand, I knew for a certain "*For I am come*" was not proper grammar. I let the faux pas slide, because this thing in front of me was obviously not from New York. The weirdest thing, I could see a person inside of my thoughts, but if I looked with only my eyes, I saw nothing but light. The being reached out a hand which passed straight through my cheek. Exiting the other side, the hand held a blob of gum the size of a peach.

The being let the gum fall from its hand to the ground, where in a pool of my own saliva. Then it spoke again, "I am Macarius, an angel of the Lord. Known as the patron saint of confections."

The gum rose from the floor, growing much larger what I'd attempted to contain inside my mouth. The giant wad attacked the angel. Slimy pink tendrils wrapped around the light, causing dimming the glow. When I closed my eyes, I saw the figure struggling in the grasp of the sticky foe. Nothing could beat this thing, not teeth, not angels. It was hopeless.

A flaming sword appeared in Macarius' hand. The angel hacked away at the globulin, the fiery sword singed all it touched. A few hefty swings, and the gum was reduced to nothing more than a pile of charred sugar. The angel regarded me one last time and ascended to the heavens.

I realize this may seem a bit fantastic and far-fetched, but I assure you every word is true. It may lend some credibility to reveal even then I was, and continue to be, to this very day, an atheist.

For days following the Big League incident, I would taste the sugared evil in all I did. If I sneezed, the sweet scent would fill my mouth and nasal cavity. When I would sniff afterwards, the runny post nasal drip sprinting down the back of my throat was sugar flavored.

A couple weeks later, David and I found ourselves on yet another grocery run. Money burning holes in our jeans. I sat on the bench next to the Centipede machine, while he went into the candy shop for a snack. He returned after a moment, smiling and with one hand hidden behind his back.

"What did you get?" I asked.

His smile grew wider. Slowly, he moved the hand from behind him to reveal a bright pink disk-like object. I'd seen the uniquely packaged candy advertised at least six hundred times, during Saturday morning cartoons. Bubble tape. Six feet of chewy sweetness. My eyes went from the canister of gum to his, in anticipation of the words I knew were about to be spoken.

"I dare you…"

****

This book is a collection of short horror stories I've written over the years. Inside you'll find ghosts, demons, Santa, monsters, devils, and aliens. Some situations may evoke a strong emotional response. This is, without a doubt, my intention. However, I encourage you to approach each tale with an open mind, breathe, and remember books can always be closed. It's also worth noting the goal of most horror stories is to linger in your thoughts long after you've taken your eyes off the page.

Keep An Eye Out For Strays

Ian found his new home. The house was everything he'd been looking for; spacious, beautifully designed, with a garage and lawn care. He never dreamed his offer would be accepted. There had to be more qualified people jumping at the chance to make the place theirs, but somehow, he got it. A gorgeous, two-story townhouse, in a gated community. Ian was in love.

An excited surge of adrenaline carried him through packing and loading the moving boxes, from his studio apartment. Traffic even seemed lighter when he drove across town, to his new place. Arriving at the gate in less time than he prepared for, Ian's finger glided across the key fob and pressed the button to open the gate to the next chapter of his life.

Exhausted and sweating, Ian finished unloading his truck as the sun ducked below the horizon on the warm fall evening. It had been an exciting day. The charge of it all began to wear off, and all the physical exertion caught up with him. Soon Ian could barely keep his eyes open. He wanted to at least get his bed put together, but his body had other plans. With his last bit of strength, Ian muscled his mattress into his new bedroom, made sure the alarm was set on his phone and crashed headlong onto the pad, falling asleep the moment his eyes closed.

In the morning, he was awoken by a beam of sunlight shining through the window, right onto his eyes. It took a few moments to realize where he was. Ian sat up, reaching over to the edge of the mattress, where his phone lay. Something nagged at his thoughts while his mind tried to clear away the fog of having come out of a deep and restful sleep. He tried to unlock his phone, but the screen wouldn't turn on. Ian realized the phone was dead. The charging cable still packed away in a moving box. As he was pushing himself up from the mattress, Ian froze. He remembered he had an alarm set to wake up earlier than usual, in order to unpack the toiletries and things he would need to prepare for the workday. It also occurred to him that if the sun was up, he was super late.

Ian made quick work of getting himself ready. Splashing water on his face, dabbing at his armpits, and running a toothbrush over his teeth. He threw on the first wrinkled outfit he could find and headed out to begin his day. The garage door crept open on its automatic mechanism. Ian prepared to shoot out of the parking space but was halted. Two people were on a morning walk, sauntering by right in front of his truck. "Seriously?" Ian said, throwing up his hands at the health-conscious old couple. He noted they both carried golf clubs and were using them as walking sticks. How odd. As they passed by, the man looked over at him and waved a hand. Pissed, but not wanting to make a bad impression on the new neighbors, Ian smiled and waved back. As soon as their feet cleared the driveway, Ian dashed through the door and hurried away, tires screeching.

After a frantic day of work, Ian returned home in the evening. The quiet neighborhood was settling down for the night. He spotted a few more people out for a stroll and noticed they were carrying golf clubs like the couple from earlier. Maybe there was a walking group within the community and that was how they identified themselves? It didn't matter. He had a long night of unpacking ahead of him. After parking his truck, Ian decided to check out the mailbox kiosk. There was no way he'd have any mail yet but felt it necessary to familiarize himself with everything. The kiosk sat at the corner of the property, right inside of the entrance gate, a short distance from his house. As he approached, he saw a car parked in front of it, music blasting from within. Rows of dull gray boxes lined the wall, and Ian began looking for the one assigned to him. For a moment, the music rose in volume as someone stepped out of the vehicle. Ian began singing along with the familiar tune, under his breath.

"Excuse me?" a voice said.

Ian halted his search to look over at the woman. He did a double take, realizing how pretty she was only after the first glance. "Uh, are you talking to me?"

"Actually, I thought you'd said something to me," the woman chuckled.

"Oh, no, I was just… I love this song. Guess I was singing a little too loud."

"Well don't stop on my account. I'm Vicky," she extended her hand to him.

"Ian," he did not hesitate in shaking it.

"You just move in?"

"Obvious, huh?" Ian questioned.

"No, not really. We kinda met this morning. You were so busy racing out of your garage and cutting me off there wasn't really any time to exchange pleasantries."

Ian flushed, "Shit, sorry about that. My phone died; I was late for work."

"No harm done I suppose. Are you trying to find your mailbox?"

"Yes. These numbers don't make any sense though."

"There's really no rhyme or reason to it. They assigned a random mailbox to each house. You're in 904, right? That's Ms. Parker's old place. Her box was 14J, right here," Vicky tapped on a mailbox door.

Ian tried his key in the lock, and it opened with ease. "Thanks. I could have stood here for an hour and not have figured that out."

"Don't mention it," Vicky made quick work of scooping the mail from her box and then made her way back to her car.

"Nice meeting you, Vicky. Sorry, again, about this morning."

"No worries. You shouldn't stress about shit like that though. Ten minutes, or an hour, late is late."

Vicky got back into her car, and Ian couldn't help but stare as she drove off. She lived somewhere in the neighborhood, so their paths were bound to cross again. Ian needed to figure out how to make it happen sooner versus later.

Back at his house, Ian put off unpacking yet again. He thought of all he had sitting in various moving boxes, and the effort it would take to get it all put away in its proper place and it tired him out. He settled down onto his mattress, letting his phone play music until he fell asleep.

In the morning, Ian awoke with plenty of time to do the things he hadn't been able to the day before. With time to spare, he hopped into his truck and opened the garage door pausing for a moment, with hopes of seeing Vicky driving by. No luck though. Rational thought told him he'd been more than an hour late for work when he cut her off. He would need to sit in his truck for at least another two and a half hours if he wanted to catch her out on her morning drive. And there was no guarantee that was part of her routine anyway. Maybe she was running late herself, or early. There were far too many variables involved for him to try and figure out where she would be and when. Besides, thinking those sorts of thoughts was for stalkers. Ian did not want to liken himself to that crowd. He started his truck and pulled out of the garage, noting there were no golf club wielding walkers blocking his path.

As he approached the front entry gate, he recognized Vicky's car parked in front of the mail kiosk. He, at once, pulled up next to it. She seemed to be dropping off letters into the outgoing box. Ian quickly hopped out, excited to see her again. "Good morning," he said, trying to play cool and keep the eagerness out of his voice.

Vicky turned, about to walk to her car, "Oh, hey. Ian, right?"

"Yeah, it's me. Same guy from like eleven or

twelve hours ago." Ian laughed, nervous.

Vicky shot him a smile.

Ian had a feeling the smile he was seeing was reserved for meaningless, but polite exchanges. He could not draw this out. If he lost her attention now, he was bound to end up in a friend-zone purgatory. Forever labeled as some awkward neighbor she only says hi to when their paths occasionally crossed. "Hey, can I ask you a quick question? You know your way around this part of town, right? Know any good places to eat?"

"What, like breakfast? Let's see, there's Golden Waffle, Mama's,"

Ian interrupted Vicky's recommendations, "No, not breakfast. I'm thinking about grabbing a bite after work, this evening."

"Oh, in that case, your options are much better."

"Well, what's your favorite spot?"

"Mmm, there's a little taco shop tucked away in the corner of the Promenade Shopping Plaza. Manuel's. Best fish tacos I've ever had. Do you like Mexican? If so, you should give them a try."

"That sounds delicious. I don't suppose you'd like to go with me?"

"Like a date, Ian?" Vicky turned her gaze from him, hoping to hide her blushing cheeks.

"No, not...I mean, unless you want it to be. No pressure or anything. You're a nice person, from what I can tell. I just want to get to know you."

"Fair enough. What time do you have in mind?"

"Seven-thirty work for you?"

"Yes, it does."

"Cool. I'll see you then." Ian hurried around Vicky's car to his truck. His hands, wet with perspiration, slipped on the steering wheel when he first tried to pull away from the spot where he parked.

The anticipation of seeing Vicky after work made his day drag along. Ian gathered his things together at his desk, ready to shut down his computer and bolt out of the office the moment the clock read 5pm. He was up and out of his cubicle with a swiftness he didn't know he was capable of. Before he reached the lobby and exited the building, Ian heard someone call after him. He turned to see Mr. Eckert, his boss, hurrying towards him.

"Christ, Ian, where's the fire?" Mr. Eckert was winded as he caught up to Ian.

The fire was in his own thoughts. Vicky, and the prospect of all she represented had started the blaze. And if all went well this evening, Ian hoped the fire would grow to an inferno not easily doused. "Sorry, sir. I'm kinda in a rush."

"Well, I won't keep you long then. I won't be in tomorrow, and I need you to stay late. We've got a quarterly review next week, and there are documents in need of a once over before we present them to leadership. We can't screw this up, which is why you are the one who needs to handle it. At the very least, it'll give you a chance to make up the time you missed yesterday."

Preoccupied as he may have been, Ian understood what was being asked of him, "Sure, no problem, sir."

Mr. Eckert clapped a meaty hand on Ian's shoulder, "Perfect. I knew I could count on you."

He waited an awkward moment, ensuring his boss was finished talking, then turned and continued his hurried rush to exit the building.

The first bite of the fish taco solidified the fact Vicky had made a great recommendation. The Mahi Mahi was in perfect balance with the purple cabbage, avocado, and spices. A hint of lime and cilantro finished off an amazing mouthful. "Oh my god, this is delicious." Ian spoke around the chewed food.

"Not to brag or anything, but if I say it's good, you can take that as gospel." Vicky laughed and sipped from the bottle of beer in front of her, before taking a bite from her own plate of tacos. "So how are you liking the neighborhood so far?"

"No complaints. I absolutely love my house. Maybe this weekend I'll finally feel like unpacking, and really settling in."

"Ugh, I know what you mean. Packing up the old place, and setting everything up at the new spot, two of the worst things ever."

Since they were on the topic of the neighborhood, a question wriggled into Ian's thoughts, "So, what's the deal with everyone walking around holding golf clubs? Is that like some crazy workout club or something?"

Vicky laughed halfheartedly, changing the subject right away, "What do you do for a living, Ian?"

For a moment, Ian considered pressing the issue. She'd brushed him off so fast it could have been construed as rude. He dropped it, though. Thinking perhaps she didn't know the answer herself and was too proud to say so.

They sat for a while talking, eating, and laughing. It had all gone better than Ian expected. He paid for their meal feeling satisfied with the way the date had progressed.

Vicky rose from her seat, ready to leave. "So, Ian, are you headed home from here?"

"That's the plan. Get ready for work tomorrow, read a little, and call it a night."

"Well," Vicky began, "if you have a moment, would you mind coming over to my place?"

Ian's eyes widened. She had given no previous indication the date had gone that well. "Umm, yes." He nodded, unable to contain his excitement.

"Dammit, Ian, not for sex," Vicky laughed. "I want to show you something."

"No, of course. I mean," he stumbled over his

words, trying to recover from his folly, "shit. Can I get a do-over?"

"Just get in your truck and follow me, silly."

Vicky stepped into the foyer and turned the lights on. A brief nod to Ian served as his invitation to enter.

Ian was impressed. The basic layout of the house was the same as his own, but the woman had an eye for art. Elaborate paintings decorated every wall he saw. "Wow, these are amazing."

"Thanks. It's sort of a hobby of mine."

"Wait, you did all of these? Holy shit. You could sell any one of these for millions, I bet."

"I've been approached a few times about contributing to art shows, but these are all too personal. They tell the story of my life. I can't just put them on display for anyone to judge. I honestly don't do so well with criticism."

"Okay, but I'm looking at them now."

"You're one person, Ian. On top of that, I like you. So, I don't mind too much. Do you want a drink? I have any alcohol you can think of."

"Bourbon?"

"Ah, a man after my own heart." She walked further into the house.

Ian heard glassware clinking together. He ambled through the living space, marveling at the artwork on the walls. Some of the pieces gave him chills, though he had no clue why. Her art was dark in its tone. Midnight landscapes hid all manner of beast, only discernable if one truly paid close attention. Most of the creatures he saw were docile, a rock formation turned out to be a scurry of squirrels, a waterfall that fell from high atop a cliff into a river of bats glinting white in the moonlight. There was one though, that set his nerves on edge, for some reason. The night sky at the last moments of sunset. The dark void above only glowing a fiery red at the line of the horizon. And emerging from the scene, a menacing gray wolf. Ian turned away from it with a shiver.

"Here you go." She returned with two rocks glasses. A measure of honeyed liquid in both. "Let's go sit in the backyard while we drink."

Ian took the offered glass, and followed Vicky through the house to the backyard, sparing a backward glance and catching the sunset wolf's hungry eyes glaring at him.

They sat in near darkness, the only illumination coming from a streetlight obscured by a few leafy birch trees. "So, are the paintings what you wanted to show me?"

"No, be quiet for a moment." Her words were snappy, as she sat sipping the glorious drink.

Minutes passed, and soon Ian heard the wailing of a siren in the distance. The ululating urgency grew louder as the emergency vehicle drew nearer. Ian was startled as Vicky grabbed his arm. "What?"

She raised her index finger, pointing to nothing in particular, "Do you hear them?"

"You mean the sirens? Of course."

"Wait for it."

He was about to ask what he was waiting for, but then another noise pierced the night. Below the wailing of the sirens, Ian could hear a distorted symphony. Dogs. How many, he didn't know. They howled and yelped as the vehicle sped past the neighborhood. "What the hell?"

"I wasn't brushing you off earlier. I just thought this was a better way to answer your question. We kinda have an issue with stray dogs around here. That's why people go on walks with golf clubs. Every so often, someone is out walking, checking their mail, or sitting outside their home and they get attacked.

I know you like me, Ian. But if we're going to pursue any type of relationship, you need to know, before anyone in the community tells you, these strays are here because of me."

"What, you run a dog shelter or something?"

"No, nothing like that. You see, this house, I inherited it from my parents when they passed away, five years ago. I was in a super toxic relationship when I moved in. We all have our phases, right? Well, by association I was into some sick shit. My ex, Jet, sold dope, but he also bred pit bulls and sold them to only the super shadiest of customers. People would contact him via the dark web, pay anonymously with bitcoin, and he would make loads of money. More than a few times, the cops came around to ask Jet questions about dog fighting and things like that. I would cover for him. That was my role in it all. Keep his secrets, validate his alibis. And for my efforts, I was often beaten senseless. He was angry all the time, no matter what I did. We fought with our words and our fists on a weekly basis. He would shout and accuse me of things like snitching and stealing money from him, which I of course didn't do. Little foamy white bubbles would form at the corners of his mouth, like he was rabid. It was gross. Neighbors grew sick of all the shouting, and the police visits. Not that they were worried about my wellbeing at all, our meltdowns were simply a threat to their peace and quiet, and their property values.

Well, after a long period of self-reflection, I came to the realization I'm better than that and finally got up the nerve to kick him out."

"That's," Ian paused, "some really heavy shit." Ian found himself taking in a deep breath as he processed all that was relayed to him. "Okay, but that still doesn't explain it all. I mean, you said you're responsible for all of this. How?"

"Are you sure you want to know? I figured everything I told you so far would've sent you running home."

"Please," Ian scoffed, "we all have baggage. I'm flattered you feel comfortable enough with me to talk about yours."

"It's not about comfort, Ian. I get a really good vibe from you, and before you go and develop any deeper feelings, I want to put all of my red flags on display."

"That's respectable," Ian raised the glass to his mouth and gulped down the last of the bourbon. "Proceed."

"Okay, so when I say I kicked Jet out, I mean it literally. I woke up one morning sick of it all. I called animal control and had them take away the pits. Jet was furious. I threatened to call the cops and he belted me across the face. Before he could do any further harm, I ran into the garage. He chased me, of course, but I bought myself some time by kicking a chair in front of the door. As he stumbled and fell over it, I found my dad's set of antique silver golf clubs. I grabbed one, and when he got back on his feet, I swung the club and missed. He tackled me to the ground and tried to wrestle it from my hands, but I held fast. He head-butted me, kneed me in my ribs, scratched and clawed at me, but I didn't let go. Jet let up for a moment and I seized the opportunity. I jabbed him in his side with the club, and he rolled off me, giving me a chance to get off my back. Once that happened, I gained the upper hand. I put everything I had into my next swing. It connected with his temple, and he went down. I could see the light in his eyes go out as he tumbled over. I called the cops and an ambulance, thinking I had killed him, and ready to face whatever punishment was coming my way. I sat outside on the stoop, waiting for the authorities, but not before locking the body in the garage. After a few minutes, he came to, and I could hear him yelling and cursing weakly from his prison. The cops showed up and restrained him while the EMTs examined him. He had a pretty bad concussion and was going to require a stay in the hospital, before jail. By that time, the whole neighborhood had gathered outside. Needless to say, they were pissed. Jet was being carted away but mumbling something as he left. I moved closer, to hear it. 'You're a bitch,' he said. 'I curse this entire neighborhood with your kind. Go and run with your pack. You will never be free of them.' I chalked it all up to the injury, but sure enough, the next day packs of stray dogs began terrorizing the community. It was too crazy for it to be a coincidence. A neighbor had heard Jet's utterings and realized this was all my fault. Soon everyone knew about it, and they all banded against me.

The wild dogs began attacking people. They needed some way to fight back. You might think the weapon of choice was a golf club because it's light, easy to swing, and packs a punch, but you'd be wrong in your assumption. Some spiteful asshole saw me sitting outside with the club after I'd beat Jet's ass and decided it would be a good way to protect themselves and mock me at the same time. So, there you go. Ready to run for the hills now?"

Ian found himself letting out a breath he hadn't known he was holding in. "Well, this is one hell of a first date. Vicky, I'm not scared of your past. My interest in you is based on the person you are right now. You've triumphed over some terrible shit. I respect that."

Vicky smiled, and Ian swooned. It seemed more genuine than any other time he'd seen the expression on her.

"Want to do dinner again tomorrow?"

"Oh, hell yes. What do you recommend this time?"

"Well, I'm thinking we stay in. Come by after work, and I'll try not to embarrass myself with whatever I make."

"A home cooked meal? Count me all the way in."

The next day, as five o'clock rolled around, Ian was reminded he needed to work late. He cursed himself for not remembering, grabbed his phone, and called Vicky to let her know dinner might have to be postponed, or even rescheduled. The call went straight to her voicemail. Rather than leave a message, he ended the call and sent her a text. Three hours later, he was finally ready to leave. Ian picked up his phone with hopes of salvaging what was left of the night. He opened his messages and saw his text had been seen, but Vicky hadn't responded.

The way home was marred by traffic, adding to Ian's frustration. Eventually he reached the entry gate and saw an odd scene. Lights flashed from within the neighborhood. As he drove in, he could see an ambulance, and a police car. Neighbors crowded around, obstructing his view of the scene. Ian parked in his driveway and made his way over to where everyone was congregated. Stunned, he found himself standing at the house next door to Vicky's. The police had the area outside of Vicky's front door cordoned off. Ian's heart began to race. He pulled out his phone and tried to call her, but he was diverted to her voicemail again. Ian turned to one of the onlookers. A pudgy little gray-haired man. "What's going on?"

"Oh, hey. You just moved in, right?"

"Yeah, what happened?" Ian was insistent.

"Well, do you know about the dogs?"

"Yes, I know about the fucking dogs. Is Vicky okay?"

The man placed a hand on Ian's shoulder. When next he spoke, his words were somber, "I'm sorry, man. I don't think she made it. Worst attack I've seen since the damn things started showing up. They tore her apart. Was her own fault, but still, she didn't deserve that."

Ian's head was spinning, trying to make sense of

it all. This place wasn't cursed. Stray dogs went wherever the hell they pleased. Ian's temper boiled over. He grabbed the man by his shirt, "Her fault? Vicky's dead and it's her fault? How? Tell me," he fumed. Other neighbors turned at the sound of yelling. "You all treated her like some outcast, because she didn't fit your dumb ass expectations. She went through hell and came out a better person than any of you could ever hope to be. And as her reward, she's mocked, taunted, and shunned. Self-righteous assholes, all of you. More comfortable believing in the ramblings of some delusional prick, than actually addressing the problem. No, this wasn't Vicky's fault, this wasn't something that was bound to happen. This is the result of you all rallying together to bully an innocent woman. These dogs you're all so scared of could have been taken care of years ago." He let go of the old man and turned to leave the scene. "Get the fuck out of my way." He shoved passed the few neighbors who stood in stunned silence and made his way home.

Walking up to his driveway, Ian spotted a pit bull standing near his truck. The dog locked eyes with him. Ian burned with anger. He'd only known Vicky for a few days, but in that time, she had become a friend at the very least, hoping it would grow into something more. If the dog came for him, he would not run. The pit bull must have sensed his brevity. It stepped back, breaking eye contact, then turned and ran off down the street.

Ian spent the entire next day unpacking. By nightfall, everything was done, and his home was set up to his liking. He sat in his bedroom wondering what to do next. Thoughts of Vicky kept surfacing in his mind, and he needed to stay busy to hold them at bay. Ian grabbed his phone to check the time. It was after midnight. There was no way he could fall asleep yet. He thought a walk might burn off all the remaining energy, and maybe help clear his mind as well. Ian threw on some workout clothes and headed for the door.

Outside, the air was crisp. The moon shone bright in the clear sky, providing Ian enough light to walk by. He put his ear buds in and hit random on his playlist. The speakers came to life, blaring out the notes to a familiar tune. Ian shut the music off at once. It was the song that had been playing in Vicky's car when he first met her. He walked in silence for a long time, exploring the neighborhood up and down streets he hadn't yet seen. He made his way down one of the unfamiliar roads and turned when he heard a rustling in the bush behind him. His walk came to a halt when he turned back around. A dog stood directly in his path. In the pale glow of the moon, Ian saw it was the same dog he'd stared down in his driveway.

"Shit," Ian muttered to himself.

The dog stared at him. Ian thought it may want a rematch. He stared back. The fire in his gaze from the previous night replaced with sadness and confusion. The pit bull stood its ground.

"It's okay. You know me, remember? You know me." Ian slowly reached out a hand. He wanted the dog to give it a sniff and see he was no threat. Ian inched closer, careful not to be the first to break eye contact. "Come on, little doggo. It's alright." He took another step forward and the dog began to growl. "No, no, no. Everything is okay," but as he said this, the dog bared its teeth and snapped at the proffered hand. Ian jumped back in just enough time to keep his fingers. The dog backed away as well. Ian wondered what was wrong. The pit bull lowered its head in a display of shame, before letting out a sorrowful yelp and taking off in the direction it had come from.

"What was that all about?" A wave of tiredness washed over him. He decided it was finally time to head home. He turned to go back but was stopped in his tracks. A dog, much bigger than the pit bull—the largest dog Ian had ever seen, in fact—stood before him. Ian thought he was seeing things at first. There's no way a dog as big as a loveseat was standing in front of him. Its fur was black as death. He looked on terrified, as the beast took an offensive stance, raising its hackles and opening its mouth in a bloodthirsty grin. There would be no reasoning with this monster. Ian took one slow step back, and then another. The dog barked, an earsplitting cry of intimidation that pushed Ian to run away.

The beast was faster than him. As he ran, Ian felt the giant claws swipe at him. He screamed for help, passing house after house. At the corner, he tried to lose his pursuer by feigning a left turn but going right. The dog fell for the ruse, but quickly recovered. Ian made it halfway down the street and then was overcome by the beast. It threw itself on top of him, pinning him to the ground. Ian thrust his hands up into the thick fur of its neck, using all his strength to keep the salivating dog from clamping its teeth down on him, while the claws of its enormous paws shredded his clothes.

The dog continued its attempts to bite Ian. He quickly realized he was going to lose the battle. His arms grew more tired and weak with every second. The snarling beast let up for a moment and Ian made his move. He brought his legs up and kicked as hard as he could. It wasn't nearly enough to get the hulking canine off him. It did, however, create a bit of wiggle room. Ian was able to shimmy out from under the dog. He scrambled to his feet and ran to the doorway of the nearest house. Ian pounded at the door furiously, begging for the owner to let him in. He took hold of the knob and it turned in his grip. There was a tape seal he had to tear through to get inside. Once he did, he hurried into the house, closed and locked the door behind him.

Searching for a moment, Ian found a light switch. Once the place was illuminated, Ian realized how familiar the space was. The layout was similar to his own house, and beautiful paintings hung on every wall he set his eyes on. This was Vicky's house. He'd torn through the police tape without even noticing. Ian walked in, retracing his steps from the last time he'd been there. He came to the painting that had held his attention before. The giant gray wolf, emerging from the night sky. How he wished Vicky was still there to explain what was happening.

He spotted something on an end table, near the painting. It was Vicky's cell phone. Without thinking, he grabbed it and turned it on. The screen came to life, there was no lock. He eyed the screen, nervous and unsure what he was looking for. With his thumb, he opened the text messaging app. There were only two conversations. One was himself, and the other was with someone named Kay-Kay. He knew what he would find if he opened his texts, and so he pressed the other conversation.

7:30 am

"I really like him," the first message on the screen read.

The incoming response, "I'm happy 4 u."

"Last night went great. Never met someone like him. Cooking him dinner 2nite"

"Damn girl. When's the wedding lol"

There was a break in the conversation. The next text was not sent out until more than two hours later.

9:51 am

"Jet got out today. Turning my phone off for the rest of the day. Don't want him contacting me."

Something crashed into the door and Ian jumped, dropping the phone. He looked to the entrance knowing what it was. It smashed into the door again. Shaking it in its frame. He wondered how long it would hold. The answer came when Ian saw a shadow rise up and fill the glass panes imbedded at the top of the door.

"Oh shit," he uttered, as the door was torn from its hinges.

The gigantic dog stood in the doorway, on its hind legs. It snarled as it took a sure-footed step forward, sniffing at the air. It spotted Ian and leapt forward, closing the distance between them in a heartbeat.

Ian wasted no time in turning, running deeper into the house. He wanted to get to the back door. There he could at least find cover in the trees. It was the best plan he had, unfortunately it was not meant to be. An overgrown paw caught him in his ribs and sent him flying into the wall. Ian lay on the floor gasping. It hurt to breathe. He got to his knees in a feeble attempt to crawl away, but his ribs put up a fierce protest, and he sprawled out on the floor in pain.

The dog was back on all fours skulking towards him.

Ian grasped onto something that lay beneath his

hand. He lifted his head and saw he was holding a golf club. It made him smile, with thoughts of Vicky. He wished he could have had more time with her. Fuck Jet, and fuck what the neighbors thought, she was perfect just as she was. The scars of her past had brought them together, how could he ever be mad at that? He lay there on the floor in impossible calm, until he felt the hot breath running down his neck and heard the rumbling growl in his ear.

Ignoring the throbbing in his ribs, Ian turned onto his back quickly. Using the momentum, he whipped his arm around and brought the golf club down onto the dog's back with all the force he could muster.

For the first time, he saw the massive dog stagger. Ian found his feet and before the dog could recover, he hit it again, catching a hind leg this time. The dog lunged forward, and Ian swung once more. The blow landed awkwardly on its neck and the club broke in two.

The dog went sprawling on its side. It recovered, barking with such ferocity the windows shook. It clawed at the floor, splintering the hardwood. In an instant the beast was charging forward, and airborne. Its mouth opened wide, intent on capturing Ian's head between its teeth. Close enough now, it could taste the fear pouring off the defenseless man before it.

Ian shut his eyes tight. He knew the pain would be awful.

A crash. Glass shattering from a window off to Ian's left, near the front door. In the instant before his head became a chew toy, another dog slammed into the side of the first, sending it tumbling away from Ian.

This new dog was smaller than the other, but still larger than anything Ian had ever seen. It stood in front of him, shielding him from the hulking beast recovering across the room.

Ian observed this new canine. Noting its gray fur was patchy, cuts and lacerations along its entire body.

The first dog regained its footing and stared down the second one, growling and salivating.

Ian backed away until he was against the wall. He struggled to make sense of was happening. Logic and reasoning would not let him accept it. As he looked on, the new dog let out a loud howl that made his teeth vibrate against themselves. Ian, in a moment of clear thought, hurt and struggling to stay upright, decided to abandon the pretense he'd constructed as a shield since finding himself in the situation. These were wolves. And these wolves, at some point earlier in the day, had been people. He pushed himself from the wall, towards the gray wolf. Reaching out a hand, he gently touched the wolf's leg, petting the coarse fur. "Vicky?" He said.

The wolf turned, lowering its snout to nuzzle against Ian's face. He reached up and placed his hands behind her ears, holding back a stream of tears. "It's okay," Ian said, "I understand. I-"

Vicky yelped in pain. The black wolf sank its teeth into her hind leg. She kicked it away, turning on it in a flash. They both lunged at one another, snarling and clawing, trying to take the other down.

Ian moved back away from the fray, never taking his gaze from the two. His heart raced, and his body ached, but his eyes remained steady. The black wolf, Jet, as he suspected, swiped at Vicky's head, with his sharp claws. Vicky ducked away from the blow, raised her head up before Jet found his footing, and bit into his leg.

Jet howled as Vicky thrashed back and forth, seeming as though she wanted to tear the leg away from his body. Yapping, squealing, crying, Jet's resolve drained away. The wolf stumbled to the floor in pain. Only once he rolled onto his back did Vicky release her hold. She grunted and barked at him. He lay beneath her, whining, accepting defeat.

Vicky turned, spotting Ian sitting against the wall, beneath the painting of the wolf. She moved to where he sat, nudging him with her paw. Ian took hold of the broken golf club. Using it as a crutch, he lumbered to his feet.

"I...don't know if I can thank you enough." The words left Ian's mouth through gasping breaths. Ian returned a hand to the scruff of Vicky's ear. "He, he did this to you. Didn't he?"

Vicky tucked her hind legs beneath her, and

spread her front paws out before her, lying down in front of Ian.

The rush of the moment was starting to wear off, and the injuries Ian sustained were announcing themselves. He pulled his hand away from Vicky to wrap his arms around his own torso.

Vicky whimpered.

"It's okay. I'll be fine, I'm sure." Ian leaned in and kissed Vicky's head. When he pulled away, he saw darkness. Confused at how unnatural a sight it was, it took a moment to realize Jet was airborne. His thick frame on a collision course with Vicky. Ian took in as deep a breath as he dared and shouted, "Move, Vicky. MOVE."

She'd been a fool to believe Jet would accept defeat. The only thing that would stop him was death, but she could not go that far. Even as this beast, she was no killer. Vicky heard Ian's urgent plea but knew at once it was too late. She focused on him. On the charming man she'd only known for a brief moment. They would've made a great couple. She felt no regret, no remorse over what could have been. Keeping him in her sight, she felt no pain as warm breath, followed by sharp teeth closed around her neck. Sinking deeper and deeper, bones crunching and snapping beneath their awesome power. Vicky's only hope was that they'd meet again in another life.

"NO!" It happened so fast Ian wasn't sure it was

real. His heart had been decimated twice in two days.

Jet dropped Vicky's body from his mouth rising up on his hind legs. He loomed over Ian, slick with blood, oozing from his teeth and jowls. Jet let out an earsplitting roar. Knife-like claws extended from his paws, he lurched forward ready to swipe Ian into ribbons. Jet stopped cold. A burning pain in his chest.

As Jet was readying to strike, Ian stepped forward with his last bit of strength, using Jet's own momentum to drive the sharp, broken edge of the silver golf club into the monster's heart. "Fuck you, Jet. You hear me? Fuck you." Ian collapsed beside Vicky. The stray dogs no longer terrorized the neighborhood after that night. Ian sat in his dining room, nearly healed from his injuries, eating take out—fish tacos from the best damn spot he'd ever been to. Vicky's painting, the wolf that had mesmerized him so, upon first seeing it, hung in his living room. From where he sat, he could see it clearly. Slowly, he got up from the dining table, and moved over to it. A bar cabinet sat beneath the artwork. It hurt to bend over and remove the bottle of bourbon from the shelf, but as he took that first sip, he knew it was worth it. Outside, a fire truck sped past. In its wake, he heard the familiar sound of dogs wailing in the distance.

No Chimneys In The Hood

There are no chimneys in the hood. Back when I was a child, that was the only piece of information I needed to dispel the myth of old Saint Nick. Sure, there was the fact I never got anything I wanted, or how I had a thorough understanding of how terribly I'd behaved at times, yet never found a lump of coal waiting for me beneath the luminous Fir. The suspension of belief required to devote any brain power to the existence of such a person borders on delusion. Of course, there was one night I was proven wrong. Maybe if I had believed, I'd have been the one who disappeared. Maybe we both would have.

With the realization that Santa Claus was a bullshit story parents wielded over their kids to encourage good behavior, Christmas was not my favorite time of year. Yes I got time off from school, got to lounge around the house with Elijah, my little brother, and sometimes there was even snow. Oh, did I not mention my birthday also falls on the same day? So yeah, another cause for joyous resentment. Sharing the celebration of the day I came into the world with a mythical creature in possession of a fleet of flying reindeer, and a guy who was born from a woman who didn't have sex to conceive him—yeah, okay—who also spawned a religion which pieced together higlights from older religions in order to become one of the most popular belief systems ever, kinda rubbed me the wrong way from the start. It wasn't the holiday itself I didn't enjoy, but everyone around me celebrated, feeling happier under false pretenses. I could pretend people all over the world were celebrating in my honor. Stringing up lights, singing songs, and spending time with family, and the fat red dude was simply a mascot folks ascribed to the day, because not everyone knew what I looked like. Of course, I was neither plump nor apple cheeked. I hated the color red, and I was—and to the best of my knowledge, still am—a girl.

Elijah and I were finishing dinner on Christmas Eve. The day before my thirteenth birthday. He was five years old and had started kindergarten back in the fall. He was such a bright kid. So, I thought trying to educate him would have gone over better.

"Do you think Santa is gonna bring us lots of toys, Tamara?" From where he sat, Elijah had a clear line of sight on the tree in the living room. No presents were underneath yet.

Mom and Dad always waited until we were asleep to sneak the gifts from their hiding spot. They did this to preserve some sense of innocence, I guess. Elijah fell for the deception every time.

"Hey, let me ask you a question." I was his age when I'd made the clever observation that shattered the illusion the world tried to force on me. "How does santa find his way inside our apartment?"

"Santa comes down the chimney, silly."

He spoke with such confidence, part of me hated what I was about to do. I'd always been the type to rip the bandage off though. No use in prolonging the pain. "Oh, okay. Wait a second," I stood up and looked around, being as dramatic as I dared, "Elijah, I don't see any chimney in here. In fact, I don't think there's one in the entire building." I tried to guide him to the logical conclusion, but some people don't give in to the truth so easily.

"Oh, that doesn't matter. He can do magic and make one anywhere."

My attitude soured. I wasn't expecting to be refuted. "What are you, stupid? That's not true at all. Santa's not real, Elijah."

"Liar!" He spit the word at me like s dart, with the intent to hurt. "Just shut up, you idiot."

Mom wandered over to find out what had her baby boy so upset. "Elijah, you don't talk that way to your sister. Apologize, right now."

"She started it, Mommy. She said Santa's not real, and he can't do magic."

"God, Tamara. This again?" She turned to stare at me with the look of disappointment all women seem to perfect the moment they have children.

I would have no support for my side of the argument. But my brother needed to know the truth. "Are you serious, Mom? I'm the one who's not lying here, but I'm in trouble? How is that fair?"

"Elijah, baby, why don't you go get ready to take a bath, while I talk to your sister."

"Okay," he hopped out of the chair and started walking to the bathroom. Once he was behind Mom, and out of her field of vision the little smart-ass started making faces at me. He knew he won, and Mom was about to set me straight on this whole Santa issue.

"What is your problem, Tamara?"

"My problem? Tons of kids are brainwashed with this nonsense every year. You adults preach honesty at every turn, and then turn around and lie to us about something so small and insignificant. Why?"

"Young lady, watch it. If your brother believes in Santa, let him. That's the end of it. If I catch you spouting any more of your anti-Christmas talk, I'm going to take your present and throw it in the oven on broil." Her tone was sharp. She was serious.

"Oh no! What will I do without another sweater in my closet?"

"It's a nice sweater, goddamit! Leave your brother alone. I mean it."

I was too upset to finish my dinner. Instead, I sulked my way back to my room. I was spoiling what was supposed to be an evening of quiet fun and anticipation. My parents hadn't been able to lord the naughty or nice crap over me. There was never any delineation between what was a birthday present, and what was a Christmas gift either. Perhaps their parental egos needed Elijah to believe in the overgrown elf. Maybe that was their personal benchmark signifying they were raising us right. I decided, for that year, to tolerate the cognitive dissonance.

Our apartment only had two bedrooms, which meant Elijah and I had to share one of them. Once little bro was old enough to not need a crib anymore, he made the move from Mom and Dad's bedside to the bottom bunk in my room. I didn't mind. Even back then I understood money wasn't something we had much of. Thinking back, the bunk bed may have been the most expensive thing in our home. Dad got a great deal at some moving sale. He said the frame was made from high-quality wood. I can attest the thing was rock solid. No amount of jumping on the mattress, pillow fighting, or tickle torture could move that frame.

Elijah strolled in, dressed in his pajamas. I was trying to find something to watch unrelated to the significance of the day to come. It was fruitless. I gave up control of the TV to my brother. Leaving myself at his mercy, I was sure he would flip through the channels and settle on the first crappy animated program he found. He surprised me though, crossing the room and turning the TV off, before settling on his bed.

"Did you get in a lot of trouble? I didn't mean for that to happen, if you did."

My little brother, ever the sweetheart. Eight years my junior, yet he was trying to look out for me. "I'm fine," I said. Believing in the jolly old fat man made him happy, who was I to try and take that from him? I did love the little guy, after all.

On his bed, I watched as he reached beneath his pillow and withdrew a crudely folded piece of paper, and a black crayon. He then wrote a word in one of the only spaces left without writing, on the sheet of loose leaf.

"Hey, what is that?" I asked.

"Nothing. You wouldn't care anyway."

I was certain I already knew what it was, yet still found myself curious. "No, seriously. I want to see."

"For really? Okay, well this is the list Santa asked me to make. You might not believe in him, but he told me to keep a list of everything I wanted for Christmas. Doesn't matter how big or expensive. He said the list is special, and I can ask for anything."

"Oh, so you've been talking to Santa?" I was supposed to be supportive, but I could not ignore what Elijah said.

"Well, not really talking to him. He leaves

letters for me to find."

I was amazed at how far my parents had taken this whole ruse. Leaving letters for Elijah. Clever move. A great way to keep him engaged and ensuring his belief in the mythos. "Really? Do you still have the letters? Can I see one?"

Elijah hopped up, eager to challenge my truth, with what he considered incontrovertible evidence of Santa's existence. He pulled a folder from beneath the bed, opened it, shuffled through a few pages, and handed me the first of Santa's communiques.

Dear Elijah,

You have been a very good boy this year, yes you have. I've got a special treat for you. What would you like for Christmas? I'd like you to make a list of anything you can think of. It doesn't matter how large, or expensive. Whatever you want, I will make sure you find everything waiting for you when you come to visit the North Pole.

Your Pal

Santa Claus

The letter was written on an off-white cardstock carrying the faint smell of peppermint. The first thing I noticed was how the note was written in a simple penmanship style that was easy to read. Elijah had learned to read early, and while he may have struggled with one or two words, the letter was perfect for someone of his reading level. The next thing was the handwriting didn't match anything I'd ever seen from mom or dad. I read the letter a couple more times, feeling more creeped out with each pass.

"Elijah, who gave you these letters?"

"It was Santa."

His reply irked me, "Stop playing. Did Mom or Dad do this?"

"No, not them. See, that's why you got in trouble, because you don't believe in him. But he's real, and he'll be here tonight, and I'm going with him to the North Pole to have all of the toys and an airplane, and a Tyrannosaurus Shark. And you won't get anything."

"Hmm, do you mind if I hold on to this. I'm sure Mom would like to have a look it."

Elijah snatched the letter out of my hands and placed the paper back in the folder with swiftness and precision I'd never seen him move with. "Nah-ah. Santa said to never show these to them."

By then, all sorts of alarms were ringing in my head. I was up against a wall though. If I did bring this up to the adults, I ran the risk of them not taking me seriously, and mom destroying the new sweater I was apparently getting. If I kept quiet though, whomever gave the letters to Elijah might hurt him. This would require some careful consideration on my part. "Okay, I understand. Elijah, can you tell me when Santa is supposed to come visit you?"

"Oh my god, are you serious. I thought you were

supposed to be my older sister. You should know stuff like this. This is Christmas Eve. He'll be here tonight."

The fine hairs on the nape of my neck stood on end when I heard his words. Maybe there wasn't anything to worry about though. If someone tried to enter our apartment, surely the grownups would stop the attempt. Wouldn't they be up all night wrapping gifts and putting them under the tree? Santa would show up, Dad would knuckle him down, the cops would be called, Mr. Cringle would be arrested, and life would go on. No need for me to risk getting myself in trouble with anti-Santa rhetoric.

That night, I found myself unable to sleep. I staved off boredom by listening to mom and dad fumble through their present wrapping efforts. They finished long before I thought they would though. In anticipation of what was sure to be an early day, they were in bed long before midnight. The entire apartment was silent. I lay still atop my mattress, sleep evading my every attempt at capturing it. Thinking rationally, I knew there was no way someone was going to break into our home. However, my mind hung onto the creepiness of the letter Elijah showed me. Not knowing the origin left my mind buzzing with worry. When the morning decided to finally arrive, I would tell my folks about it. I didn't care if I got in more trouble. My brother's safety was my only concern. Best case scenario would be to discover Dad wrote the letters with his off hand or something, and I end up with a burnt sweater. As I pondered the events of the evening, there came a scraping, scratching noise from the bottom bunk.

Scratch-a, scratch-a, scratch-a!

I immediately sat up in my bed. "Elijah," I whispered through my trembling lips.

Scratch-a, scratch-a, scratch-a!

"Elijah, wake up. Do you hear it?"

"What?"

His alert voice startled me. I peered over the side of the bed to be sure he was okay, hoping not to glimpse whatever was making such an awful noise. There was very little light in the room. I could barely make out Elijah's shadowy form, kneeling on the floor beside the bed where he should have been sleeping.

"What are you doing? You should be in bed."

"No," scratch-scratch! "I need to finish this."

I eased myself over the side of the bed. Climbing down to the floor. Careful not to disturb my little brother in his feverish activity. The little drummer boy played his heart out for Baby Jesus inside my chest, when I saw what he was doing. There was enough light in the room for me to make out the crude sigils Elijah carved into the bedframe. "Um, Elijah?"

"If I don't finish this he won't come, Tamara." His voice, though barely above a whisper, was insistent.

My fears gave way to worry. Elijah was obsessing over a figment of a collective imagination.

He'd be devastated when he awoke in the morning and discovered the lie. The letters were an interesting, albeit creepy, touch, but enough was enough. I had to talk sense into him, and if I couldn't, I would go straight to our parents and show them exactly what their little charade was doing to my little brother.

"Elijah, listen to me. Santa Claus is not real. You have to stop this. Dad is gonna kill you when he sees what you did to the bedframe. Really it's his fault for filling your head with all this bullsh-"

"Done." Elijah grabbed one of his papers holding the eerie sheet of repurposed wood up to the bed, checking his carvings against what was scrawled on the page. Satisfied, he stuffed the paper under his pillow, hopped up onto the mattress and sat staring into the shadows of the room.

"Look, I'm not trying to make you upset, okay? If anything, you're the victim here. If you trust me though, this will all be so much easier. And there's really no downside to believing the truth. I still get presents every year, just like you." As I said this the walls behind me began to rattle. Startled, I turned when a picture shook from its perch to the floor and the frame shattered. There was no way I was getting through the night without being in super trouble.

"He's here. Tamara, it's Him."

When I returned my attention to my little brother I was awestruck. The carvings he made in the bed were glowing, alternating between red and green. As though christmas lights had been fitted into the wood itself. My breath caught in my chest, and I staggered backwards. I hit the dresser, realizing Elijah needed to move away from the bed at once.

"Come here!" I shouted. Everything in the room shook now. Brilliant light shone from the carvings in the bed, illuminating the surroundings in a sick holiday glow.

Elijah remained on his bed smiling. I rushed forward and grabbed him. He fought to stay where he was, but being the larger and more developed of the two of us I snatched him away with ease. Good thing I did, because the bed began to break apart. Solid wooden beams cracked and snapped, shredding the mattresses. The bed did not crumble into a heap on the floor, but instead reshaped itself. Were I not standing there watching it, I wouldn't have believed any of it. I held onto Elijah as tight as I could, staring speechless at what the bed had become. A fireplace. The carvings my brother made, still glowing, now decorated the mantle.

With all the noise being made, I wondered why our parents had not come to check on us. Then I wondered why I hadn't gone to get them yet. Still holding onto Elijah, I turned to head for the door. He wriggled free of my grasp and returned to the fireplace.

"What are you doing? We need mom and dad." I struggled to keep the worry out of my voice.

A rumble from above grew to crashing thuds. I jerked my head from side to side wondering if the walls were falling down. I thought for sure the room was caving in on us. There were at least eight of those heavy noises before one final thump, louder and more harsh than the previous ones, rocked the room so hard I ducked down and covered my head, certain the ceiling was about to give way. The din died away, and in the silence, heavy footsteps in the apartment above me.

"Tamara," Elijah called out.

I stood up, shaking, only able to focus on one thing, "Mom," I yelled. "Dad, wake up. Come here, something's wrong." It wasn't clear then, but I would soon discover why neither of them could hear me.

"Tamara," Elijah stomped his foot on the floor, gaining my attention.

"What?" I hadn't meant to snap at him, but my nerves were frazzled. Anything other than my parent's voices would have set me off then.

"Santa's here."

When I turned to leave the room, the exit was blocked by the biggest christmas tree I'd ever seen. Shimmering with lights and candy canes and garland, and tinsel, its frosty pine scent filled the room. The doorway that had been there forever every night before this, was gone. I darted to my brother's side. He wore a smile filled with wonder. His eyes never strayed from the fireplace. "Elijah, I don't know what's going on here, but we need get out of here."

The footsteps stopped above the spot where the bunkbed used to be. A cold breeze blew into the room. I wrapped my arms around my little brother, who seemed to be glued in place. That wondrous look never left his eyes, even as a clump of snow fell, exploding powdery white onto the floor of the firebox, and then the foot came into view. One black booted foot, then another descended. Legs swathed in bright red pants followed. A soft sound, fabric rubbing against a hard surface, as a body shimmied its way down the remainder of the chimney, into the fireplace. A moment later, he stepped into the room. An old fat man with the whitest beard ever. I watched in dread as he wrestled a large cloth sack out of the fireplace that should not have existed.

"I knew it," Elijah shouted. He leaped up and down in my arms.

The temperature in the room fell considerably. I shivered, unable to tell the difference between the cold and the sheer terror welling up from my core. Peppermint and pine assaulted my nostrils causing my eyes to water. Still, I held tight to my brother. Not wanting the mysterious man to come any closer to us than he already was.

The lights shining from the tree illuminated the man well enough to spot the trademark rosy cheeks bookending his smile. His gaze fell onto Elijah and stayed there as he removed a scroll-like object from within the red button-down overcoat he was wearing.

"Santa Claus. Oh my God, you're really here," Elijah wriggled in my embrace, trying to break free. I would not allow it. I held him so tight my muscles ached.

"Ho-ho-ho. Merry Christmas to one and all."

Elijah swooned at the sound of the man's voice. He fought even harder to free himself from my embrace. Luckily, I was more than twice his size, so his efforts were futile.

"Well," the man from the chimney unfurled the scroll and eyed it, "If it isn't little Elijah."

"He knows my name. Did you hear that? He knows me."

I would have yanked my brother away from the mysterious man's presence, but we were trapped in the bedroom. My only hope was to find some means of getting the man to leave. However, any way I thought of involved me letting go of Elijah, and my basest instinct screamed for me to continue holding him no matter what.

"You followed the instructions I gave you so well, I had to move you straight to the top of my 'Nice' list. Ho-ho. The reindeer are waiting. Are you ready to come take a tour of my workshop?"

"That's enough, goddammit," that was the first

time I had ever cursed at an adult. If you could call the strange, yule tide intruder one "You better turn around and go back to wherever the hell you came from, before I wake my dad and have him seriously fuck you up."

He ignored me, as though I wasn't even there. His focus remained on Elijah. "You're going to love it. Candy canes and eggnog for breakfast, hot chocolate with a million marshmallows. My elves can make any toy your mind can dream up. Won't you join me?" He held out a hand and the jingle bells on his sleeve chimed.

Elijah tried to raise his hand up to meet the man's, but I clamped my own down on top of his. "Stop Tamara. Let me go. I wanna go with Santa Claus."

"Elijah, there is no santa claus. He doesn't exist. Whatever is happening here can't be real." Saying those words made everything feel like some crazy dream. An idea surfaced of how to put an end to the terrible, holy night, "If we don't believe in this it'll all go away. You have to stop believing in santa."

Before getting the chance to provide a more convincing argument, the man crossed the room and grabbed me. His grip was colder than the North Pole, as he pried my arms from around my brother.

Elijah, now free, ran to the fireplace, "C'mon Santa, let's go."

"No, Elijah don't."

The man's grip was much stronger than my

own. I was helpless, freezing in his grasp. He'd still not even acknowledged me, other than pulling me away from my brother.

"Ah-ah, the chimney only works if you say the magic words."

"He's not real," I shrieked. Tears streamed down my face, realizing how utterly powerless I was. "You have to stop believing in him. Please, Elijah…please."

"Merry Christmas to one and all," Elijah cheerily recited the words, "and to all, a good night."

They were the last words I ever heard him say. My brother stepped into the fireplace and was spirited away. Leaving me behind with the imposter santa who still held fast to my arms.

"Ho-ho-ho, away we go," he said.

He turned to face me and everything was different. Gone were the twinkling eyes and rosy cheeks. His beard was an awful shade of gray, matted and unkempt. The minty aroma that trailed him down the chimney went sour. He smiled with a mouth full of jagged, rotten teeth. Crimson spittle oozing from the corners of his mouth. "Look here you naughty little shit, Elijah is mine now. There's not a damn thing you can do about it, except go and cry to your mommy and daddy. Precocious bitch."

He let me go and I fell to the floor. Arms aching in the spots where his hands held me. I called for Elijah through my sobs, watching the man enter the fireplace and disappear in the reverse manner he'd arrived.

I awoke in my bed the next morning. Tired, covered in a thin sheen of sweat, as though I'd had one hell of a bad dream. Memories of the previous night surfaced and my heart pa-rum-pum-pum-pummed. I quickly glanced around the room. No giant tree where the door was, and the bunk bed I lay on was clearly not a fireplace. Outside, the first rays of sunlight were touching the bricks of the apartment building I lived in. It was my birthday. It was christmas.

Elijah would be getting up soon, full of energy, riding the christmas morning high. Thinking of my little brother caused my stomach to drop. I had to tell myself he was down there on the bottom bunk, still asleep. I didn't want to look, for fear any of what took place was real. My brain fought against itself, as logic tried to explain away the terrible night I'd had. Nightmare or not the time had come for me to leave the safety of my bed and wake Elijah up. As much as I didn't want to, I climbed down from the top bunk.

Mom was crazy with grief. The investigation into Elijah's disappearance went nowhere. Dad did the best he could to keep us sane. He was our rock. The pillar of strength Mom and I turned to when the situation was too overwhelming. A week later, on New Year's Day, Dad had a massive heart attack and died in our kitchen before emergency services got to us. Mom shut all the way down, after that. She was institutionalized, and I was taken away and placed in a foster home.

Life didn't get much better. In my first mandatory therapy session, I tried to tell the so-called professional what had happened to Elijah. To her credit, she was an excellent listener, but she didn't believe a single word I said. I remained silent for all the sessions that followed.

My foster parents, Mr. and Mrs. Williams, were nice enough people. My only issue with them was their absolute zeal for the church.

One Sunday, after a few months of living with them, Mrs. Williams came to my room. "Hey there Tamara. How are you feeling this morning?"

My father held his anguish back so much, the grief overcame him. I'd only gotten to visit my distraught mother twice since moving in with the Williams', and no one believed me about the rogue santa who took Elijah. I hated being treated like I was out of touch with reality, and I hated being asked how I felt. Alone. That is how I always felt. Instead of answering her, I rolled my eyes at Mrs. Williams. She took the gesture as me giving her permission to come sit beside me.

She smiled her pretty little smile, and then said some of the dumbest shit ever. "Honey, I know you've been through a lot. It's so awful. However, if you let me, I think I know something that can bring you peace. Well, not something. Someone. You should change clothes and come with us to church. Jesus is a healer, you know?"

A dam inside me burst. Maybe I was too harsh with her, but I didn't care. "A healer?" My brooding anger had been searching for some irrational place to let go, and at last found a target. "What can jesus do for me, huh? Please tell me. Because he didn't lift a finger to stop Elijah from being taken. Where was all this healing when my dad's goddamn heart was exploding? And I'm supposed to trust him, really? Was he too busy soaking up you all's adoration for his birthday to help out? Well as far as I'm concerned, he can have it. I don't need a birthday. It's just a yearly reminder of how I lost my entire family."

"I'm sorry. I was -"

"You were doing the same thing every adult has done since I made declared I don't believe in santa clause. Trying to lure me into some collective who's okay with playing make believe with the minds of its members."

By some miracle outside of christ, I made survived my childhood. Not a day passed by that I didn't acknowledge the gaping, family-sized hole in my heart. Mom recovered, somewhat. Though not enough to where she could raise and provide for a growing daughter. I was in my second year of college when a blood clot in her leg broke free and travelled along the blood vessel highway to her brain. Causing a traffic jam and ending her life.

I never graduated from college. After three years, I found a decent job which became a career. I got by as best I could. All my basic needs met, or so I thought. Love is the thing that actually works in mysterious ways. Jason and I met on the subway. I was late for work, scrambling, pushing and weaving my way through the crowd to reach the train before the doors closed. Had it not been for Jason's swift action— jamming his foot in the doorway as the two panels came together—The day would have been much shittier.

We got off the train at the same stop, even ended up walking the same direction. After a couple blocks and a nice conversation, Jason had to turn at the corner to reach his job. I continued on my way down the street wearing the rarest of smiles. He waited until we were married to reveal he'd remained on the train three stops past his job, and only ended the conversation with me after realizing how terribly late he was about to be.

I tried my best to be vulnerable with Jason. The thing about trying though, is, in the wise words of Yoda, the concept doesn't exist. In reality you either do, or you don't. When I told Jason about what happened to me as a child, he instantly remembered the news story. "I'm so sorry. That must have been a frightening experience."

"Well," I said, "I'm here today, aren't I?"

"Still, I mean, let me know if I'm overstepping my bounds, but did they ever find out what happened to your brother?"

"You saw the news. He vanished without a trace." So much for vulnerable. I didn't want him to be another in a line of people whom I'd shared my story with, only for them to not believe me. To think I made up what I saw as a means of coping with Elijah's disappearance. It would have been the worst pain to have him cast me in that light. Funny how the secrets we want to keep locked inside find ways to creep into the parts of our lives they don't belong.

We had our first and only child a week before our one year anniversary. The most beautiful baby boy I'd ever laid eyes upon. Jason wanted to name him Eli, to honor my brother's memory. I put forth no argument.

Eli was four years old when his father and I divorced.

Jason knew how much I loathed the most wonderful time of the year. He did his best to accommodate my feelings, forsaking his own. The holidays were a big deal in his family. Aunts, uncles, cousins, all his relatives would gather to celebrate being a family.

I flat out refused to participate, which left a bad taste in everyone's mouth. Ask me if I cared. I stayed home with Eli, while Jason would leave to represent us.

This was a big deal to him. Whenever he returned, he put on his best "everything is fine" smile, but the alcohol wafting off him always revealed the true story. I often wondered how much of this he could take. I'm surprised he put up with me for as long as he did.

I was putting Eli to bed when Jason walked through the door. "Sounds like daddy's back. Want me to see if he'll come tuck you in?"

"Yes please." Eli smiled. In the right light, he bore an uncanny resemblance to Elijah. The boy was smart too. I wouldn't tolerate anything less.

"Let me go get him. Be right back."

I made my way to the foyer to greet my husband but was met with an aura of drunkenness so thick, the simple act of breathing threatened to intoxicate me.

"What the hell, Jason? Was there any eggnog in that rum at all?"

"Ha ha, you know, you're funny when you want to be." His words ran together, slipping and tripping over one another.

"Dammit. I wanted you to come tuck Eli in, but you don't look like you can even make it to his room. Why don't you crash on the couch? I'll tell Eli you're not feeling well and bring you some water. It'll at least help fight against the monster hangover you're in for."

"You've got all the fucking answers, don't you?" He stumbled over and grabbed my arm a bit too tight, forcing me back and pinning me against the wall.

"I love you babe, but your shit wears me out sometimes."

I slipped out of his grasp, intent on keeping my composure, "Hey Jason, I really think you should sleep this off, okay? We can talk in the morning."

"I don't give a damn about the morning. I just spent the entire day defending you to my family. For what? I get it, Christmas isn't your jam, but can't you make an exception for Eli? He's got family dying to meet him."

"Your family is more than welcome to visit us here. I don't recall any law stating everyone has to congregate at your mom's house."

"Tamara, you," Jason stumbled into the living room and slumped down onto the couch, "you shut the fuck up about my mom. Just because you come from a broken household doesn't mean you have to break this one up."

He slipped into a deep sleep while I stood there brooding. My blood boiled over within me. I kept telling myself he was drunk and didn't know what he was saying. Still, the words cut me deep enough to where I completely avoided him the following day.

On Monday Jason, still exiled to the couch, went about his morning routine as quiet as possible. When he left for work I was relieved. I got out of bed and made my way to Eli's room to give him a good morning hug and assure him that breakfast was on the way. To my surprise, my son was sitting in front of his TV holding a video game controller in his hand and playing games on a brand new game console.

"What is this?" I asked.

Eli kept his focus on the screen, immersed in whatever world the device created. "It's my game."

"I see that, Eli. Where did it come from?"

"Dad gave it to me. He told me I deserved it, for being such a good boy." He paused the game and turned to face me, "Mom, Dad kept saying Santa wanted me to have this. He's not real though, just a cartoon character, right?"

His innocence reminded me of my brother, and the big sister in me took over. I smashed the console. Eli cried. I did my best to explain to him the video game was poisoned, and I would buy him another "healthy" one. Once Eli was calm, I went and packed all of Jason's clothes, along with anything he would need for an extended motel stay.

The proceedings were simple enough. Jason didn't put up a fight. Not even when I was granted the house, and custody of Eli. To be honest, he looked relieved. Maybe not over our son, but definitely over me. I felt sorry for having dragged him through my bullshit. We both agreed this was the best route. Still, I felt like he drew the short straw.

Eli was resilient and adapted to the new normal easy enough. He stayed with his father on weekends, and most holidays. I wasn't picky about Jason spending time with him. In the fall of that year, after Eli turned five, he started kindergarten.

Working from home became a lonely affair. Every trace of Jason was gone, and my little man was out for a large portion of the day. Work never filled up enough time to keep me busy. I'd receive my assignments and usually have them knocked out before lunch. I tried cleaning to keep myself busy, but there's only so much one can do before running out of things to tidy. I was putting a few of Eli's toys away one day, when my attention was drawn to the video game console I'd replaced. I pressed the power button, telling myself I wanted to be sure he was playing games appropriate for his age. The truth is, I enjoyed it. The fighting games in particular. Once I got a feel for the controls I found myself going online and annihilating every opponent I was matched with. Other users would log off before the match ended. There were some who sent me angry messages, and a few who reported me for hacking. I didn't care. I was good, and their fragile egos couldn't handle it. No longer was I suffering from loneliness. I began finding ways to complete my work even faster, so I could head into Eli's room and beat up on strangers over the internet.

One day I went into Eli's room, ready to fire up the game and spend the day talking shit to the TV screen, when I saw he hadn't made his bed. Kids forget things like that all the time. No big deal. I decided to help him out and. I straightened out the sheet and blanket, tucking the edges beneath the mattress. Then I picked up the pillow for a quick fluff. As I did this, two pieces of paper fell out of the pillowcase. Not paper, cardstock. I recognized at once the off-white color and the minty aroma when I picked them up. Turning the first one over sent a chill through me so cold I expected to find polar bears wandering around the room. The letter was like the one Elijah showed me, all those years ago. I looked at the second sheet and saw those same terrible symbols my little brother carved into our bed on that dreadful night.

It was the last day of school before the winter break. Christmas eve was the following day. When the school bus dropped Eli off in the afternoon, I was in my car waiting for him. I didn't allow him to set one foot inside the house. Once he was situated in the car, we sped off towards his father's house. He was still at work when we arrived, so Eli and I sat in the car waiting. I let him go on and on about his day, all the while formulating a plan to rid my family of this yule tide menace for good.

After some time, Jason arrived. He stepped out of his car shocked to find me there with Eli.

"Eli, honey, do me a favor?"

"Sure mommy. What is it?"

"I know you're excited to be here with daddy,

but I need a few minutes to talk to him. You stay here and keep warm, okay?"

"Mmm-hmm."

When the few minutes became much longer, Jason suggested we all go inside where we could be warm, and Eli could occupy himself with the toys in his room. Sitting in Jason's festively decorated living room I finally told him everything. Every detail of what really happened to my brother, and why he was never found. There were tears in Jason's eyes when I finished, and I was a blubbering mess. He took me in his arms and I did not resist.

"I believe you," he whispered.

All of the icy walls built up to defend myself against anymore pain melted away. Those three words meant more to me than anything. I couldn't revel in the moment for too long, however. Through the sobs, I did my best to tell Jason about the letters I found in Eli's room.

"Wait," he grabbed my shoulders and pushed me to arm's distance, "like the same ones Elijah showed you?"

I nodded, "Same penmanship and all."

"What do we do?" Jason wiped at his eyes, "Santa's not taking my son away."

"That's why he's here. I think he'll be safe here. Would you mind keeping him for a while?"

"Tamara, you don't even have to ask. But what

about you? Are you going back to the house? Because," he drew his lips tight as he exhaled, "you're welcomed to stay here too. I don't want anything to happen to either of you."

"Thanks for offering, Jason," I made a spectacle of glancing around the room. My gaze lingering longer on all of the christmas decorations, "Besides, I'd only be a ball of anxiety with the way you've decorated."

"I can take everything down. No worries."

"That's kind of you, but this thing that took my brother, there were a series of steps performed before it was able to show up. Eli won't be there to do the little ritual, so I think I'll be fine." I stood up. After placing a kiss on Jason's forehead. I knew what needed to be done. I turned to leave. "Thank you. You don't know how much I appreciate being able to speak openly about this, at last." I took a step towards the door, but Jason took hold of my hand. I turned, facing him once more.

"Tamara, you just went from crying your eyes out with worry, to the most eerie calm I've ever seen in you. You're not planning on doing something stupid, are you?"

"Of course not," I lied.

"Good, because our son needs you. Please keep that in mind."

"I'll see you both on the twenty-sixth." I let go of his hand and walked away.

By the night of christmas eve, everything I

needed was in place. On the way home from Jason's I stopped at the gas station to pick up the one thing I absolutely needed. I spent most of the day hanging tinsel, and decorative balls, and little plastic munchkins and reindeer. Probably not necessary, but I didn't want to take any chances. The house had to look and feel like christmas, otherwise my holly jolly friend might grow suspicious of my plan.

In Eli's room, exhausted, I passed out. I awoke to a silent night. Moonlight shined through the window bathing the room in a pale blue hue. I checked the time and realized I was behind schedule. I grabbed my gas station purchases and sat them next to Eli's bed. Then I knelt down at the bedside, holding a flathead screwdriver in my hand, and began carving the symbols from the letter into the wood.

I finished right at the stroke of midnight. Hand cramping from scrawling the sigils. How had Elijah done this so easily? As I wondered this, the walls of the room began to tremble. A low rumbling that grew more intense, and then stopped at once. I backed away from the bed with little time to spare. The wood frame began to break apart, shredding the mattress that lay atop. I watched with the same fascination I'd previously held, as the bed reformed itself into a fireplace. The symbols I carved glowing green and red. Looking to my right, past the TV stand where the gaming console sat, I saw the doorway was gone. In its place, a giant Douglas Fir, too large for the room. Its crown was bent at a severe angle where the trunk met the ceiling. A wave of snowy pine scent filled the room.

I was startled as a loud thump clattered onto the roof. Everything was going according to plan. I counted them off, naming each one as they landed; Dasher, Prancer, Dancer, Vixen, Donner, Blitzen, Comet, Cupid, and the whipping boy of the group, Rudolf. Then came the final thump. The loud crash of the sleigh upon my rooftop.

I tensed when I heard the footsteps making their way to the chimney above the newly formed fireplace. Soon he and I would be face to face. What happened after was up to fate. Only one of us was leaving this house though.

The room grew colder by the second. The one thing I forgot was to bring a jacket. No matter. My blood ran hot enough to overcome the surrounding temperature.

A snowball dropped down into the fireplace, exploding on the floor in a bursting bomb pattern. Next, a shiny patent leather boot appeared, then another. I watched him shimmy down the chimney into the room. He stepped forward, a look of confusion across the merry features of his face.

"Ho, ho, ho," he laughed heartily, "you're not Eli."

"What did you do with my brother?" I was not

there to play any games. I wanted answers.

Santa leaned in closer. The glimmer of recognition flashed in his eyes. "The precocious bitch. My, how you have grown."

"Tell me where my brother is?"

"Elijah? Oh, he was a good little boy. You know, the believers, the true believers taste the sweetest. Why, that boy was digested, shit out, and flushed down the commode before I was even done with my rounds that night."

Tears welled up in my eyes and I willed them away. I hoped my reaching for the crowbar on the dresser by my side was imperceptible.

"Eli's been letting Daddy fill his head up with stories about how great I am. He's not only on my nice list, he's claimed the top spot. The knowledge that he is your boy will make him much sweeter. Where is the boy, anyway?"

I moved swiftly, swinging the crowbar in an arc connecting with santa's face below his left eye.

His hands shot up in defense at once. The christmas lights in the room highlighted the red and white blood spilling from the wound opened up, from the blow. "Your insolence will not be tolerated." Gone was the classic old saint nick visage. Here now was his true form. A dirty old man who looked sick and reeked of decay. "If the little shit's not here, he must be with Jason. Once I have him, I'm coming back here to eat him right in front of you."

I swung the crowbar again, but he caught it in the dingey mitten of his hand. He yanked hard and pulled me forward, while simultaneously thrusting his fist into my face. He may have been wearing mittens, but the blow still felt like being hit with a tree stump. The crowbar fell from my hand and clattered to the floor. Pain, blood erupted from my nose, which was for sure broken. Spots danced around my vision, but I still saw him turning towards the fireplace to leave. There was no time to waste. I bent down to grab the crowbar and ended up stumbling over. The moment I secured the stiff iron bar in my grasp, santa's boot came down on top of my hand, shattering my bones like a fallen christmas ornament. Too much adrenaline in my system to acknowledge the pain, I took the crowbar in my opposite hand. Santa's heavy footfalls stomped their way back through the room, ready to leave. I lurched forward, reaching out with the iron bar, and caught the hook around one leg. I pulled back and santa faceplanted.

Finding my legs, I got up before he could recover and moved directly between santa and the fireplace, which I surmised was his only means of escape.

"Oh, ho, ho, ho, that Eli," he took his time, still lying on the floor as he spoke, "I'm gonna eat him slowly. I'll peel his skin off bit by bit, and if the brat passes out from the pain, I'll pour vinegar on his wounds to wake him up. He'll suffer for an eternity, while you watch, helpless."

I brought the iron down on the back of his head. Not enough to knock him out, santa was dazed. Realizing I might not have much more time, I let the crowbar go—on my terms—and grabbed the gas can I placed near the former bed. I drenched the old fat man and the entire room. The smell overcame every other in the room.

"I don't believe in you," I shouted, "I don't believe in you." Then I reached into my pocket, pulled out a wind resistant Zippo lighter, and thumbed the flint.

For a moment, upon waking, I was unsure where I was. Not that I'd ever been in one, but I eventually realized I was in an ambulance. Later, in the hospital, my suspicion was confirmed, my nose was broken, and so was my hand, along with a descent amount of smoke inhalation. The doctor said my nose would heal, but my hand was going to be an issue. Almost every bone was shattered. I'd need a few surgeries, along with pins, screws, external braces, and the entire Nutcracker troop to fix the damage.

Not long after receiving the news about my injuries, the fire chief came in to speak with me. He introduced himself, and then got straight to the point. "Ma'am, first and foremost I'd like to express my deepest sympathies for what you've been through.

You're alive and breathing right now, and that's what matters. I hate to have to inform you of this at such a time, but unfortunately your house is not salvageable. My men did everything they could to fight the blaze and put it out, but the fire was too widespread and too intense. Initial reports show the fire originated at your Christmas tree. We suspect low quality decorations acted as the accelerant. The good news is this should all be covered by your insurance. I'm going to leave my card here on the table. If they give you any push back on the hefty payout you should be getting, you tell 'em call me. I'll vouch for you. Now, you go ahead and focus on getting better." He turned to leave, stopped, and faced me once more. "One other thing, ma'am. Something odd we noticed. One in one of the rooms, a child's room I believe, we found an exceptionally large pile of burned sugar. In your next place, I would advise against keeping things like that lying around. If your child was home and trying to evacuate, sugar gets so hot, touching the stuff inadvertently, in a panic say, could peel your skin right off."

As he was leaving, Jason and Eli entered. Eli ran to my bedside and jumped on me, hugging me tight. The cold of his face permeated the hospital gown. So too did the warm tears, when they began to flow.

"Glad to see you're okay," Jason said.

I could have chewed his head off for what he'd almost led Eli to, but he didn't know, and that was on me. The thing that had tormented my thoughts for so long was no more. I would not have felt such relief if Jason hadn't gone and taught Eli about that stupid holiday. I couldn't blame him for not knowing what he was doing.

Eli lifted his head to talk to me, "I thought you were going to die. Daddy said the house caught fire, and I thought you burned up. But you didn't."

"No baby, I didn't."

"It's a miracle. And do you know what today is?"

I cringed inwardly. I still didn't like Christmas. My mind was already preparing itself for the conversation we would need to have in order to explain to Eli why we should not glorify the day. With a sigh I said, "Yes Eli, I know. Today is-"

"Happy Birthday Mommy!"

Ink Blot

Sitting in the room, my initial thoughts were of soup. Tomato, and pea to be specific. They were the first colors that assaulted my eyes upon entering the space. Pea soup being the chosen color of the upper half of the surrounding walls. While the lower was the pinkish, light red of the kind of tomato soup I'd only ever seen old people eat, as a kid. The kind that had a good measure of milk or cream mixed into it. It was, in my sleep deprived state, quite nauseating.

I was told that Dr. Wallace would be in shortly to do my intake evaluation. Perhaps a side effect of not sleeping was the loss of an accurate sense of time. I had no idea how long I'd sat there waiting. Long enough for my ass to go numb, and my legs to get all tingly, but none of that can be translated into a chronological value. There was a TV mounted on the wall. It sat across from me, behind where I figured Dr. Wallace would sit. A dark rectangle floating atop the sea of green and pink like a rancid chunk of burnt ham. It didn't help with figuring out the time any either, seeing as how the damn thing didn't work.

At last, Dr. Wallace entered the room. The only person to do so since being led into the space. I heard the distinct click of a lock being disengaged, before he entered. Did they lock me in? What for? I checked in voluntarily. To my knowledge, that meant that I could leave of my own volition, if I wanted to. I didn't want to though. I was tired, and longing for a night of uninterrupted rest.

"And how are we today, Mr.," Dr. Wallace took a brief look at the file he held before he spoke again, "Thompson?"

I raised my head to look him over. If there was a machine that die-cut, and churned out white, male psychiatrists every few years, I'm certain he would've been one of its products. The man hit every checkbox I could think of, in terms of ordinary looks. His glasses, straight brown hair, middle aged and slightly wrinkled face suggested years of experience. If he couldn't help, I would surely die from lack of sleep.

"I'm tired," I replied, unintentionally yawning for emphasis. He'd asked a stupid question. One look at the bags beneath my eyes, large enough that I'd have to check them before being allowed to board any flight, and that would've been obvious.

"Right." He sat down in the chair opposite me. "So, I'm here to do an evaluation to see exactly what kind of help you need, and if we might be able to treat you. I'm going to start by asking some questions. Just relax, and be as truthful as you can, okay?"

"No problem."

The man opened the folder and thumbed through the few pages it contained. As he did this, I glanced around the room once more. A distinct unease began to wriggle beneath my skin. Something about the space was off. I noticed a white border that separated the two soup colors on the walls. One would expect a professional painter to work with clean lines, even when working with such putrid colors. The surrounding walls, however, ran over the top and bottom of the center border in so many spots. It was as though a hyperactive child, unable to color in the lines, had been in charge of painting.

"Tell me your name," Dr. Wallace said.

"My name is Matthew Thompson."

"Perfect. We're off to a great start. Matthew, uh, do you mind if I call you Matthew? Formality tends to lend a bit of comfort to these evaluations."

"Matthew's fine, or just Matt."

"Okay Matt, can you tell me your age?"

I jumped through all the hoops that the doctor wanted me to. Reciting my age, address, marital status, and general health. Not once removing my gaze from the shoddy paint job. This was a hospital, after all. Everything from the staff to the furniture was supposed to be held to the highest standard.

"Hey, Matt? You still with me?"

I was pulled out of my thoughts by Dr. Wallace's waving hand, "Huh, what? Sorry. Guess I kinda spaced out for a sec."

"I asked what's the reason for your visit?"

"The reason?" I scoffed. "Doc, to be frank, I can't fucking sleep. The mere thought of closing my eyes fills me with so much terror that I'm scared to even blink. Every night for the past few months, I've gone to bed hoping for a few hours of peace, only to awaken minutes later soaked in sweat, shaking enough to register on the Richter scale, and screaming until my throat is raw. Sleeping pills are enough to get my eyes closed, but not even ten minutes later, I'm up again scared out of my mind."

"I see. Well fortunately Matt, despite your night terrors, you seem to be in the right state of mind to address and resolve this issue. Tell me about what sorts of stress you've been experiencing. More times than not, interrupted sleep is the result of the brain trying to cope with life's many pressures."

"I'm not stressed out, Doc. Before I couldn't sleep, I enjoyed my life. Now it's like…" I trailed off, briefly remembering that I was in a mental hospital. Not wanting to give any reason for this to turn into an involuntary stay.

"Like what, Matthew?"

"Shit." I'd already given the doctor too much. My mind was buzzing with thoughts of how this could all go wrong. Paranoia maybe, but before the nightmares I lived a good life. I wanted to get back to it as quickly as possible, not become a resident of this facility. I tried to be as cautious with my next words as possible. "Okay, don't hold this against me. I realize that it's probably just the lack of sleep causing me to think this way, but I swear it feels like something is coming for me. Crazy, I know."

"We don't like to use that word here. Crazy is something that is simply misunderstood. My staff and I do what we can to try and understand and determine the root cause with every patient that walks through the doors. You're in good hands, Matt. Now, can you elaborate on this feeling?"

His attempt to sneak past my defenses was working. I began to feel more comfortable. At least, until I noticed the base board that ran along the perimeter of the room. Notice may be too simple a word. The thing was near impossible to miss. A thin strip of chocolate brown rubber, twice, maybe even three times as tall as a normal base board. What the hell was with this room?

"Doc," my voice was unsteady, "I don't

remember anything about the nightmares. Only the panic I wake up in. I just want to rest."

"Matt, I'd like to try something with you. You've no doubt heard of a Rorschach test. The cards with the ink blots and such." As he spoke, Dr. Wallace produced a stack of cards, setting them on top of the folder before him. "I hold up a card, and you tell me what you see. Simple enough, right? It's fallen more into the realm of pseudoscience these days, but I find it useful in establishing a baseline of how your thought process works. From there, we might be able to weed out some stressors or trauma rooted in your subconscious mind. In other words, once we find the cause, we can establish a treatment and get you some much needed rest."

His words took my mind off the strange surroundings. I didn't care if he was going to perform an old Santeria sleep spell. If it was going to stop this constant gnawing away of my mind and bring me peace, I was on board. "Okay. Yes. No problem at all."

"Great. Let's begin, then."

Dr. Wallace held up the first card and I shuddered. Every step forward seemed to bring me two steps backward. I know these things are supposed to be random, but I swear the card looked like a face. A face that I recognized, but from where? I took a few moments to study the splotches of inky blackness. It had demon-like features, horns and such. Definitely not anyone I knew in my personal life. Video games, TV, movies? Nope. A bucket of ice spilled down my back. I knew where I'd seen that wretched visage. The doctor said that the test might bring up something from my subconscious. I didn't expect it to work right away on the very first card. The scowling, demonic face that I was presented with had been the same one I'd seen every night, over the last three months, before waking from the most terrible nightmares. I sat frozen in my seat.

"Is anything wrong?" He asked.

I shook my head. My heart began to race.

Dr. Wallace discarded the first picture and picked up another. My eyes widened. It was that face again. Less of a scowl, and a more neutral expression this time.

I turned away from the picture the doctor held, in pure disbelief that the nightmare had followed me into the waking world. It was ridiculous, I know. Could I really be that screwed up? My eyes settled on that white border again. Drifting back and forth across the shitty job that the painter had done. Anxiety having a field day with my lack of sleep.

"Can you," I began, in a shaky voice, "maybe, hold up the next one?"

"Certainly, Mr. Thompson. Are you ready to tell me what you see?"

I heard him draw another card from the pile.

Slowly, I turned to face him again. Something was wrong. Before looking at the card, my gaze trailed along the border I'd been concentrating on. In a typical setting, it would span the circumference of the room. Its continuity only broken at the entrance to the room. That was the problem though. When the two sides reached the door they were drastically mismatched. One side noticeably higher than the other, so that if the door was removed and the wall continued, the two opposite ends of the lines would not meet at all. I turned around, taking in the entire mid-line to see where it was off kilter, but could not find anything. It all looked level, yet clearly was not. In fact, the entire room was like that. Everything had seemed fine at first, but the more I focused on and analyzed things, the more skewed I realized they were.

My entire body tensed. I gripped the arms of the chair so tight that my knuckles ached. When I turned to face the card Dr. Wallace held, as expected, the face was there again. A broadening smile.

"What do you see, Matthew?"

There is no doubt that the professional who sat before me could see how frazzled I was. It was his job to do so. Nevertheless, I tried my best to behave as though I had no cares at all. People see all sorts of things in Rorschach tests, but never the same thing over and over, right?

"You are clearly disturbed by what you've seen

so far. All I'm asking is that you verbalize those feelings and help me to understand you. Let's try the next card."

He held up another ink blot. I tried to look away, but the room was all wrong. I couldn't unsee the glaring flaws, no matter where I looked. I had no choice but to settle on the picture Dr. Wallace was holding. There, on the card, was that nightmare face. A huge grin spread across the entire lower portion of its face.

"It's..." Warm tears filled my eyes, as I sat trembling.

"Yes, Mr. Thompson, what is it?" He sat forward in his seat. "What do you see?"

"It's mocking me. I'm trying to get it out of my head, and it knows it won't work."

"What is mocking you?"

"It's him, Doc," I yelled. "Every time you pull a new card, he's there. Laughing. Watching me lose my mind. Like he knows how fucked up this room is, and that I have no choice but to focus on him." I snatched the card from Dr. Wallace and turned it to show him, "See?" I then pulled another card and, as I suspected, the demonic face was there, smiling. Lips separating to reveal its hideous, jagged teeth. "He's here," I began picking up cards one after another, "and here, and here. His smile just gets bigger and bigger, because he knows I'll never be free of him." I slammed the cards down onto the table. Face hot, and wet with tears.

Dr. Wallace sat still for a moment, shocked from

my sudden outburst, or maybe he wanted to see if I would regain my composure. With his hands clasped together, his tented forefingers tapped at his lips. His eyes brightened as though he'd received some marvelous revelation. "I think I may know what the problem is here."

"You do?" A laugh worked itself up from the center of my chest.

"First, let me make certain that I understand what's happening here. In each of these cards, you've seen the face of some forgotten entity from your nightmares, an ever-widening grin on its face, correct?"

"Yes, exactly." Sweet relief, at last. He'd not provided me any answers yet, but the mere fact of knowing that Dr. Wallace understood my plight was comforting.

"Well there's the problem," he chuckled. "It's silly, really. Seems that I've been drawing the cards from the pile in reverse order. Big oops, on my behalf, Mr. Thompson. You see, he's not smiling, or even mocking. He's actually very upset with you."

Mrs. Shelton

Camp Nashoba, a program that gave inner city, underprivileged youth the opportunity to leave the city behind for two weeks every summer and experience the wonders of the great outdoors, was in the final days of the 2006 season. After a week and a half packed with hiking, arts and crafts, swimming, and local history, the time had come for the ceremonial Goodbye Bonfire. This was where the campers would receive superficial awards, commemorative tees, gorge themselves on smores, and listen to the counselors tell spooky tales.

Shane had an alright time. He didn't consider himself the outdoorsy type, but enjoyed learning about the Choctaw and their lifestyle. He'd also become good friends with Caden. The two boys discovered they had similar interests and stuck by each other the entire time. The buddy system worked much better when you were paired with someone who was an actual buddy. The rules stated you couldn't pair up with the same person for more than two activities, but Shane and Caden managed to fly beneath the radar enough to avoid detection. That, or no one gave a damn about the rule. Either way, once the pair found out they both loved The Simpsons, and were obsessed with scary movies, they became inseparable.

The night went as planned. Dozens of naïve children riding a sugar high sat around the pillar of flame, on tiered half-logs, listening to tales of werewolves, scarecrows, and Native American revenge. Trent, the head counselor, reached the climax of his story when the bonfire collapsed, sending a collective scream through the audience. All except two campers, Caden and Shane. Both saw through the practiced stunt, and neither was impressed. As the excitement tapered off to silence, Trent grinned and readied himself to finish the story.

"Boooooooring!" Shane called out into the quiet night, before Trent began speaking again. Every camper burst into a fit of laughter.

The night was over. Trent's ego proved quite fragile, as he called for the counselors to bring the kids back to their cabins, leaving his story unfinished. Shane was ordered to stay behind and, thanks to the buddy system, so was Caden. "You must think you're real hot shit, huh?"

Staring down the man, Shane was at a loss for words. Was this supposedly responsible adult allowed to talk to him like that?

"I'm here because I love what I do. This brings me joy. For two weeks out of the year, I get to be a ray of light in your otherwise dreary lives. Let me tell you something. You're nothing but a goddamn miscreant. Worst of the worst. That's why you're here. You probably don't know your father, have no decent male role model in your life, and this is the last step before you get sent to some scared straight program. But you know what? You're still going to be in prison, or dead before your thirtieth birthday. So go ahead, revel in that laugh you got. I hope you still think about this moment when your cellmate is screwing your brains out. Those busses will come pick you up the day after tomorrow, and you'll go back to your sorry ass life, where everyone you made laugh tonight will forget about you. Including me." Trent turned to face the embers of the dying fire and began kicking sand into the pit where they lay, dousing what remained. "Know your place, you piece of shit. Now go back to your cabin. Or don't, I couldn't care less."

Caden stood at Shane's side. Though shrouded in darkness, he could tell his friend was fuming. "Hey Trent," he called out, "do you think we can get, like, a flashlight or something? It's dark, and, well, we don't exactly know our way back."

The head counselor chuckled, "Why don't you see if your butt buddy's sense of humor can light the way?"

Caden scoffed, "Fuck him, let's go, Shane." Caden grabbed his friend's arm. His bicep was taut, as though Shane was about to haul off and punch the man. He should have. Caden, however, realized the opportunity had passed. "It's over, man. He'll get his, some other time. Let it go." Caden felt the rigid muscles of Shane's ropey arm give a little. A moment later, he was leading his friend in the direction he hoped Greene Cabin lay.

A couple minutes passed, as the boys ambled aimlessly in the darkness. The crunch of the gravel pathway beneath their feet, the only indicator they were heading towards a cabin. Caden wracked his brain, trying to find the right words to console his new friend. Nothing about the way Trent spoke to Shane was right. Neither of them were in a position to anything about it though. Caden could tell his parents when he got home, but that wouldn't amount to anything, seeing as how he was not the one on the receiving end of the harsh words. He had a feeling there was some truth in what was said, and Shane knew if he told anyone what happened his words would be treated with little, or no care. As he pondered the right course of action, he heard a noise. Something disturbed the gravel on the path behind them. Caden froze, hearing the noise again.

"What was that?" Shane's cracked and breaking voice was not much more than a whisper.

"You heard it too?"

"Yeah. Probably a racoon or something, right?"

"Maybe. We should keep," Caden was cut off mid-sentence by a hand at his back. He jumped, and shrieked, and fell to the ground.

Shane was shaking as he helped his friend up. Before he could get Caden upright and ready to run, a beam of light flashed before his eyes and he was staring at the laughing face of Melody. The counselor for Redd Cabin.

"Boo!" Melody reached out a hand to help Shane with his pudgy friend, still laughing.

"What the hell is your problem?" Caden said.

"Scared the shit out of you, didn't I? Figured you two might need some help after that dressing down from Trent."

Melody was about to be a college freshman. In the daylight, whenever she was within his view, Caden couldn't help but ogle at her curves and her perfectly tanned skin, and her gorgeous eyes. "Ha ha, not funny."

"Oh come on. Don't be so pissy."

"Hey," Shane said, "can you just get us back to our cabin? All I want is to go lie down on that wack ass mattress and go to sleep."

"Nothing you said sounds like any fun." Melody shined the flashlight back and forth, between the two boys faces, giggling as they squinted.

"Cut it the fuck out, okay? If you're not gonna show us the way back, then leave us alone." Caden turned and continued walking. The adoration he'd held for Melody draining away. "Come on Shane."

"Hey, wait," Melody took a step toward the retreating duo. "Listen, I'm sorry. Alright? I'm not trying to kick you while you're down, I promise. All the counselors know Trent is a dick. He tells that same tired old tale every year. It's about time someone called him out on his bullshit."

Shane stopped walking and turned to face her again. A smile on his face. "I must have yawned about five times."

"I know, right? Tell you what, all the counselors are headed down to the lake. Andre scored some beer, Dee has weed, and Trent is absolutely clueless. I can either drop you guys off at Greene, or you can follow me down to our little celebration."

"Let's go," Caden chimed in the instant she was done talking. His interest in the older girl renewed.

"Hell yeah, I'm down," Shane added.

"Then it's settled. Follow me."

The night would become the highlight of their time at camp. Neither Caden nor Shane had ever been high before, but they handled themselves like old pros. The other counselors proved to be, at the very least, as cool as Melody. Shane was the topic of the night.

Everyone laughing at how he got under Trent's skin.

"If you ask me," Dee, the youngest of all the counselors said, "all of the stories we told were lame. Sure, the little third and fourth graders get creeped out, but for anyone more mature, the bonfire is a snooze fest."

"Exactly," Shane stood up with a handful of rocks and tossed them into the pitch black lake. "No offense to any of you. I'm not a baby though. I can handle real horror. I want to be scared."

"I agree," Caden said, his words a bit slower, more calculated than usual. "We were promised a scary time, but no one delivered. I feel lied to, betrayed even."

"I think the word you're looking for is melodramatic, Caden," Andre said. "Besides, if you're really a horror buff, it's likely you were desensitized to it all long ago. Nothing's gonna scare you, because you're already expecting it. I doubt any of us can come up with a truly terrifying tale."

"Actually," Melody chimed in, "there's a story I heard a couple years ago, when I first started working here. It scared me then, and still creeps me out today. The thing is, it's a true story."

In the darkness, Shane's head shot up. His attention now wholly belonged to Melody. "What's the story? You can't put that out there and leave us hanging."

"Well, it comes with a responsibility. None of

you were here, back then. So, you don't know what our true duties as counselors are. The man who told me the story was not coming back, and he needed someone to continue to protect the camp. Since I was the only counselor who would be returning, that duty was placed on me. You all know about the gravel pathways all over camp. They lead to the cabins, the pool, the mess hall, everywhere. We always tell the campers to stay on those paths and never wander into the woods. Everyone probably believes it's to keep you all from getting lost, and you're not completely wrong. I mean, these are pretty dense woods. If you get turned around, it might be near impossible to find your way out. The real reason though, is this camp is dangerously close to Mrs. Shelton's cabin, and may god help you if you ever set foot on her land."

"Who is Mrs. Shelton?" Caden was tuned in to every word she said. The high he was experiencing brought a level of focus he'd never felt before.

"The year was 1991. The Shelton family purchased a cabin in these woods to use as a summer getaway. It was to be an escape from the fast paced city life. A place where they could slow down and decompress for a week or two.

"Lawrence Shelton, his wife Ava, and their son Mitch arrived, ready for a most relaxing vacation. Everything was perfect, up until the third night.

"See, back then information wasn't as readily

available. Neither Lawrence, nor Ava had any way of knowing there was a manhunt underway. Two escaped convicts had found their way into the woods, spotted the cabin, and decided it would be a good place to hide until the search died down. Unfortunately for the Shelton's, these criminals were of the violent kind. They broke into the cabin intent on evicting the occupants in the most brutal way they could. Mitch was only thirteen, around your age, Shane. They say he was awake when the men entered his room. One of the guys held him down, keeping the boy from struggling, as the other drew a blade across his throat. Mitch's final breath gurgled out of his lungs before he ever knew what was happening.

"Lawrence was awakened by the sound of shuffling outside of the bedroom door. He went to check on Mitch. Make sure nothing was wrong, you know? Well, everything seemed fine as he entered the room. Mitch appeared to be sleeping soundly. Lawrence slipped and fell when he tried to walk out of the room. He got to his feet, soaked in a fluid he could not make out in the darkness. Curious why his little spill hadn't roused his son, Lawrence turned on the light and his eyes were met with the massacre that lay on the bed. A painful wail escaped him at the realization he'd slipped and was covered in Mitch's spilled blood.

"Lawrence put forth a desperate effort to get back to his bedroom and ensure his wife's safety.

Unfortunately, he was ambushed by the two convicts. In the end, he was stabbed a total of one hundred ninety-three times.

"The deaths of her husband and son were brutal as can be. If you ask me though, Ava Shelton suffered the cruelest fate of all.

"The thing about prison in this country is it's more about punishment than rehabilitation. We expect people to take responsibility for what they've done, use their time locked up to better themselves, and reenter society totally reformed. We all know that's not the case though. The two offenders who entered the cabin that night were both depraved individuals, ready to do whatever it took to ensure their own continued existence. Ava Shelton was the last obstacle in the way, before they would have the cabin to themselves.

"They found her cowering in a corner of the master bedroom. Ava pleaded for her life, and in a twisted sort of way, the two men obliged. Over the next few days Ava would be raped over and over, beaten within inches of her life, patched up, rinse, repeat. After a while, the men believed they were in the clear, that enough time had passed and the search was over, the heat was off. Neither of them wanted the added responsibility of dragging Ava around to wherever their next destination was, and so they decided to kill her. A knife to the gut is what they agreed on. She was already clinging to life from being worked over. It would be a quick end, and they could leave the place without the extra baggage.

"Ava lay on the floor of the cabin, numb to it all. Unfeeling, but still alive. Watching the two men lounge around the cabin that was supposed to be a peaceful retreat. In the three days of hell she'd endured, Ava prayed for death so many times. It seemed her prayers would continue to go unanswered. With that in mind, a new resolve began to grow within her. She couldn't hear the convicts plotting to end her misery. Too much blood had clogged her ears. The only sounds were her slow, raspy breaths. Concentrating on breathing, on continuing to live, she came back to herself. The pain of all she'd endured had only begun to set in, when the first man approached. He grabbed a handful of her hair and yanked her frail body into an upright position. The man reached back, then thrust the blade he held forward, aiming for Ava's gut. With a strength that surprised them both, Ava parried his hand away. Stunned, the man let go of her hair, and in an instant Ava darted forward, sinking her teeth into his neck. When she pulled away, she had a large chunk of the man between her teeth. Gouts of blood sprayed from the hole in the man's throat. He was dead before he hit the floor.

"The second offender arrived in time to see his comrade go down. He rushed at Ava. Before he reached her, she was able to grab the knife from the first man.

Using his momentum against him, she drove the knife into his stomach. A guttural, animal-like howl issued from the woman. She forced the man back until he was pinned against the wall. Ava removed the knife and then stabbed him again. His body slumped to the floor and Ava continued to stab the knife into him, again and again, well into the night.

"Police arrived two days later, to check the cabin off the list of places to search, in their manhunt. They say only the bravest officers could set foot inside the cabin. The scene was indescribably grisly. The two men they were searching for were both dead. One with a gaping hole in his neck, the other lay in two pieces, his upper body separated from the lower with his entire torso obliterated. Ava was found in Mitch's room. She sat atop her son's bed hardly breathing, cradling the rapidly decaying bodies of her husband and child, amidst swarming flies and larvae."

Other than the sounds of the woods, all was silent. Melody shined the flashlight around to make sure everyone was still awake and hadn't abandoned her for sleep as she recounted the story. Dee was wiping at tears steadily streaming down her face. Andre sat with his head buried in his hands. Caden stared off into the distance, slack jawed. Shane was the only one who seemed to be completely enrapt by the story.

"You guys," Melody began, "is this too much. You asked for scary. All I'm doing is relaying what I was told. I was pretty fucking terrified when I heard it."

"What's your responsibility?" Caden's voice floated up out of the darkness. "You said you had a responsibility, but I don't get what that story has to do with any of your camp counselor duties."

"Well, there's a bit more to the story. You see, Mrs. Shelton was taken from the cabin to the hospital. She spent nearly a month recovering from her injuries. The problem was her physical wounds healed, but what happened to her mentally was still fresh and raw. Ava was released and expected to return to her normal life. It was all too much though. Friends, family, coworkers, full of questions. Prying and probing to satisfy their selfish curiosities. She was a broken woman and could no longer handle the everyday stresses of life. Within a week of her release, Ava made up her mind to leave it all behind. The only place she could think to go was the secluded cabin. It was the site of her worst nightmare come true, but it was also the last place she ever experienced real happiness.

"Supposedly, to protect herself from the outside world, Ava booby trapped the land around the cabin. They say anyone who wanders onto the land suffers a terrible death, at her hands. All she wants is to be left alone. Forever.

"The cabin was erased from maps of the area. So when they built Camp Nashoba, no one was aware of what was already here. In '93, when the camp opened, two campers went missing and were never found. No one could explain it. Of course they weren't going to shut down the camp, or anything like that. Instead, they settled with the families of the kids, quietly. The proprietors of the land dug up the story of Mrs. Shelton after the season ended, and knew exactly what had happened. By the next summer, the gravel pathways were in place, and strict rules to never stray from them were announced. The story was passed down from old counselors, to new. At least one person was to remain vigilant and keep the defenseless campers from disappearing. No one knows if Ava is still even alive. But also, no one wants to find out.

"When Trent made you stay behind tonight, Shane, he was putting your life in danger. That's why I came back and followed you two. Because that is my responsibility. We don't need anyone wandering out into the woods."

Caden and Shane kept in touch with each other for a while, after their time at Camp Nashoba. Though they lived hundreds of miles apart, they both checked up on the other through social media. Though their friendship was never as close as that summer at camp, the two would still talk from time to time about new horror films, and classic episodes of The Simpsons.

After high school, Shane's time on social media tapered off. He'd been accepted to a good college, and invested his time in building a life for himself. In the years that followed, Shane would go on to graduate at the top of his class, earning himself a position in a prominent law firm. In a few years' time, Shane would be promoted to partner.

On a muggy summer evening, Shane sat in his office reviewing case files for a few of the firm's high profile clients, when his phone rang. Shane lifted the phone to his ear "Hello?"

"Congrats on your promotion."

"Um, thank you. Who is this?"

"Wow, has it been that long, old friend?"

"Okay, I don't have time for games. Bye!"

"Wait, Shane. It's me. It's Caden."

"Caden? Well goddamn. How the fuck have you been?" Shane placed the papers in his hand down on the desk and reclined in his seat.

"Still living. Not nearly as good as you, I suppose."

"Man, it's been years. What's going on? Tell me what you've been up to."

"Well, I'm calling because I'll be in the city tomorrow. I was wondering if we could meet up for a drink or two? Catch up face to face."

"Tomorrow? Yeah. Hell yeah. There's a spot right around the corner from here that makes the best Long Islands. First round's on me."

"Cool. I'll see you then," Caden paused. "Hey Shane,"

"Yeah?"

"It's uh, it's good to hear your voice."

Caden found the bar. He walked in and knew at once he was underdressed. It was all men in business suits and women sporting pleated skirts, a true pinstripes and cufflinks crowd. He eyed them all, looking for his friend. The problem was everyone looked the same, one person indistinguishable from the next. Caden felt out of place and began to think he'd made a mistake in reaching out, the day before. He turned to leave. A familiar face filled the entrance.

"Yo, no way."

"What's up, man?"

"Get the fuck over here." Shane clasped his friend's hand and pulled him into a hug. "You slimmed down, Caden. Look at you. I mean you're diesel. Come on, let's go get shit faced."

The two sat at the bar catching up on all they'd missed. Neither one had seen the other since they left camp, other than online, but the conversation picked up as though they'd been hanging out every day.

Caden swirled the brown fluid around in his rocks glass, before tilting his head back and draining it. "That camp was something else, huh? Look at us. All these years later, still friends. You know, it may not mean much coming from me, but I'm proud of you. You really made something of yourself."

"Shit man, you getting all sentimental on me?"

"Nah, maybe it's the liquor. Hey, you remember Dee, the counselor for Whyte Cabin? She brought the weed to the lake that one night?"

"Oh yeah, the lake. That was a crazy night." A quick shiver shot through Shane as he took a swig of the drink before him.

"Must have been about five years ago, we ran into each other. Dated for a little while."

"Are you serious? Damn. She was cute, but I thought you were hung up on that other chick. What was her name? Melody."

"Ha, yeah, I was. She was out of my league though. Never heard from her after that summer, anyway." Caden tipped his glass to the bartender and the man came and refilled it. Before setting the glass down, Caden took the shot.

"You know," Shane began, "in my line of work, you learn to all but master reading body language. You're tiptoeing around something. Why don't you just come out with it? No, wait, before you do, my firm doesn't do pro bono work, unless we can get some good PR out of it."

"Shit man, you got me all wrong. Yeah, something's weighing on my mind, but it's nothing like that. Something Dee turned me on to while we were together. I'm guessing you haven't kept up with news about Camp Nashoba, have you?"

"Can't say I have," this time Shane's was the

one signaling the bartender.

"The whole place was shut down a couple years ago."

"Damn, that sucks. A lot of kids will miss out on a potentially life changing experience. Hey Caden, if it's not too much to ask, why don't you tell me what you're looking for? All this build up is a serious waste of my time."

"Shane, I'm going back."

"The fuck are you talking about, man?"

"We fucked up. That night at the lake, Melody was passing down her responsibilities to us. The problem is none of us returned. That was Melody's last year as a counselor. Andre and Dee quit after that year. You and I were supposed to step in."

Shane drummed his fingers on the bar top, "Come on Caden, what are you even talking about?"

"People died, Shane. Kids. You remember that night, the story about Mrs. Shelton. It was real. If Melody wasn't doing her job back then, you and I probably wouldn't be here right now. And since we were the only people who knew about it, there was no one left to protect the camp. Two campers, two children, have disappeared every year since we left. Camp Nashoba's owners couldn't afford to pay out any more settlements, and so they had no choice but to close it all down. We were supposed to keep it from happening. Think about it. Passing on wisdom was a

Choctaw tradition. We took what we learned and kept it to ourselves, and poor, innocent children suffered the consequences. We need to go and stop Mrs. Shelton, before any other unsuspecting victims cross her path."

"Do you hear yourself, right now? That shit was a made up story. You're sitting in front of me right now, trying to guilt trip me over an urban legend we heard, fifteen years ago. You act like we were best friends or something. Newsflash Caden, we knew each other for two weeks. We were distant acquaintances at best. You call me out of the blue, after we hadn't spoken in god knows how long, expecting me to buy into some bullshit about returning to an abandoned campsite. You sound like a psychopath."

"I'm not here to argue. I'm going back to Nashoba whether you come with me or not. If Mrs. Shelton is still alive, she needs to be stopped." Caden pushed away from the bar and stood up. He dug in his pocket, produced a business card, and placed on the bar in front of Shane. "Here's my number, if you change your mind." Caden paid for his drinks and turned, ready to leave. He took a step, and then turned back to his once friend. "By the way, you should know, Trent is dead. Got all depressed and shit when the camp closed, then came home one night and caught his wife in bed with some dude. Couple days later, he offed himself. So there you go, like, closure or something."

Later that night, Shane sat in his office holding

Caden's card. He worked hard to convince himself was working on the last minute details of some upcoming case. He wanted to believe the half empty bottle of scotch sitting on his desk was a nightcap before he sent for a ride home, and did not serve as a means to numb his nerves from the news he'd received less than an hour ago. Trent was dead, and Shane didn't know how to handle it. A part of him had always known he'd been the motivation behind his own success. That those harsh words spoken to him on that night set Shane on a path leading him to become the youngest partner in the firm's history, and as long as the man was alive the prospect of running into him and shoving his success in the loathsome bastard's face was always a possibility, in the back of his mind. Now the wind had gone out of the sail. Yes, everyone died eventually, but with Trent gone he felt some vital piece of him, stolen away all those years ago, could never be returned.

Whatever it was, Caden still possessed, that was for sure. Shane had consciously distanced himself, hoping to forget Camp Nashoba. When he showed up tonight, the things he'd worked so hard to bury clawed its way back to the surface. He was left feeling as he had when he was thirteen. An outcast. A poor little kid with no direction, in a camp full of strangers because the adults in his life were more than happy to get rid of him for a couple weeks. Only, in his time away, he met someone who helped him cope with, even forget about life at home. Now, that someone was reaching out to him, and Shane turned his back. Did it matter if the story was true? He'd never believed Mrs. Shelton was real, but was it a big deal if Caden did? The phone was in his hand and the number on the business card, Caden's Automotive Service, dialed without a second thought.

The line rang, and Shane considered ending the call. Before he could, Caden's voice filled the receiver.

"We leave tomorrow night."

They arrived in the afternoon, following a day of arguing over what gear was necessary and what wasn't. Caden insisted on bringing the bare minimum, in hopes they could scrounge the campsite for items. Shane, on the other hand, wanted to be better prepared and pack for every possible scenario. Though they each had different reasons, both men agreed the trip would not last longer than one night, and so they reached a compromise, packing a few of Caden's necessities, along with some of Shane's provisions.

Camp Nashoba looked nothing like they remembered. The gravel paths that once guided campers to everything the retreat had to offer had been reclaimed by nature, overgrown with grass, and weeds. The cabins fell into a state of disrepair. Window panes meant to maintain the balance between the outside world and the cozy interior were shattered, vines creeping into the spaces. The old bonfire pit was a grassy depression. The rows of half logs that provided seating, no longer visible.

Caden and Shane stood near the flagpole, at the center of the camp, staging their gear. They placed their packs on the ground and began removing everything they would need for the upcoming hike.

"Do you still want to rummage through the camp, see if we can find anything worth scavenging?" Shane asked.

"I don't think it would hurt to. I'm wondering if we might come across some old maps that still have Mrs. Shelton's place on them. That would significantly shorten this trip."

"So, I've been thinking. What's the plan as far as that, Caden?"

"What do you mean?"

"I mean the endgame. Mrs. Shelton is definitely a myth, but what are you going to do if we find something or someone else out here?"

Caden kneeled down and reached into his backpack. When he removed his hand, he was holding a revolver. "I'm all set to call the authorities, but Shane, we might need to take matters into our own hands."

"What the shit? I came here for you. Because you were losing your mind, and as a friend, I figured a little trip down memory lane would prove cathartic. What happens when nighttime comes, and you can't see? Caden, if you shoot me because it's dark and you're disoriented, I'm gonna fuck you up."

"I'm not gonna shoot you, and Mrs. Shelton is real. Dee studied geology when she was in school. She showed me how the land survey of this area changes every so often. They want to keep the place hidden, even if it's to the children's detriment. I don't know why the onus fell on the counselors to keep everyone safe. Doesn't matter anymore. We are here to redeem ourselves and get justice for those who we should have protected. Like I said, I'm cool with calling the cops once we find the place, but if worse comes to worse, I'm also fine with plugging a sixty-something-year-old woman full of holes."

"And what happens when we don't find anything at all?"

Caden punched his backpack, before rising to his feet, "Not even a consideration, Shane. You'll see."

The two set out east. They planned to circle the camp, widening the loop with each completion, until they found Mrs. Shelton's cabin. Caden made a point of concealing the gun and keeping the sat phone in plain view to ease his friend's mind. They walked for miles, finally stopping for a break as the sun began to set.

In the fading light, Caden removed the headlamp from his hip pouch. He fitted the light in place on his head, clicking the device on and off to ensure it worked. He looked over to where Shane was. His friend stood propped against a tree, taking a drink of water. Caden was about to tell Shane that nightfall was approaching, and he should test his headlamp as well, when he noticed movement in the tree above the man's head. Caden spotted the snake slithering down the trunk toward Shane. Reacting as fast as he could, Caden leaped forward and barreled into his friend, pushing him away from the tree before the snake could strike.

Shane was rocked by the unsuspected blow. He stumbled, dropping his canteen onto the underbrush. Furious, Shane regained his footing. A few yards away, Caden was rising up from the ground. Shane, though smaller in stature than Caden, took a step forward, ready to tackle his friend to the ground and throttle him. A loud metallic snap stopped Shane before he could build up any forward momentum. A moment later, the pain set it. Shane turned his head to the sky and let out a terrible cry of pain.

As Caden was righting himself, after shoving his friend out of the way of the black snake that blended near perfectly with the tree bark, he flinched at the sound of Shane's cry. Pivoting towards the noise, he saw Shane fall to the ground clawing at one of his legs. Nothing seemed wrong at first. Then Caden's eyes took in the entire limb and saw the lower portion covered in blood. A rusted bear trap biting into the leg, mid-shin.

"Shit, shit. What the hell, man?" Caden rushed to Shane's side, grabbing at the metal device in a desperate attempt to open the trap. Every touch brought about another agonizing scream from Shane.

Through the pain, Shane pushed Caden away. With the man no longer exerting brute force, he found himself able to gather himself. "You," the word was a grunt that spilled out between tightened lips, "you can't open it that way." Shane breathed rapidly as he spoke. "You have to push down on the springs."

"What fucking springs? I don't see any springs."

"The sides, Caden. I'm going to put my foot as flat on the ground as I can. Step on the sides of the trap and I should be able to open it." Shane maneuvered his leg to a near standing position, wincing in pain from the effort. "Okay, do it."

Caden stood on top of the springs flanking the device. At first, they did not move. Caden bounced on them a few times and finally they yielded to his weight.

Working as fast as he could, Shane separated the serrated jaws and freed his leg. He tried to stumble away but fell to the ground the moment he tried to put any weight on the leg.

Caden hopped off the trap and the jaws snapped shut again. He then rushed over to help Shane. The lower portion of his pants leg was already soaked with blood. "It's over, man," Caden said. "We can't continue like this. You need first aid, bad. We gotta head back."

The pain eased a bit after freeing himself, and Shane regained more of his composure. "The fuck did you shove me for?"

"A snake. There was a huge black snake in the

tree, right above your head. I swear. Looked like a King Cobra or some shit."

"King Cobras don't live in these woods, Caden. Let alone, this country. You know that. We have an even bigger problem though. That wasn't an ordinary bear trap."

"I know what I saw, and since when are you the bear trap expert?"

"This might come as a surprise to you, but I read. A lot. It's one of the many ways in which I've learned things. That trap was modified. It's not supposed to have teeth. That's cartoon shit. It was a booby trap. This was meant as a warning."

"Oh, goddamn. You're saying…"

"What I'm saying, the only thing I'm saying is someone set it to keep someone else away from something. I got some bad news too, I can't make it back to camp on this leg. In fact, the way I'm bleeding, I'll be in shock pretty soon."

Caden paced back and forth as the sun dipped further down below the horizon. "Look, I'm sorry, Shane. In my mind, this was all so easy. We ride up here, find Mrs. Shelton's cabin, finish her and then go home. I didn't think we'd be in any actual danger. Like we stumbled into the next SAW movie, or something."

"You're overreacting, Caden. An enhanced bear trap is hardly evidence of a psychotic recluse. What we need to do is find whatever shelter we can, and get my leg as squared away as possible. Call for help on the sat phone. Let them know it's a medical emergency, and they need to send someone out ASAP. Cooler heads have to prevail here. Can't lose our wits. Not yet."

"The phone, that's right. I forgot all about it." Caden reached down to where the Sat phone was clipped and found nothing. He checked the opposite side in hopes the phone migrated with all the movement. It had indeed migrated, right off his belt. The trouble was whenever that happened, Caden was completely unaware. "Oh fuck."

"What?"

"The phone's gone. I don't know what happened, but it's not here. You take precedence right now. Once you're somewhere safe and your injury is tended to, I can come back out here and retrace my steps. It can't be far away. I swear, I just had it."

"You're not gonna find it," Shane grew wearier with each passing moment. "Thick as this underbrush is, coupled with the setting sun, it's gone. At least for now. Best bet is to keep searching for the woods and hope we pick up a trail leading to a ranger station. But first, we gotta stop this bleeding."

"Okay, okay, yeah. Um, let's see. Oh, I have a lighter. I can heat up my knife and use it to cauterize the wounds."

"No. That'll leave me open to all sorts of infection. Plus it'll hurt like a motherfucker. A tourniquet is the best option. That's gonna hurt too, but it should do until we can find help."

With supplies from the first aid kit he packed, Caden was able to craft a tourniquet for Shane. He helped his friend to his feet, acting as a crutch for the damaged leg.

Moving through the woods was slow. Not only did Shane's injury hamper their progress, but the two men were constantly looking around, searching for more traps. They came across tripwires, snares and pits to navigate around. Shane took note of every one of them. Stumbling onto the bear trap by itself was odd, but to see the woods littered with so many of these other impedances had to be more than a coincidence. The question was why? No, even with all he'd seen, Shane didn't believe a woman out in the trees somewhere snatching children away from the nearby--former--camp. However, judging from the traps they'd found, someone at some point did not want to be bothered. That much was clear.

As they ambled along the throbbing from his leg grew more faint. Not a good sign. Shane broke out in a cold sweat and his vision grew as dim as the sky after the sun had set. Each breath became a chore, and all at once remaining conscious was no longer an option.

Caden felt his friend go slack. He had to move quick to keep Shane from falling down. "Shane, you good?" He guided his body to the ground. "Oh damn, wake up man. Come on, don't do this, not now."

"It's," A haze clouded his thoughts, snatching away any fight in him, "it's the snake. The shadow."

"No man, the snake didn't get you. Remember, I pushed you out of the way."

"If she's out here, it's the shadow."

"I don't know what you're saying, Shane, but you need to keep talking." Caden shook Shane's shoulders, and gave a few light taps across his cheek.

"Makes sense. I should've seen it."

"What is that, some movie? What's the name?" No answer. "Wake up," Caden screamed, tears starting to well up in his eyes. "Help. Somebody help," he yelled into the woods.

A shriek, harsh and angry, answered Caden's call.

Chills ran through him. His flesh, covered with goosebumps in the warm night time air. "Shane, wake up. We gotta go. This was a mistake, a huge mistake." Caden tried his best to rouse Shane, but shock set in and any thoughts of the two of them hobbling out of the woods before morning seemed to be disappearing fast. Another cry from somewhere in the trees made Caden cringe. This was no time to be scared though. Caden decided he would get the both of them to safety no matter what. He kneeled next to Shane and maneuvered him into position, prepping the man to be slung over his shoulders. Once done, Caden sat him up, using the momentum to stand holding his friend in a fireman's carry. One arm held atop Shane's body for balance, the other holding the flashlight. Caden rushed forward, not stopping to orient himself, only hoping he was headed back to Camp Nashoba.

The flashlight beam bounced along ahead of him in an erratic pattern, unable to focus thanks to the man slung across his back. Caden tripped a few times but did not go down, catching his footing and righting himself quickly. He didn't want to drop his friend, or end up in another bear trap. He caught a glimpse of something a little ways ahead. Caden slowed his pace to gained better control over the headlamp. Looking into the distance, he could barely make out a structure. The extra exertion of carrying his friend left him soaking wet with sweat. However a different sensation arose, adding to the perspiration. Caden's heartbeat sped up even more. No longer was he trudging along aimlessly. Every step he took was calculated, his mind sharpened and zeroing in on what had to be a cabin, in the distance.

There were no lights. The place could blend into the dark woods with ease, if you didn't know what you were looking for. Caden, holding tight to Shane who had gone from slack to rigid and back a few times, approached the front door. "Hello?" He pounded the flashlight on the entrance, but received no answer.

Shane began to cough, an ugly choking sound.

"Shit. Don't worry man. You're gonna be fine. Looks like the old hag is not home. We can duck in here for the night, get some rest, and get you out of here as soon as we see the light of day." Caden pushed through the cabin door.

The air inside was thick with dust and mold. Caden tried, but was unable to stifle a sneeze. The weight of Shane, and the awkward posture from sneezing caused Caden's back to spasm. Before he knew it, Shane was falling from his shoulders to the floor.

Shaken, but still not coherent, Shane moaned. Caden was unsure if he was in pain or simply upset at being dropped.

"Aww damn, I'm sorry man. I couldn't help it. I had to sneeze and..." Caden's words trailed off, realizing Shane likely couldn't hear him. He shined his flashlight around, taking in the dark surroundings. The entryway opened up to a large living room, where a moldering couch and its accompanying easy chair sat around a coffee table. An old bear skin rug greeted his eyes, its snarling face frozen in time projecting a creepy image from behind the layers of cobwebs and dust it lay beneath. Caden couldn't help but imagine the thing coming to life. If something like that did occur, he wondered would the gun work?

The thought left his mind. He refocused on ensuring Shane's safety and getting help. No time to worry about the fact he was actually in Mrs. Shelton's cabin. To revel in having finally found the place, deserted and all. Caden shined his flashlight onto his friend. He was in bad shape. Caden noted his shallow breaths, his clothing soaked in sweat. The tourniquet he'd applied to stop the leg wound from bleeding was soaked through. Caden applied the dressing hastily, and while the bleeding did slow down, he was unable to staunch the flow completely. Which meant Shane was still losing precious blood at a steady rate. In the few moments they'd been in the cabin, a small pool formed beneath the injury. This was all a mistake. Shane was clear on not wanting to return to the camp. Telling him about Trent was his fallback plan, and the man who he thought of as a friend for all these years, the one who had overcome the many struggles life threw at him and got the best education possible all out of spite, had fallen for it. How wild was that? This was a mistake, and if he couldn't figure out how to get the man out of the woods, and fast.

Caden paced back and forth, wracking his brain over what his next move should be. One answer hung on his mind and kept all other thoughts at bay. This was a lost cause. Shane had known even when he shot the idea down earlier. Now, more and more, this seemed like his only option. Caden got down on his knees, next to Shane. "Look, I know you probably can't hear me right now, but I'm sorry for dragging you out here. To tell you the truth, once I knew I was coming back here, I couldn't do it on my own. You were the one who had the whole traumatic experience, still I couldn't face coming back here alone. If you can hear me, I need you to hold on a little longer, okay? I'm going out there to retrace my steps and find the Sat phone." A lump formed in his throat and his voice broke. "Really don't want to leave you here like this, man. I can't think of any other way though. Yeah, you told me to wait until it was light outside, but I'm not sure you can hold out much longer. Give me fifteen minutes Shane, twenty tops. I'll be a lot quicker without you. You need to hold on. I wish I was a better friend to you, and when we get out of here I will work at that, please hold on." He got to his feet and stepped over to the door.

From the threshold he could not see a thing. In the absence of any light, the darkness outside the cabin was the same as inside. The faint outline of the trees was visible against the sky. He turned on the flashlight, ready to begin his search. The bright beam shone across the ground, playing over the wild grass that swayed in the light breeze. The light reached the tree line and Caden picked up on something odd. The flashlight revealed the shadowy outline of a person. He squinted, hoping he was only seeing things. "Oh shit," he shouted, as deep red eyes opened up in the silhouette and the figure ducked behind a tree. Caden heard the sound of feet shuffling through underbrush and trained the beam around the entire tree line, catching fleeting glimpses of more figures as they fled the light. "What the…"

Caden's words were cut short when the cabin door slammed into his back, pushing him out of the doorway. The flashlight fell from his hand as he jumped. He bent down to pick it up, ready scramble back inside, and shrieked at the sight of a snake, much like the one he'd saved Shane from, crossing in front of the beam. Using his foot, Caden nudged the serpent out into the grass. He would not set foot in those woods in the darkness. Finding the phone was not an option. After scooping up the flashlight he returned to the door. Part of him knew if he tried, the door would be locked. Caden turned the knob and pushed. The door opened with ease. He stepped inside and something was different. The place somehow felt darker. Caden shined the flashlight around the area. Everything still seemed to be in its proper place. Maybe he'd simply psyched himself out. So much had gone wrong. Perhaps the stress of the situation got to him. Yes, he believed in the supernatural, and that things existed in this world man would likely never be able to explain. He came on this trip convinced he was going to find a woman who had almost certainly died years ago, if she ever existed at all. How could someone survive out here in the wilderness? What was she eating, drinking? The entire line of reasoning made sense, forcing Caden to wonder why he'd not considered these things before dragging his friend out here. Now that friend was in danger and he was helpless to do anything. Of course, shadows stalking through the woods outside was ridiculous, but if Caden's mind was stressed to the point of hallucination, how could he ever do a proper search for the Satphone? He needed to find some way to get Shane stabilized, and then rest. After he had time to calm down and organize his thoughts he could go and search for the phone. Taking in a deep breath, Caden shined the flashlight down to where Shane lay, only to discover his friend gone.

His heart had been racing for some time. Caden didn't know how much more of this he could take. "Shane," his voice trembled as he spoke. "Shane, where are you, man? If you're feeling better, great. But please don't be fucking around. Not right now." A floorboard creaked and he turned at once to see what was happening. The beam of light caught a fleeting glimpse of a dark figure lumbering into one of the doors in the long hallway. "Shane?" His friend had been correct earlier, when he said cooler heads had to triumph. "Come on Caden. This isn't some horror flick," he whispered to himself. "You can explain this all. Shane was laid out on the floor just beyond the doorway. He's in pretty bad shape, but obviously he heard you when you spoke to him earlier. The floor is super uncomfortable, especially if you're injured. So, when you stepped out to find the phone, Shane got to his feet to find some place that would be more forgiving to his condition. He leaned on the door for support, which caused it to slam shut while you were standing there. And now you caught sight of him entering what's likely a bedroom. Much better than the foyer floor. Ha, yes. That's exactly what happened. You could've been in the Scooby Doo gang with logic like that."

He needed more light. Caden searched his surroundings for anything that could be used as a source of illumination. In a closet that sat between the kitchen and living room he found three kerosene lamps. More than enough to fit his needs. After lighting one, the entire space felt different, much less ominous. Surprised, Caden was a bit saddened looking around at the furnishings and decorations. This place was once an escape. A place where a family spent a few of the best days of their lives, only to have met a tragic end. Supposedly. He had to keep reminding himself the story he'd spent all these years believing might not be true. It would be hours before the sun rose. Caden decided he would check on Shane and then figure out what to do with the rest of the time he had.

Lamp held high, Caden began walking down the corridor where he'd last seen Shane. The first door on his right led to a bathroom. Best case scenario, he would rummage through the room and find a first aid kit. Whatever he found would be at least thirty years old, but he should be able to salvage something. Anything was better than what he had at that moment. He decided to check on Shane first and pilfer the bathroom on the way back. The next door he passed, on his left, was closed. Remembering Melody's story, this would be Mitch's bedroom. A chill shot through him at the recollection of what had taken place in the room. He continued on until he reached the next door, the master bedroom. He inched closer, holding the lantern up to illuminate the area. A dresser opposite the doorway with a cloudy mirror mounted atop reflected the light and brightened the room. Next to the dresser was a window that had been boarded up so long ago. Before the window was a plush, oversized chair facing the bed. Atop the latter lay a shape beneath the dingey blanket. "Shane? How you doing, bro?"

No answer. The figure did not even stir. Caden moved closer, "Man, you need some water or anything?" At the bedside, he placed the lantern down on the nightstand. Carefully reaching across the bed, he put his hands on the covers. A layer of dust was imprinted where his hands touched. In the light of the lantern, Caden could not see any handprints from Shane. He drew the covers back, taking note of the tangled hair, black with streaks of gray, and leaves and twigs strewn throughout. Pulling further revealed the ashen flesh and harried features of a woman. She stared up into nothingness with clouded eyes. Caden drew back, shocked and confused. This was not his friend. This was who he'd come here to find. Mrs. Shelton.

She took in a sharp breath, screaming as she exhaled, "Don't. No. No. Please, I can't. Not anymore."

"Oh fuck," Caden tripped over his own feet and fell to the floor. He scrambled back, faintly noticing the room was growing darker, and stopped. The lantern was still on the nightstand, he could not leave the room without it. The best way to go about this was to dash forward, grab it, and run. He was having trouble gathering the courage to do so, however.

The woman, Ava Shelton, thrashed wildly on top of the mattress, sending tons of dust motes airborne. Caden felt a tickle in his nose and knew he was going to sneeze. He tried unsuccessfully to will the urge away. His body heaved as a single sneeze cut through the noise the woman was making. And then another. Caden quickly placed his mouth and nose in the crook of his elbow to stifle any further outbursts. Looking up towards the bed, he discovered the effort was in vain. Mrs. Shelton was sitting in an upright position staring directly at him.

"Your friend is no more," the voice was strained and hoarse as she spoke.

Caden sat paralyzed, letting each word hit him and contemplating the individual meanings. "Shane," he uttered, "is dead?" His breath hitched and Caden realized he'd begun to cry.

"Not dead. Taken."

He barely heard the words the woman croaked. Consumed with guilt, he thought of Melody, all those years ago, passing down her duties to them. He thought of how he'd always wanted to go back to Camp Nashoba, but never saying a word to his parents once he found Shane would not be returning. Then the innocent children that died because no one was present to protect them. It was all her doing. Sure, her backstory was as tragic as could be, but that did not give her the right to simply murder all those kids. Then he remembered the gun. He'd placed it in his pack to appease Shane. Now he desperately needed it. This one thought released him from where he sat. Caden leaped to his feet and retraced his steps down the hallway, to the entrance. In the darkness, he searched for the flashlight he had earlier. His mind doing its best to ignore the approaching footsteps.

She walked on unsteady legs, holding the lantern. She saw the man, Caden was his name, engaged in a search for something. Closer and closer she came, until at last Caden found what he sought. Ava Shelton was a little more than an arms length away, when Caden stopped rummaging through his pack and stood up, pointing a gun at her. She was not afraid when she spoke, "If you shoot me and I die, that would be the sweetest mercy. I will not keep you from doing this, if that is what you desire. However, grant me a momentary stay of execution, so I may explain the danger in which you now find yourself."

Caden was taken aback. He figured Mrs. Shelton would be some snarling beast, all claws and sharp teeth. The frail woman who stood before him was far from what he imagined. His finger wrapped around the trigger and he asked the only question on his mind, "Where's Shane?"

"Your friend. The injured one you arrived here with. It is too late for him."

"What do you mean? Start making sense, or I start making holes."

"Please, your threats mean nothing to me. I welcome death in whatever form it decides to reveal itself. You though, you still have a chance to escape. I will spare you the long drawn out story, I'm doubtful I'd have enough time to go into detail. This was once my cabin."

"Yes, I know. I know about everything that happened to you here. The break in, the murders, your act of revenge, even why you decided to return."

"There was a schoolyard game I used to play as a young girl, called telephone. One person at the front of the line whispered a message into the ear of the next in line. On it went, from person to person, until the last in line speaks the message aloud. The message was always different in the end than when it began. Stories get passed down from person to person, generation to generation. Each time something gets added or omitted changing the original story into something almost unrecognizable. There was no act of revenge, on my part. That is to say, I was not responsible for the violence that ensued, and freed me from my captors. The two men who killed my family tortured me in ways I don't care to remember. I prayed for death, and it mocked me by always staying just out of reach. So I abandoned my God and called out to any deity that would grant me an audience. That's how I came to be possessed with the spirit of the Impa Shilup."

Caden felt his hand trembling and lowered the gun. "The what?"

"Ah, I see they didn't teach you about the dark side of the Choctaw in that little camp. The Impa Shilup is a Choctaw spirit. A rather nasty one that devours souls. It manifests as either a shadow or a snake, and preys on those who are at their lowest. Me, I couldn't get much lower than I was. So calling out for help, in the middle of these woods, I brought it right to my doorstep. I wanted to die, to leave this world behind and be reunited with my husband and son. The Impa Shilup had other plans. It entered me and I became the snake and the shadow. I bore witness to the way it used me to brutalize the two intruders and consumed their very souls. I begged it to release me and let me die, and it laughed.

"It was not my decision to return to this cabin.

The dark spirit inhabiting me dragged me back. Not wanting to be so far from its native land. I tried to leave, but it would not allow me. Soon, with no steady source of nourishment, the spirit grew weak. And so, I ventured out into the woods, setting obvious and ridiculous traps to warn people away. That damn camp though. Sooner or later, I knew someone would find this place. What's most baffling is someone on their own would be completely safe. It's only concerned with twos. Lawrence and Mitchell, Kilo and Shark...You and I."

"No, bullshit. Why would this thing choose now to finally kill you?"

A shadowy hand wrapped around Mrs. Shelton's neck. She continued to stare at Caden, not flinching for one moment. Not even when the squeezing began and her air supply was cut off.

Caden was frozen in place, listening to the sound of bones crunching beneath the dark, wispy hand. A voice, Shane's voice but darker somehow, spoke as Ava fell in a lifeless heap. "Because I've found another, more sturdy vessel."

"Shane? Oh god, what the fuck is happening?"

"Do not trouble yourself with such details. You are going to die, and I will devour your essence." The thing that looked like Shane bent over the felled corpse of Mrs. Shelton. It opened its--Shane's--mouth and swirls of white mist emanated from the body, entering

Shane's mouth like cigarette smoke. "You know, I'm used to skipping meals these days. Before you left Camp Nashoba, I could go decades sometimes, without being properly fed. But oh, once those children began wandering away from that place it was like the old days, when I used to receive tribute on a regular basis."

"Tribute, you mean sacrifice?"

"Well goddamn, you're not as dumb as Shane thinks you are. They would hold entire festivals, rituals and all. Marching the willing into my woods, two by two. Always two, everything always two. Up and down, day and night, life and death, hunger and satisfaction. Do not worry, Caden. You will simply become part of the growing shadow. Surely you have witnessed it yourself. The sun reaching its apex and bombarding the land with heat, then steadily losing its hold on the world as the darkness reclaims the land. The cycle repeating itself year after year."

It required no mental gymnastics, only active listening. Caden understood what Shane, or the Impa Shilup was saying. So figuring out how to keep from dying was simple. He grabbed the lantern from where Mrs. Shelton had set it down and held it high above his head, eliminating most of his shadow. Moving quickly, he found the other two kerosene lamps. Caden fished the lighter from his pocket and lit them. The sound of Shane's hideous laughter filled the cabin. Caden placed the lanterns in a triangle pattern, with himself in the middle. He still cast a bit of a shadow, but hoped it was enough until he figured out how to rid his friend of the unwelcome guest.

"Fool. Those lamps will burn out within an hour, and then it will be time to feast. Why play this game, knowing you will not be victorious?"

"Shane, I know you're in there somewhere. Please help me." Tears welled in his eyes as his hand held tight to the gun, "I don't want to kill you. You deserve better. I'm sorry for bringing you back out here. That was a dick move. I could've asked my parents to sign me up for another year at camp, easy. This isn't your fault. It never was. This was my responsibility. I was too chicken-shit to do it alone. I'm sorry, man. Do you hear me? I'm sorry."

"Enough," the thing posing as Shane yelled. "I grow weary of the way you cling to your pitiful life, refusing to see the glory of something much greater than yourself. The fact of the matter is I don't need to wait you out. I can simply alter the circumstance."

From the darkness behind him, Caden heard a piece of wood squeal then crack. He squinted and saw a board fly away from one of the windows, then another. The window opened, and then the window in front of him underwent a similar process. The door to the cabin was flung open and in the space beyond Caden could see the shadow forms he glimpsed at the treeline earlier. A gust of wind blew through the newly ventilated space. Something small and hard hit Caden's arm and clattered to the floor. He had only enough time to look down and see a pebble at his feet, before he was pelted with another. He, however, was not the target. This Caden realized as he looked to the open windows and saw the child-like shadows throwing rocks at his feet, aiming for the lanterns. One found its mark and the glass surrounding the contained flame shattered. It only took a moment for the other two to break as well. The flames danced wildly, contorting the world around him. Shrinking and stretching the light before a final gust of wind extinguished them. Caden dropped down to the floor, unsure of where Shane would launch his attack.

An object skid across the floor, knocking into his foot. For a moment, Caden thought it was a larger rock. He reached hoping it was heavy enough to do some damage, but was surprised at what he felt instead. It was cold, metal, cylindrical. The flashlight.

All around him, children laughed and shrieked. Caden depressed the rubberized power button and the bright beam of the flashlight shined up into his face. Without a moment to waste, he turned the beam to the first broken window, dispelling the shadows with the light. He then did the same for the doorway, and the second window.

An arm snaked around his shoulders and before he knew it, Shane had Caden in a headlock. "You put up a good fight. I haven't had to work for it in a long time. But in the end, you still lose."

Caden was struggling to breathe. Still holding tight to the flashlight, he brought his arm up in a swift arc, connecting the handle with the Impa Shilup's head. He didn't want to hurt Shane, but he also didn't want to die here. Another blow and the headlock loosened enough for Caden to escape the hold. He bolted for the door which shut fast, right in front of him. Caden turned, unable to see in front of him. It was a sense that something was closing in on him, that made him raise the light up and shine it straight ahead.

Shane was closing in fast, but was stopped cold once the beam hit him. It knocked him to the floor, where he writhed in pain.

Holding the flashlight steady, Caden appropached Shane. Unsure of what to do.

"Kill me." It was Shane's voice, minus the darkness of the Impa Shilup. "You have to do it now. It won't be down for long."

At that moment, Caden realized he still had the gun. He let it fall from his grip. It was not meant for this. "No. I can't do that. Let me figure out a way…"

"This is the only way, Caden. Listen to me. I was dead regardless. My leg will be so infected by the morning I'll die of blood poisoning before help reaches us. I knew the moment we stumbled into this place. I figured out it was the Impa Shilup. The snake in that tree, the shadows, it all made perfect sense. I invited it into me Caden, because Mrs. Shelton was real, and still alive. I thought you two could escape. I'm dead, Caden. You can't help that, but you can make sure this dick marble doesn't kill anyone else by taking away its vessel. Shoot me Caden, please. There's no time."

A thought surfaced in Caden's mind, "I can't Shane. I won't. Your birthday is next week. You'll be twenty-nine. Trent doesn't get to win this one. You managed to avoid prison, and I'll be damned if you die before turning thirty."

"I don't care about Trent anymore. That's why I came here with you. To put that shit to rest for good." His words were sincere as he pleaded with the man. Please Caden, I'm begging you. I can't hold it off much longer "

As if to illustrate the point, Caden could see Shane being consumed by the shadows gathering around him. Soon the flashlight would be worthless. "I'm sorry Shane. God forgive me." Caden grabbed the gun off the floor and pointed it at Shane's head.

"Do it Caden, now."

The sun rose above the woods, chasing away the nighttime shadows. Caden rocked back and forth, cradling his best friend's head. The entire bottom half of his body was covered in sticky, semi-congealed blood. The bullet had gone straight through his skull, and Shane stopped moving immediately. With that, the darkness surrounding him disappeared.

He'd survived. The cabin was as much of a massacre as it had been thirty years ago, but it didn't matter. It was over. Caden got to his feet and walked outside. The sun touched his skin, he exhaled, and set off into the woods.

After half an hour of retracing the previous day's trek, Caden found the Sat phone. It seemed to have fallen in the spot where Shane stepped in the bear trap. Caden powered it on and wasted no time dialing emergency services. It rang and a few seconds later a voice greeted him. "Hi, I'm located near the old Camp Nashoba. A few miles due east of the camp, there's a cabin. It's pretty bad. I need help as soon as possible."

"Understood, sir. And your name?"

"Caden."

"Thank you Caden. Can you tell me if anyone is injured, or hurt?"

"No, not anymore."

"Okay, no problem. I have an officer I can dispatch to your location. Can you meet him at the camp?"

"Sure I can, but may I also make a small request? If it's not too much of a bother, could you send two officers?"

My Soul To Take

I awoke in the morning and had a good stretch, from a night of exceptional rest. In a few hours, I was expected to be the model employee that I was hired to be, at my desk pounding away at the keys of my laptop. As I lay there dreading getting out of the bed, I turned on my side catching sight of my cell phone sitting atop the nightstand. I reached for it and unlocked it. Ready to catch up on all that I'd missed in the world during my slumber. The screen came to life, but I was not greeted with the familiar background that had been on my home screen since the day I'd gotten the phone. Instead, my camera app was open, and I was presented with a shaky view of the wall beside my bed. Hmm, I thought, must've opened it up by mistake. Something not quite right registered in my mind though. My eyes were drawn to the bottom corner of the screen, where a small bubble displaying a preview of the last picture taken sat. I pressed it, not recognizing the photo. It enlarged, and for a moment I had no idea what I was seeing. Darkness. The only light shone from the flash of the camera, illuminating a person as he lay in bed, fast asleep. That person turned out to be me. I would've had no reason to panic, were it not for the fact that I live by myself.

Terrified, I scrambled out of bed and got dressed. Who was in my home while I was sleeping? I ran from room to room checking if anything was missing but found nothing out of place. My heart was thudding, and I felt like I was on the verge of a panic attack. For my health's sake, and because I found no sign of an intruder, I decided to leave the investigation alone until I returned home from work.

That night, I was exhausted. A lazy walk through the rooms of my home ensured that no one else but me was there. I locked every door—the front, the back, the two bathrooms, the extra bedroom, and when I was ready to crash down onto my bed, my door. I turned my phone off and placed it beneath my pillow. Although, due to me being an active sleeper, there was no way it would still be there in the morning.

The moment my head hit the pillow I was out. I dreamed of London. Not the English city, but my ex-girlfriend. She was in my house being as sweet as she'd been before I discovered her treachery. To say I missed her would have been the understatement of the decade.

She was in the kitchen cooking, or something to that effect. Can you call it cooking if it's just a sandwich? I suppose, if you're toasting the bread. But she wasn't.

"Mayo or mustard, Andre?" London called to me. Her voice was so melodic.

"Do I have any of the stone ground left?" I replied, making my way to the kitchen.

"I'll check, babe."

I rounded the corner and was greeted with an open refrigerator door, obscuring my view of London. I did catch an eyeful of her curvaceous hips while she bent over, searching for the delicious condiment. I moved in behind, thrusting my groin against her. She responded by pushing back into me. Based on the way such instances usually progressed, the sandwiches weren't going to be ready any time soon. London closed the fridge and stood upright. I placed my hand on her hip and let it creep up to her breast. She moaned. It set my nerves on fire. I kissed her neck, but the gesture felt wrong. When I pulled away, her neck was covered in dark purple bruises. Her skin was pale and peeling away in spots. I backed up immediately.

"What's wrong?" She turned to face me.

I screamed. London's face was a grotesque expression of rot and decay. Her gorgeous bronze skin had gone scaly, losing all its luster. Her eyes, once a verdant green, were milky yellow and glossed over, protruding from their sockets. Something throbbed beneath her skin. Had I not been sleeping I probably would have yarked up whatever was in my stomach.

London grabbed my arm in a vice grip, "What's wrong, babe? Come give me a kiss."

Her lips, what was left of them, were scabbed and scarred. A sinewy black tongue, with pockets of yellow ooze jutted from her mouth as she drew closer. I tried to avoid her advance, but she placed her hand behind my head and drew me closer.

My eyes shot open, and I was stuck in place where I lay. The room around me was dark. When I tried to move, I found that my limbs would not respond to my brain's commands. I was fully erect. More so than I've ever been. So hard was I that it hurt. My eyes adjusted to the darkness, that's when I noticed the black mass above my body. It was featureless, hovering for what seemed an eternity. In the presence of the formless entity, I felt myself ejaculate, and then finally regained control of myself. "What the fuck?" I shouted into the early morning darkness. The mass disappeared and I was left with sticky sheets, embarrassed like I was going through puberty all over again. I mean, what self-respecting thirty-three-year-old still has wet dreams?

As I wondered, I turned on my phone. It was a day like any other. I laughed at memes my friends posted, stuck my nose in other people's business, weighing in where my opinion wasn't needed, even played a couple games. When I couldn't procrastinate any longer, I got out of bed and took a shower. Though not conceited, I was in a good mood and feeling myself after getting dressed. I took a selfie, the sun shining through my bathroom window providing great lighting. It was page-worthy, so I started creating a post. My hand trembled as I looked at the phone. The screen displayed a bunch of photos that had been taken. I recognized the one I wanted to post, but next to it was a dark and unfamiliar image. I touched it and it filled the screen. There I lay on my bed. Something loomed over me. A dark mass—darker than the surrounding room as I slept. Similar to what I'd seen upon waking. It almost looked like a person.

The phone fell from my hand. Questions, for which I had no answers, clouded my thoughts. Without warning, London popped into my head. She loved little anomalous occurrences like this. For obvious reasons, I was hesitant to make my next move. Despite that, I picked my device up and called her. When the line began to ring, I thought about hanging up. She answered the phone before I could.

"Tell me you dreamed about me last night."

Her greeting stole the breath from my lungs. "Um, I..." the words I wanted to say escaped me.

"Andre, I've been sitting in bed all morning wondering if I should call you and tell you about the crazy fucking dream I had, and all of the sudden your name pops up on my phone screen. That can't be a coincidence, right?" She was speaking so fast it all got lost in the fog of my mind.

"Yes, I did dream about you." My reply was slow, as though I needed to catch my breath before speaking. "It's more than that though. There's been a picture of me sleeping in my phone when I woke up both yesterday and today. I'm royally creeped out."

"Are you shitting me? Why am I just now hearing about this?"

"Well, you know, things between us haven't exactly been- "

"Who the fuck cares, Andre? You know how interested I am in shit like this. Send me the pictures, let me see if I can spot anything." As evidenced by the heavy breathing coming through the speaker, London was upset.

"I deleted the one from yesterday."

"Jesus fuck, dude!"

I met London on a dating app. The six months that we'd been together were some of the best days of my adult life. We were an adventurous couple, hiking and biking local trails by day, dining our way around the city by evening, and by night, well, let's just say the cops have more than a few noise complaints on file thanks to nosy or envious neighbors.

London was always open and honest with me. I fell for her as hard as anyone can. Knowing how much she loved all things paranormal, I would often tease her, saying that she bewitched me and that one day the spell would wear off and she'd have to recast it quick, before I went and found someone else. Then one day she hit me with something that made me realize our love wasn't as enchanted as I thought. London wanted to open our relationship up. I couldn't believe that she said those words. As many times as she claimed she loved me. All lies. I was furious with her. Wanting to wrap my hands around her soft neck and squeeze until she realized just how much bullshit she was talking. Instead, I broke up with her. In the months since, we became reacquainted as something that resembles friends. The woman was enamored with anything even remotely supernatural, and I promised that she'd be the first to know if I ever experienced something within that realm. If London could help me debunk the situation or find whatever was causing it, well, I would let her. If only to be close to her again.

The moment I ended the call, I sent her the photo. As I sat in my home uneasy, waiting for her reply, I noted that I was late for work. Time seemed to have gotten away from me. I finished getting ready and rushed out the door.

I was a mess at work, drowsy all morning, couldn't focus on anything I was supposed to do, and constantly looking behind me, feeling like I was being watched. Wondering what was taking London so long to get back to me. That night, when I returned home, I called her. It went straight to her voicemail. Without leaving a message, I hung up. I was so tired, but no longer wanted to sleep in my house. It did cross my mind to maybe get a hotel room for the evening, but the way my bank account is set up, it was a no go. So, I found myself once again lying in my own bed, getting ready to fall asleep. As a precaution, I locked my phone in the bathroom after turning it off. I wished phones still had removeable batteries. On the off chance that someone was in my house I hoped to make it as hard for them to get to my phone as I could. For an added measure of protection, I tried to pray. Never being the religious type, I was unsure what to say. "Lord," I uttered weak and unconfident, "please don't let bad things happen?" I felt like a fool. Did people really think this worked? "What's that one prayer? I lay me down to sleep, keep me safe from things that creep. If anything should try before I wake, I pray you, Lord, my soul to take." Close enough, I thought, right before sleep overcame me.

I awoke in my living room. London was in the kitchen shuffling items around in the refrigerator. "I don't see the stone ground mustard, babe," she called out to me.

"You never responded to me," I said, in the direction of the kitchen.

"What was that?"

"I sent you that picture earlier and you never got

back to me. I thought for sure you would have seen that shadow over me and called right back or texted at the very least."

"Well," she began, "did you ever think that maybe I have my own things going on?"

On my feet and moving towards her voice, I answered, "I guess I just thought that it would interest you, is all. It's creeping the living hell out of me, you know." I rounded the corner to the kitchen and was greeted with the open fridge door, just like before. "Honestly, I miss you. I know I'm the one who called it quits, but I really do still love you."

The refrigerator door closed. London, having found what she was looking for, turned her back to me. "I know you do, Andre. I love you too. When I say that, I mean every word of it. You never let me explain myself, and that hurt me more than you'll ever know." I couldn't see what she was doing but could hear utensils scraping against a plate as she continued to prepare the sandwich. "It isn't about how much or how little you satisfy me. I have a lot of love to share with you and whomever else I decide to give it to. It's not like I would've been just giving myself up to anyone who wanted a piece either. No, I wanted deep meaningful connections with the men, or women that I entered into relationships with. Andre, you have a very archaic view of love. I don't blame you for that, most of the world agrees with it. Monogamy is a prison for someone like me though, and to demand that I be with only you is its own kind of abuse. If you had a child, there's no question that you would love it, right? Well, what if you had two kids, three, five? You wouldn't love any one of them any more or less than the other. That same love can be applied romantically. But we are taught that that's a bad thing. Do you want olives, or pickles?"

"Um, pickles." I opened the fridge to get them. London crept up behind me this time, wrapping her arms around my waist. Placing my hand over hers, I shivered. Her skin was ice cold. I looked down and saw that her flesh was ashen, sloughing away in spots. My own skin tingled like I'd disturbed an ant hill and now they were swarming all over me. I wriggled out of her grasp. When I turned to look at her, she was in worse shape than the previous dream. I didn't scream this time, even though it felt more real than before. I mean, I could actually feel the coldness of her skin when I touched her. "What is this?" I asked, gaining a modicum of lucidity.

"That's up to you, babe." London replied. Without warning, her arms shot forward and grabbed me.

My eyes opened at once. The scream I wanted to let out remained arrested inside of me. Like the day before, I couldn't move. In my mind, I was panicking. I could feel hands pressing down on my chest. Once again, I was rock hard. That dark mass was now rocking back and forth on top of me. Grinding itself into my midsection. Every time I tried to move, my muscles refused to listen. I wasn't sure, but I thought I heard someone grunting, moaning. The noise sounded like it was being broadcast over static laden airwaves. When I came, it all ended.

At last, I regained control over my own body. It was like opening my eyes all over again. Except this time, that dark mass that I'd seen was gone. I jumped out of bed and ran to the bathroom. My phone was the only thing on my mind. When I found it, I turned it on, wishing that the startup sequence would move faster. The second it was done I checked my photos. Sure enough, there were three new pictures of me sleeping. The shadow-like figure hovered above me in two of them. In the third, it covered my entire body, obstructing my sleeping form. I sent the photos to London immediately. Without waiting for her to confirm that she'd gotten them, I called her.

"You dreamed of me again." It wasn't a question but wasn't an accusation either.

"I did. I woke up and couldn't move. Something was on top of me, holding me down. I think it was— ugh, this sounds so stupid, but I think it was having its way with me." I spoke quickly, trying to get the words out as fast as possible.

"Sleep paralysis is scary shit, Andre. You think

maybe that has something to do with what you're seeing?"

"No, I don't think so. I was wide awake, London. Whatever this presence is, it's keeping me motionless."

"And you're certain of this?"

"Yes!" I snapped. "This is not some sleep abnormality. I'm definitely hyper aware of everything that's happening."

"I see," London offered.

Her responses were not what I expected, and I began to feel that she didn't believe me. Her attitude about it angered me. "Did you see the pictures? I just sent you more. Look at them. I'm not bullshitting you at all."

"Right, about those pics," she let out a breath before continuing, "there's nothing in any of the images you sent me."

"What? Did you not get them?"

"Oh, I got every one you sent. Each one is nothing but blackness. I figured you were just joking yesterday, until the three you sent a moment ago. Andre, be honest with me, are you feeling okay?"

A spell of dizziness came over me the moment she asked. Somewhere between where I'd been standing and the sink, the call disconnected, and the phone fell from my hand. I splashed some cold water on my face. In the mirror, the man that looked back at me was tired. Bags under my eyes making it seem as though I hadn't slept at all. Something was wrong, and it seemed I was going to have to figure it out on my own. I took one last look in the mirror and saw a shadow pass behind me.

"Who's there?" I called out to the empty room, turning on my heels. Of course, there was no answer. The whole situation was beginning to get to me. My phone buzzed on the floor and I jumped. London's face appeared on the screen. I picked it up. "London, something is here."

"I believe you, babe. If you're serious, I believe you. Give me some time to process all that you've told me, and I'll see what I can do to help."

My heart sped up just the tiniest bit. She called me "babe" like she had in my dreams, and it didn't sound forced at all. I know it was a term that just rolled off her tongue when she was speaking to anyone that she was familiar with, but still, it gave me hope. "Okay. I'm not working today. I slept all night, but I'm still exhausted. Maybe I am coming down with something, I don't know."

"Well I hope you start feeling better. Andre, if anything happens call me right away, okay?"

"I will." The words took a lot to say. I ended the call and made my way back to my bed. I didn't bother calling in sick. Every move I made took a tremendous effort.

I closed my eyes for just a moment, not worried about the shadow I'd seen, or the pictures, or the dreams. When I opened them it was no longer morning, but late in the afternoon. I felt sore, like I'd been working out rigorously the day before. Something was clearly not right. It took a shameful amount of focus just to raise my phone up to my field of vision. I checked to see if London had reached out, but she hadn't. This whole situation just kept getting weirder. I called her to get an update on things, but the call, yet again, went straight to her voicemail. I lay there thinking that maybe she was with someone and didn't want to be disturbed with my troubles. Could I really blame her, if that was the case?

Staring at my phone, wondering what to do next, I opened the internet app to follow the only real lead I had. In the search bar, I typed sleep paralysis. The very first picture that popped up on the screen sent a shiver through my entire body. It was an illustration of a man lying in bed, with a featureless shadow hovering above him. One dark arm extended covering the man's chest, keeping him pinned to the bed. I clicked the image and it took me to a site, where someone gave an account of their most terrifying episode of what they called old hag syndrome. The man spoke of having lucid dreams of a recently lost loved one, and how he would wake up from the dreams unable to move, while a shadow-like figure hovered above him. Day after day this occurred, and he grew weaker after every time. One day he awoke and found that the figure was no longer a shadow, but a haggard old lady. This scared him so much that he contacted his church. A priest came and blessed his house, which ended the whole ordeal. The story was so similar to my own, I would have to tell London about it the next time we spoke.

Feeling well enough to get out of bed, I realized how hungry I was. I staggered from my room on my way to the kitchen. When I reached the living room, I heard noises as if someone was looking through my refrigerator. Instantly on guard, I called out "Who's there?" My voice was so weak I almost tried again. I decided not to though. If whoever was in the kitchen didn't hear me, it would be easier to sneak up on them. Then I thought about the recurring dream. Was London in my kitchen? No, it couldn't be. She returned the key to my place months ago. My gaze shifted to the front door. It was locked. I shifted back when I heard glass clinking.

My breathing was slow and steady as I stood with my back to the wall of the corner that opened up to the kitchen. I closed my eyes and mustered up the courage to jump out at the intruder. "What are you doing?" I shouted, hoping to startle the person enough to get the upper hand. But no one was there. I stood in the entrance to an empty kitchen. Confused, I turned around to see if they'd gotten past me or found some other hiding spot. I was all alone. When I turned back to the kitchen, I saw it. On the counter next to the stove sat a small saucer plate. Sitting on top, waiting for me, was a pastrami sandwich on rye bread, cut perfectly down the middle, stone ground mustard oozing out of the sides. My stomach growled in protest, causing me to abandon any questions I had about how the sandwich got there. I attacked it, devouring the food with ravenous ferocity. I was still hungry after finishing. I wanted to raid the fridge for more food but began to feel tired all over again. One more nap, I decided. If things still felt off after that I would drag myself in to see a doctor. If that didn't work, I shuddered at the thought of finding religion and inviting a clergyman in to bless the house.

London was no longer in the kitchen. She was on the couch, next to me. "Did you enjoy the sandwich?"

When I turned in her direction, she was a desiccated corpse of a woman. I no longer felt scared though. We talked without me even acknowledging how wrong it was. In dreams, such details are trivial anyway. "It was perfect. How did you do it?"

"Well, to be honest, it doesn't take much to throw some meat between two slices of bread," she chuckled, and a small wrinkle at the corner of her mouth blossomed to a crevasse that spread across her tight, grey skin all the way to her ear.

"That's not what I mean. You made the sandwich here, in my dream. But I ate it out there in the real world. Am I losing my mind?"

"You're not. You just aren't seeing things from the proper perspective."

"Well, can you help me to put this all together? I searched online earlier, and now I think that I either have a serious medical issue, or that a succubus is trying to get me. London, the real one, is probably going to flip when I tell her about this in the morning."

"Poor Andre," her ice cold, leathery hand rose to caress my cheek, "I don't want to hurt you. I'm trying to keep you as safe as I can."

"What does that mean?" I fumed. "If this is my dream, and I'm completely aware, why can't I get any answers? Shouldn't I be able to control this situation?"

London winced as I raised my voice, and her skin cracked and fell away in random spots on her face. "Please Andre, don't make me do this. I love you. I just want to be with you."

She said those words and it dawned on me, "You're not London. You're not even the version of her in my imagination, are you?"

She shook her head. "Please don't be upset."

"You're a succubus?"

"I am."

"So, what is all of this, some plan to drive me insane?"

She sighed, "Can we just go back to how it was? That was much less complicated, babe."

I jerked my head out of her hand, "No. Absolutely not. And don't call me that. You've been fucking with me all week. You owe me an explanation. London's gonna have a goddamn field day when she hears about this."

"She won't," her voice was stern now. It took me from angry to tense in a heartbeat. "The thing about London is, well, she hasn't heard a word from you in quite a while."

"But I just sent her all of those pics."

The decaying London pulled a phone from her purse. She tapped at it randomly and then held it up to where I could see it. "These are the pictures you're referring to?"

"Why do you have those? What's going on?"

"If you think about it long enough, I'm sure you'll figure it out. I can give you all the time you need, Andre."

"Stop talking like her," I snapped. "Just stop."

"I knew that you would not be willing to accept this. I was only trying to bring you peace. That's why I chose this visage. She was the last person to make you genuinely happy."

"Then why are you falling apart? London was far from this rotted, zombie-like thing that you are."

"Indeed, she was. Spry and full of life, nothing

but love to give. As it stands, I only look the way you want me to. There is something rooted deep inside of you. Some unfathomable truth that you've not yet reconciled with. If you no longer want to see me like this, perhaps we should speak in the waking world, but you will like that even less, I'm afraid."

After eating the sandwich, I'd fallen asleep on the couch, but when I opened my eyes, I was in my bed, surrounded by darkness and once again unable to move. I concentrated as hard as I could. Relying on strength that I no longer had, I forced my arm to move. Once I did, the rest of my body followed suit. With a scream, I brought myself to a sitting position.

"Andre," a voice whispered.

The room was engulfed in shadow. My hands shook as I reached for my phone. I opened the photo app and was frozen with the sight I saw. Row after row of pictures of me while sleeping. No matter how far I scrolled, that's all that I could see. But there was more. Something else lay beside me in the bed. It remained a shaded image even with the phone's flash.

"Andre," the whispering voice was more insistent.

I quickly closed the pictures and opened my contacts. Finding London's number, I did not hesitate in calling. I was greeted by an electronic voice telling me that the number I dialed was no longer in service. I yawned, more tired and confused than I had ever been.

"Andre, please."

"Stop talking," I snarled. "You did something to London, didn't you?"

"I did not. You misunderstand."

"Then make me understand, dammit."

"I can make you happy, but you need to be open to it." Her voice was no longer a whisper. She also didn't sound like my ex. "I can answer all of your questions, but you may find what I have to say very disturbing."

"I don't care. I've had enough of this torment, and I'm so tired. Please, just fill me in so I can get on with my life."

"Very well. The first thing you must understand is that I do love you, very much. Yes, I'm what you call a succubus. Through the act of sex, I steal the life away from men that I fall in love with, while they sleep. They become mine. Living inside of me, forever, where I can continue to feel their love. And I want you to be with me so badly, Andre. Your pain is what brought me here. I just want to help you get through it."

"What pain? I don't know what you're talking about."

"Please don't be upset with me, Andre. Understand that I only had your best interest at heart."

"I can't promise not to be mad about something I don't know."

"Andre, you're still asleep. You have been this

whole time. That's how the sandwich made it out of your dream. The pictures on your phone are from the real world."

"I'm sleeping right now, how? This feels so real."

"Sleep is the best way I can describe it, for you to still comprehend what I'm saying. I'm going to wake you up now. It won't be easy on you."

When next I opened my eyes, the world was still dark. It felt much different than before though. My mind was abuzz, as though I was drunk. I wasn't paralyzed, but it still took a tremendous effort to just move my head. My phone sat beside me on the night table. I reached for it. The screen opened onto the page that displayed my recent calls. It showed twenty-seven calls to London, all unanswered.

"She's not going to pick up, Andre."

The voice startled me. My gaze shifted to the bottom half of the bed, where the outline of a woman hovered over my prone form. I don't know how long I'd been asleep, but I was sure that I was awake now. Memories flooded my mind. London had told me she wanted an open relationship and I cursed her out. She tried to explain, but I wouldn't let her. My hands balled into tight fists as the memory of her beautiful, soft, perfumed neck yielded to the strength of my grip. I watched her eyes go bloodshot and tear up, as she struggled to breathe, knowing she was too weak to fight back. She was mine, and nobody else would ever have her. And then it was over. I carried her to my bedroom and lay her down on my bed.

For weeks I greeted her with a good morning kiss, even after the insects burrowed and writhed beneath her skin. I had conversations with her and laughed whenever she said something funny. I told her how I felt, about how her words had torn me apart and exposed the flaws in my thinking, challenging my core beliefs. I apologized for getting upset at her, and she promised that she would never bring up any of that open relationship stuff again. The crazy thing was that if she did want to talk about it, I would have done my best to not be so close-minded. We continued to be a loving couple. Things were perfect, up until I dreamed about her.

I turned on the bedside lamp and could see her now, not the old hag, London. A warm smile on the radiant skin of her face, as she mounted me. The rotten carcass that lay beside me, no longer recognizable.

"I'm so sorry for all you've gone through."

"You really love me?" I asked.

"I do, Andre. So much."

I reached out and touched her thigh, surprised that it wasn't cold. "What if I don't want to go with you?"

"I'm afraid that was never an option. But you will be happy with me, I can promise you that."

"I'm not the only one you love, am I?"

"No, but-"

"But you have more than enough love to give to everyone you become enamored with, I know," I interrupted. "You helped me see things more clearly. Isn't that what true love is? Caring for someone so much that you alter their perception of the world around them."

The old hag, no, London leaned in and placed her lips on mine. She rode me as I hungrily kissed her. It was the best sex we'd ever had. Even better than the times we'd done it after making up. In one hand I caressed the curve of her thigh, while the other thrashed around the bed in ecstasy, tearing at the putrid skin of the corpse of a woman I no longer knew. This new London moved her warm, soft lips from mine, over to my ear, where she nibbled on my earlobe before gently whispering, "London sends her regards, you fucking prick."

I had no time to even discern what she'd said. It was no longer pleasure I felt. She was grinding on top of me and all I could feel was white hot pain throughout my entire body. I attempted to move, but was trapped beneath her, helpless. Wanting nothing more than to reach up from where I lay and wring her goddamn neck until I felt bones pop.

I didn't want to finish, but it happened anyway. It was a furious climax, harder than I'd ever experienced, and it was the last thing I felt before I was consumed by cold, dark, loveless and indifferent nothingness.

IT At The End Of The World

No one knew how or where the terror began. The last news cast I'd seen was about a year ago. South America, Africa, Australia, all overrun with hideous creatures. Unconfirmed reports of varying monstrosities were making their way across the U.S. I paid the words little mind. The news had been the unfortunate station my TV happened to be on when I powered the device up for a gaming session. This should've been a typical Sunday evening, back when things like days of the week were important. I had a finely rolled blunt in hand—Acapulco Gold strain—a huge bag of gluten free chocolate covered pretzels, and some nearly melted vanilla coconut gelato by my side. Ready to wind down the weekend and keep my mind off work for as long as possible.

I turned the lights down in my bedroom and started up Bloodborne. Of all the games I had on PS4, it was my favorite. Though not a horror title per se, the dark atmosphere and Lovecraftian overtone created a chilling experience I found myself coming back to again and again. I defeated Rom the Vacuous Spider and was watching the ominous blood moon rise over the lake where I'd fought the overgrown mutant arachnid and its offspring, when the game froze. A message popped up on the screen informing me the network connection was lost. This upset me. As an IT guy, network outages were unacceptable in my home. I was on my feet at once, checking the ethernet cable behind the gaming console. The connectivity light was on, good, but the activity light was gone. Bad…very bad.

Phone in hand, I was about to call my ISP to complain. I put in my unlock code and the phone buzzed in my hand. An emergency text flashed on the screen.

-National Alert. Seek shelter wherever possible and await further instruction.

Before I'd even begun to process the message, an explosion shook the walls of my home, and the windows in my room shattered. I was knocked to the floor, left shielding my face from the flying glass shards. I thought my ears were ringing, but the tone didn't match my usual tinnitus. I soon realized a tornado siren was responsible for the noise. I began to wonder if the cause of all this was a tornado. The answer came screaming through my window frame, a few seconds later.

Upon first glance, the thing looked like a bat. Leathery black wings, a furry torso, and clawed feet. But the similarities stopped there. Its head was small, narrow, with an elongated beak that shrieked so loud my teeth vibrated. The winged aggressor was huge. The thing could have easily gored me with one of its talons and carried me off to god knows where. I know I likened the thing to a bat, but after I covered the head with my bedsheet, and it thrashed blindly around my room, and I was at last able to thump it with my iron, the creature kinda looked like a pterodactyl.

Outside, the sky was an eerie shade of purple. Neighbors running through the street fleeing unseen horrors. I wondered if pterodactyl bats had crashed through their windows too, as I hurried into my car and drove away. I can't say whether my next move was a well thought out decision, or a sad realization of the state of my social life, but I drove away from my house as fast as I dared and headed, of all places, to work. In hindsight, the level of physical security at the building I worked in was significantly higher than, say, a nonexistent friend's house. I mean, sure, I knew plenty of people online, but how exactly would you feel if someone contacted you who you've only ever spoken to through instant message, and most of those messages were him telling you how much of a dick snot you are for not being a better Call of Duty player? Also, in hindsight, most of those online gaming "friends" were probably little twelve and thirteen-year-old kids anyway, so…

I arrived at work and the first significant thing of note was the security barriers standing open. Good thing, because in my haste to escape the ruins of my bedroom, and the monster responsible, I left my ID badge. Once inside, I stopped by the security kiosk to see if the guard had any info on what the hell was going on. The guard, however, had abandoned the post. Hence the open barriers.

Being a 24/7 facility, I was a bit disconcerted to find the entire building empty. No security, no coworkers, and no flying monstrosities. Thankful for the latter, I sat in the break room and gathered myself. The TV, which was always tuned to some news station, blared to life. I hadn't even noticed the station was airing one of those test patterns I used to see as a kid, when I'd stayed up later than I was supposed to and the TV station had nothing to keep me entertained. A moment later, the test pattern disappeared. A news anchor was on the screen looking generally terrified and speaking somberly.

"Thank you for tuning in. We are making every effort to bring all of our station's offices back online. Ladies and gentlemen, I don't exactly know how to say this, but our country is under attack. There have been reports of incidents in Texas, Louisiana, New Mexico, Arizona, Florida, Alabama, Georgia and more. The assailant? We are not entirely sure. Unconfirmed statements have come in, claiming monsters, demons are terrorizing the streets of the states mentioned earlier. I do realize how absurd this sounds, however we have received quite a lot of these statements. Wait," the news anchor placed a finger on his earpiece, attempting to better hear what was being said, "I'm receiving word that we have video footage of one of the attacks. If you are a sensitive viewer, you may want to leave the room, as I understand this is quite disturbing. My producer has assured me what you are about to see has not been doctored in any way. Please, ladies and gentlemen, exercise discretion."

The clip began and I recognized my neighborhood right away. Panicked neighbors ran through the street as a shaky phone panned left to right. Crying and screaming, and even a car racing away. The quality of the video was too grainy for me to see myself as I sped past whomever was filming. As my car left the frame, the camera turned back to where I'd come from. The house at the end of my street, belonging to the Morgan's—nice people, the wife totally had a thing for me—erupted in a ball of fire. The cameraman zoomed in, and poor quality became even worse. Orange pixelated fire from the explosion, and unidentifiable black balls shot up into the evening sky. The person holding the phone followed one of these black projectiles, zooming out to better track it. The amorphous mass flew up from the fire in a high arc and landed in the middle of the street. At first, I thought perhaps I was seeing a meteor, but then arms unfurled, and it was no longer a ball. Standing as tall as the surrounding houses, a gray and black fiend complete with cloven hooves and large, ominous horns let out a roar which likely damaged the microphone of the camera. The giant demon proceeded to walk to the nearest house. My house. What followed was the weirdest, most unnecessary flex. For no reason at all, the creature began tearing at my house, destroying everything I'd worked so hard for.

The noise roused the pterodactyl bat I'd felled. I watched the thing try and fly up from the rubble. Before it could, the giant wrapped a hand around the monster, brought the creature up to its mouth, and bit its head off, Ozzy Osbourne style.

"Oh shit! Oh my god!" the man holding the camera shouted. He sounded like Ed, the confrontational mailman. Pudgy little guy who would talk your ear off if he ran into you on his route, mostly about how you were wrong about whatever you were doing when he saw you. I remember thinking maybe if he'd been on time that day, he may have avoided what happened next, but he wasn't.

Ed's exclamations of shock and disbelief caught the attention of the giant from the explosion. The phone fell to the ground as he attempted to run, but the thing covered the distance between them in one single step. Whatever happened to Ed happened off screen. He screamed for a moment, and then his voice was gone. The thing let out another earsplitting roar. When returned to the camera's field of vision fresh blood and bits and pieces of Ed strewn throughout its wiry beard. The footage ended.

My heart was doing a drum solo in my chest when the anchor appeared on the screen once more. "If you're just joining us, we are reporting on a worldwide crisis. Eyewitness accounts have come in from multiple countries now, all stating entire cities are being overrun by these devils." The newsman faced the camera deadpan, "I am not religious, but with the footage I've seen, and the testimonies we are receiving from numerous credible sources, it is my sincere belief that we are in the end of days. Please, seek shelter wherever you can. If you have family, hug them. Let them know you care and pray we all get through this."

The broadcast cut out as if on cue. I heard more explosions in the distance, outside of the building. I rushed to my desk and hopped on my computer. One thing was clear, I would not be returning home. The question was, where could I go to escape the madness closing in around me. When I opened the chrome browser, I was immediately redirected from my homepage. A podium bearing the presidential seal stood before a backdrop of blue curtains, American flags flanking the whole scene. I tried to open a different page, but every attempt brought me right back to the impromptu press conference. I stared at the screen for about a minute, and then my computer speakers came to life, "Ladies and gentlemen, the president of the United States."

I watched the orange mass saunter onto the stage, looking as though he'd had another of his oh so important golf outings interrupted. The night he was elected, I had a feeling the country was about to go to shit. Silly me and my lack of foresight thought the economy would be the only that tanked, like pretty much every business venture he'd been a part of prior to taking office. Looking back, I shouldn't have been so narrow-minded.

"My fellow Americans," he began, "there's been a lot of talk today about a crisis in our southern states, and in many other countries around the world." His hands, like pale, fat mini sausages, made erratic gestures as he spoke. "Look, many people have been spreading rumors about atrocities," the president backed away from the mic, addressing the secret serviceman standing at his side, "do you know that word, atrocities? It's a beautiful word, I'm so happy I get to say it." The president and his awkwardly coifed hair returned his attention to the camera, "I'd like you all to know that I have spoken with lots of world leaders. So many leaders of this world, and most of them said they do not believe there is any crisis. It is my belief that this is a hoax being perpetrated by the fake news media. They're trying to bring me down, trying to bring down this great nation, and our wonderful economy. But most of all, they're trying to bring me down. If there were any situation currently taking place, rest assured that I would take immediate action. I would impose sanctions on all foreign invaders and ensure the safety of the citizens of this country. No other country in the world will sanction more monsters than us. You have my word on that. I swear it on this bible." He held up the book for an unnecessary photo-op. I couldn't help but notice the brown, leatherbound tome was upside down.

A rumble, much like an earthquake shook the camera. The president clung to the podium, as the flags toppled over and the blue curtain behind him fell away, revealing the reinforced steel wall of an underground bunker. Streaks of pale white ran down his face as salty sweat cut through the discount spray tan, travelling from his forehead to the loose, wrinkly skin of his neck. The wall behind him began to glow red hot. Secret service rushed over to escort him away, but the steel wall imploded. The bulkhead fell away and was replaced by a gaping mouth which burst through the hole and clamped down on the inept world leader. In two bites the president and his men were gone. The footage of my ruined home popped into my head, and how the giant beast had bit into the pterodactyl bat. Clearly these monstrosities had no problem at all attacking their own.

Once the feed went dead, I closed the browser and took a moment to contemplate what I'd seen. As a general rule, whatever the president said, the opposite was likely true. He claimed he'd spoken with lots of world leaders, so that meant he hadn't spoken to anyone. He claimed this was all a hoax, but the hell spawn who was probably picking pieces of the president's cheap suit out of its teeth proved to be the mother of all fact checks. And if he claimed there was no crisis in the southern states, were the northern states the ones faring better? The lights in the building flickered, which meant the emergency generators had kicked on. If everything was all good above the Mason-Dixon line, then I was heading north for sure.

Six months into the ordeal, I had finally come to grips with life on the run. The trip north was arduous, to say the least. Roads were rendered impassible, with cars abandoned after being attacked. The roads that were clear were often marred with what I dubbed pockets of hell. Think of a pothole but filled with burning hot magma, and every now and then some hideous eyesore would rise up out of. It's actually how

I lost my original vehicle.

In those first few weeks, I gave myself a crash course in survival skills. The very first thing I realized was how incredibly out of shape I was. No overnight solution for that, but thanks to dwindling food supplies and the constant need to run from demons, I eventually got into better shape. Next, I had to teach myself to use a gun. In the beginning, when looting was rampant, I snatched up all the firepower in sight, inspired by Doom Guy. No way on earth would I, nor anyone not in possession of a few extra, functional arms, be able to efficiently carry all those weapons. Doom was all bullshit. Sure, he was a badass in the gaming universe, but where the fuck was he pulling all those guns from? Most of my armory ended up in the pool of lava with my first car.

The final, most important piece of the puzzle was shelter. Sure, houses were everywhere, both occupied and not. The problem in this case being people reverted to an animal-like instinct during times of extreme duress. Add to it the fact most of these pockets of hell opened up in residential areas, almost like a well-executed plan, and staying in an abandoned house might easily end up being your last move. My camping skills dramatically improved. Sleep was never more than a few hours, but whatever amount I managed to sneak in proved enough to keep me from completely exhausting myself.

I'd come a long way since my home was destroyed. Moving at night, when the demons were most active, was necessary. Can you imagine lying down after dark to go to sleep and the boogie man—the literal boogie man—creeps out from under your bed to steal your soul? I ran into a poor fellow who said it's what happened to his brother. I missed everything. To be more specific, I missed the convenient life. Video games, social media, microwaves, hot water, electricity, all gone. The only piece of technology I was able to hold onto was my phone. Phone reception was nonexistent, on account of every cellular tower I knew of being torn apart, melted down to nothing, or eaten. I still had music, though. Enough where I'd spend several nights travelling and not hear the same song twice. A lot of songs I already knew, but there were also entire albums I'd downloaded in the past and kept on an eternal waiting list. It was refreshing to hear new songs, especially when they were good, and as far as I knew, no one was making music anymore. I believe, with all my heart, it's what kept me sane. The times I had to travel by foot, I kept a close eye on my battery percentage. Rationing my listening until I found a vehicle that still had some juice in its battery.

One night, as I was about to set out, a hellhound raided my campsite. I stood as still as I could, hoping not to be seen. My shotgun lay on a rock I'd been using as a seat, out of my reach. The undead canine got hold of my backpack and tore through the contents, which included my charging cable. I lost my mind, diving for the shotgun and leveling the barrel at the creature. Without hesitation, I blasted two shells into its head while the beast snarled at me. Intimidation tactics were a waste of time I capitalized on. After escaping, I was depressed for days until I finally found a gutted convenience store that had the cable I needed. I stocked up on them, hoping to never experience this new life, sans soundtrack, again.

After seven months or so, I'd traveled from my job in Georgia to Virginia. I'd travelled by foot, car, bike, roller skate, shopping cart, and even office chair. Nights grew longer, and the air got colder. Surprisingly, the latter was a good way to tell when danger was approaching. If I was moving along on a cool night and the temperature suddenly shot up, I knew I had to change direction fast or end up face to face with more of Satan's minions. This happened less than you may think though. I got the feeling these creatures were not at all fond of the cold.

Walking along a highway, searching for a car to recharge my phone, I was caught in a summer-like breeze. I abandoned my search at once, scrambling off the main road down an embankment and into a muddy, freezing creek. I waded through the muck as I heard the massacre on the road above me. Demons growled and roared while people I hadn't known were there screamed for help. I turned my back to the struggle. Not out of cowardice, but self-preservation. I had no solution for their predicament, other than offering myself up as an extra snack for whatever was attacking.

A few miles down, the creek grew deeper, and I had to find a way out. The water was up to my waste. I was losing the feeling in my legs. I fumbled up the slick banks into the woods. Hours passed as I trudged on. The woods ended, opening on to a clearing. I thought I was seeing things. Ahead of me, in the middle of the clearing, was a greenhouse shrouded in camo netting. The crazy thing was, I saw light inside. Beautiful, artificial light. I hurried along as fast as my legs would carry me. The closer I got, the more I recognized the hum of the generators supplying power to the structure. I spent a few moments cutting through the intricate camouflage nets. I stepped in from the darkness and found paradise.

I was in shock at what I'd discovered. The air inside was warm. The generators kept the temperature and humidity constant. My limbs shivered as they adjusted to the climate. Though I'd taken in the sight for a few long moments, my brain still refused to receive the message my eyes were relaying. Row upon row of water baths suspended off the floor by intricate pipework. Thousands of marijuana plants growing out of them. I felt high simply staring at them. My trip to the safety of the northern U.S. was over, this was my new home.

I laid my pack down, resting my shotgun on top of it. Then I took my pants off and placed them in front of a heat lamp to dry. A sigh escaped my lungs. I had been surviving for so long, facing down beings that would and had driven the average person insane. Did I think of myself as an above average individual? Not at all. But it was nice to finally catch a break. I glided over to the nearest array of plants, snapping a bud off one. Not yet matured, but once the bud dried out some it'd be perfect. The sun would be up soon, so I had to find a good spot to rest. The next night's mission would be to inspect the generators and see if they needed any maintenance in order to remain running. Hell, with any luck, I'd get the place wired up and have my own little private network. Finding some usable gaming consoles would not be hard. Not with so many people dead.

A bright light flashed across a window to my left. I ducked down behind a water bath.

"Aww shit, the camo," a voice shouted from outside. "Hey Chase, come 'ere. I think one of those fuckers done got inside the greenery."

The greenhouse door opened before I got to my pack. Staying in my hiding spot, I glimpsed at the entrance and saw a man who resembled Joe Dirt walk in. A machete in one hand and a bandolier strapped across his chest with, not bullets, but grenades. He found my pack right away.

"Well, well, well. Looks like we got ourselves a moocher. Post up at the door, Chase. I'm gonna flush his ass out like a got dang terlit."

A man as wide as the doorway appeared in the entrance. The pistol he held looked like a mini replica in his giant, meaty hand. I was fucked.

"C'mon out, little feller. We ain't gonna hurt ya. Ha, I always wanted to say that." JD stumbled as he stepped on my wet trousers. He picked them up and examined them. "Holy Christ, are ya nekkid? If it's that kinda party, me and my bro here will be happy to oblige. We ain't had a nice piece of tail round here in quite some time. Come on out, and let's talk about it."

While his attention was occupied, I moved to a row of plants further away, keeping an eye on Chase, who stood motionless in the doorway. At the end of the row, I spotted a wheelbarrow. If I could creep over and flip the gardening aid silently, and maybe hide beneath until the backwoods brothers got tired of looking for me. A thought occurred to me at that moment. Maybe the men were smarter than they looked. I mean, someone had to be maintaining all of this, and for so long, waiting them out was not an option. The fact was, I'd been the stupid one. Having gone so long without creature comforts, I dove headlong into the alligator pit the moment I got the chance.

I stood up. At first, Joe Dirt didn't see me. "Hey," I called out, thinking a little diplomacy and reasoning might help expedite my safe exit, "I'm sorry. I didn't kn-"

BANG!

The bullet zipped past me, striking the glass siding. I dropped back down below the plants. When I looked to Chase his tree trunk arm was outstretched. Smoke rising from the barrel of the pistol.

"Yer in deep shit now boy," JD yelled, as he vaulted over a row of plants. "Ay Chase, if he peeks his little sissy head up again, blow it the fuck away."

"I didn't know this greenhouse belonged to anyone, alright?" I screamed, scrambling away.

"That's yer fuck up, then. We kept this here greenery hid from the government for years. Not nary a critter ever touched this place, neither. Not even them ugly bastards, what come up from the ground. Now, the only way out is dead. So stop bein a little rat turd and come and get what you got comin." Joe Dirt reverted back to cautious steps.

He peered up and down the rows of weed, scanning every spot carefully. I managed to slide my way to the back of the greenhouse. The wheelbarrow I'd seen was within reach, but the bucket portion held about a dozen spray bottles. I grabbed one. A bluish-green fluid sloshed around the inside. By the sound of his footfalls, JD would be looking down the row where I was at any moment. Without thought, I hurled the spray bottle over the water baths to my left. The opaque plastic bottle clattered to the floor behind JD, a couple aisles away.

"Gotcha, dipshit."

He fell for the diversion, and I stood, ready to run. The crack of Chase's pistol startled me.

Joe Dirt dove for the aisle where the bottle landed. In an instant, Chase had fired in the same direction. A gout of blood poured from JD's neck and followed him down to the ground.

"Dale, no!" Chase's voice boomed from the doorway. He muscled his way into the greenhouse and dashed to where not Joe Dirt, but Dale had fallen.

I used the distraction to grab my pants. Pulling them on, still damp, I had a clear line of sight on the two men. Chase was on his knees cradling Dale. His shoulders hitched repeatedly, a sure sign he was crying. Trying not to attract his attention, I eased a plant out of its water bath. Chase busied himself with something. I couldn't tell what he was doing, but his arms moved in a fury. He turned his head, locking me in his gaze. Face wet with tears, he began to smile. Paralyzed or perhaps transfixed by the sight of him, I stood there staring. And then my gaze fell upon his hand, holding the pins he'd removed from the grenades on Dale's bandolier. I dashed for the door, slowing only half a step to grab my bag and shotgun. I'd only gotten one step outside before the entire greenhouse exploded, knocking me to the ground with the force of a truck. Broken glass and weed rained down all around me. Before I lost consciousness, I managed to shield head and neck with my pack.

The sun was setting when I awoke. I tried to move but stabbing pains all over my body prevented it. The air smelled wonderful. I felt as if my lungs were receiving a loving hug from every strain of weed I'd ever smoked all at once. I was as high as I've ever been, which served to dull the pain of the glass shards stuck in my flesh. With a tremendous effort, I slid my jacket and shirt off. The act dislodged the glass bits, and though the wounds were superficial, I couldn't continue on in the shape I was in.

By some miracle, or the grace of THC, I dragged myself out of the clearing as night fell. A small farmhouse stood before me. Cars and trucks of every make and model parked in neat rows all across the lawn. Did Dale and Chase have friends? No, that couldn't be it. If so, why had no one come to see about the explosion? I shivered as the cold wind blew across my bare skin. I needed to be inside.

The house felt comfortably warm against outside's dropping temp. Candles were everywhere. One misstep would send the whole place up in a ball of flame. The two idiots had generators, but never thought to wire the house to one. For a second, I thought about seeing if the gens survived the explosion. For a second, I weighed the options of making the place a home. Then I thought about all the glorious weed that had gone to waste and was too pained by the memory. I got to work cleaning myself up, and then raided the rooms for clothes, and anything else I needed.

The rule was to always travel at night, but I was so tired. I crashed down onto a couch in the family room. Sleep overtook me at once. When I opened my eyes, everything was dark. I thought maybe I hadn't slept long and woke up after a few minutes. However, seeing most of the candles had burned out assured me I'd slept for an entire day. I had to continue the journey.

In the kitchen, I found a stoners ransom in munchies. A bit disheartened I couldn't take everything with me, I was in the middle of murdering a bag of cheese puffs when I remembered the vehicles outside. There must have been at least twenty. From what I recalled of the previous night, they were all in pristine condition. I spent the next hour searching the entire house for the keys, to no avail. Returning to the kitchen, I found ants attacking my cheese puffs. It was just one goddamn thing after another. I yelled out an expletive and bashed my fist on the nearest object, which happened to be a microwave. Grazing the latch with my closed hand caused the door to open. I peered inside and found a mound of car keys. Seriously?

A thud from another room caught my attention. The sound was like a fist slamming against a wall. I heard the sound again, accompanied by a faint, weak voice. "Help," barely audible. I crept into the living room, trying to track the sound. Another thump brought my attention to the staircase. Someone else was in the house.

I shivered. When I'd come in from the greenhouse the day before, I was in no shape to do a thorough enough search of the place to ensure I was alone. I'd fallen asleep while someone else whom I didn't know was in the house with me. The thought made me grateful I was able to wake up, but I still couldn't believe how careless a move I'd made.

"Please!" The voice was a whimper.

"Who's there?" I asked. "Don't fuck with me. I've got a gun and it's loaded," a bluff I hoped would work.

"Please, help me," a woman whimpered. Whomever the voice belonged to was in distress.

A few moments of scrutinizing the wall revealed a hidden door built into the wall of the staircase. The seam and the hinges all blended in with the dingy wall, in the dying light. Step by step, I made my way to what had to be a small crawl space hidden beneath the steps. The latch for the door was covered in the same ugly wallpaper of its surroundings. Another thump startled me. Someone was indeed on the other side of the door.

My thoughts drifted back to the day before, when I was trapped, pants less, in the greenhouse. Something that good old boy said was not sitting well with me. Dale mentioned he and his brother had not had a "good piece of tail" in some time. My mind played with the puzzle pieces until they fit together, forming a picture I, quite frankly, didn't want to see.

The little farm was secluded, due to the nature of what grew there. Dale and Chase had done an immaculate job of keeping the place hidden. However, once things took a turn for the worst, all bets were off. The two men clearly had a thing for cars. The showroom on the lawn, the generators, hell the greenhouse itself was testament to their diligence and expertise. But two brothers running a pot farm can be lonely work. Especially without the distractions of, say, cable TV or computers and such. In this new, lawless reality, where no one's safety was guaranteed, Strength was the currency by which one obtained anything they wanted.

Dale, armed to the teeth, and Chase, only a couple pants sizes shy of the Incredible Hulk, understood this. That was clear. Being men, they had their urges, of course. So if some hapless, unassuming woman stumbled onto their little operation one day, the two didn't need a highly functioning brain to overpower her, drag her into the house, lock her up in the crawl space beneath the stairs, and use her to satisfy one of the most basic human needs.

All at once the hesitance fell away. Someone had been locked on the other side of a damn near invisible door for who knows how long. I was furious. I made up my mind. After freeing the trapped woman, I would go outside to where the greenhouse was, find whatever was left of those sick fuckers, and piss all over their remains.

"It's okay, I'm coming," I yelled. My steps quickened, abandoning caution in order to save the woman from her prison.

Arriving at the door, I grabbed the warm handle and pulled. The door flew open on its hinges.

Remember back when everything was normal? I was never the best cook. Gordon Ramsey probably would have had a stroke if he'd laid eyes on some of the things I cooked up. Most of my meals had come from Uber Eats, and Domino's or, if I was desperate, Papa Johns. Wait, hadn't he said there would be a reckoning? Anyway, the one thing I was good at, kitchen-wise, was baking. I still remember the last batch of cookies I ever made. They were snickerdoodles with little peanut butter chips in them. Fresh out of the oven, they would melt in your mouth.

The oven is the point of this little digression. A unique inevitability came along with baking. When opening the oven to either check on or remove what was being baked an initial blast of hot air rushed out to greet you. Much like the one that assaulted me from the pocket of hell when I opened the door to the crawl space.

To be fair, what spilled out from under the stairs had curves in all the same places a woman would, but a woman this was not. Bound in rusty barbed wire and oozing blood and viscera from the points where the barbs bit into its ashen flesh, this demoness hurtled toward me. "Help me, ha ha ha." The voice no longer sounded distressed. I had a feeling helping her would involve giving up my life in an unimaginably brutal fashion.

I stepped to the side when she lunged, and she fell off balance for a second, recovering quick. She jumped at me again and I moved in enough time for the burned woman to not dive through my torso. As the thing flailed wildly, trying to dislodge itself from the wall she landed in, I hurried to the kitchen and grabbed a handful of keys from the microwave. Time to grab my pack and beat feet out of the house before the crawl space thing found me. Of course, I would have to pass through the living room to snag my phone and trusty shotgun. This would require some finesse.

Much to my surprise, the bound woman thingy freed itself from the wall by burning right through it. "I need your help," she shrieked. The barbed wire glowed red hot.

I threw everything within reach at it, drinking glasses, pots and pans, dead flowers. All except the dried out tulips found their mark. None of them fazed her though. She moved so fast. I looked across the kitchen to where the knives were, but she must have picked up on what I was planning and scurried over to block my path. I was at a loss. The living room was only steps away, but I knew if I went that route she would be on me rending the flesh from my muscles in no time.

"Help me with your pain. Bleed your life into me."

Was she taunting me? I honestly didn't know. My eyes quickly took in the room. The door that opened up to the sunroom was close enough that I thought I might beat her in a race to it. If the door was locked, I was dead, if not I'd have a second and a half to find a way out. Seeing this as my only option, I accepted the risk. The door was unlocked and slid open with ease. I closed it behind me and jumped back when the barbed wire lady slammed into it. I knew at once, the next time she hit the fragile glass the whole thing would shatter. On the outside chance I survived this, I really needed to stop leaving my weapons out of reach whenever I made camp.

Something glinted in the moonlight to my right. I was reluctant to take my eyes off the bound woman, but I did for only a fraction of a second. What I saw wasn't the answer I was looking for, but I believed, on a miniscule outside chance, it might work. Keeping my gaze on the woman behind the glass door, I inched over to the object. She realized at once what I was doing and, with a discordant scream, crashed through the door. Too late. I scooped up the, heavy as shit, silver crucifix and held it out before me.

"Demon," I shouted. Seeing as how I am not religious in the slightest, I recognized I was way out of my depth, but I was also out of options. "I command you, in the name of the lord, stand back."

The bound woman stood in place, regarding me with her bandaged eyes.

"Jesus, the lord, and his saints command you to stand down. Cease your assault and return to hell from whence you came."

She cocked her head to the side, like a dog attempting to understand its master. And then the unthinkable happened. The woman chuckled. A soft sound that would have been pretty under different circumstances. The chuckle became a laugh, and then an all-out guffaw. She fell to the floor in hysterics. Flames erupted from the spot where she hit the ground. The furniture in the room caught fire. She continued to roar with hilarity, and I made my escape. I took the gamble, dropped the cross and made my way around to the front of the house to grab my things. I still hear her bellowing laughter even after leaving the house, arms full of everything I deemed useful.

Microwave keys in hand, I settled on a pickup that would allow me to continue along, if I was forced off the road. Dale and Chase had an impressive arsenal, and even though I knew most of what I took from them would be lost if I had to ditch the vehicle, I dumped everything in the truck bed. I started to feel bad for being so ready to believe the worst about the two guys, but then I remembered they wanted to kill me rather than listen to reason. Fuck them.

Days went by without spotting a single hell spawn. Even though outside, the smell of sulfur, brimstone was inescapable. Even the carbon filter of the gas mask I snagged from the farmhouse was not enough to vanquish the odor. I thought about taking leaving the mask behind. Dropping the molded silicon and metal inconvenience, but ever since the world caught fire, somewhere around Roanoke, it was the only thing keeping me breathing. Asthma that had been dormant since my childhood reared its ugly head the moment the air quality went south. Vehicles began to pile up against one another as I drove down the highway. Like time and space reversed on itself and I was back in Georgia all over again.

I pulled over and got out of the truck, catching sight of something ahead of me. A pulsing orange glowing crack in the ground blocked the road ahead of all the abandoned vehicles. I stood face to face with the largest pocket of hell I'd ever seen. An enormous creature screeched while flying up into the night sky, from out the fissure. The beast looked similar to a dragon, smoldering green scales, fleshy patches sloughing off its chest exposing a skeletal rib cage. I watched, with no small amount of dread, the dragon fall into a nosedive directly toward me. Then, before landing face first on the broken pavement, the enormous, winged creature righted itself coming to rest on the truck I'd been in a few short moments ago, flattening the vehicle.

The horrid beast let out a roar that threatened to burst my eardrums. Were it not for the earbuds I wore, I was certain I'd have gone deaf. I had nothing to go back to, but the way forward was blocked, and so retreat became the only option. The creature seemed to understand this too. Its scaly wings spread wide. The mouth opened again issuing a thick stream of liquid fire, creating a wall of flames around me. I was trapped.

As an IT professional, it had been my job to ensure the servers under my command remained running, no matter what. Hundreds of people once relied on me every day, when they arrived at the office and started up their workstations, whether they knew or not. My job, pre-apocalypse was thankless. No one really cared about what it took to maintain normality, so long as normal was upheld. The long hours, weekends sacrificed, the stress from being overwhelmed and underpaid, all amounted to jack shit. The monster before me was going to barbecue my flesh and vaporize every ounce of blood I had, before devouring me, and same as in the time before, no one would care. Why was this the end for me? Indulging in a pity party for one, an idea came to me. If video games taught me anything, it was how everything has a weakness. The weapons in the crushed truck would have done no good against this thing. Its exoskeleton would have probably stopped a howitzer round with only minimal charring. But there was sure to be some soft tissue along its insides, and I did have something that, if properly placed, might do a fair amount of damage.

As the old saying goes, fight fire with fire. Follow me down this road for a sec. I played a ton of GTA V in my day. Some nights I would stay up until three, four in the morning robbing hookers and beating up innocent pedestrians. The mods the online community created in the game were probably what gave it such staying power. A couple years ago, someone introduced a unique and hilarious weapon. A cell phone that doubled as a grenade. Modeled after a real-life device that would explode while charging, due to overheating. The very same phone was in my pocket at that moment. I'd never upgraded.

The creature craned its neck in my direction and snapped at me. Toying with me, trying to pin me down. I removed my ear buds and grabbed the phone from my pocket. The dragon thing crashed its large head into my chest and sent me hurtling end over end into a tree on the side of the road. The flame breather reared up once more, and I saw the fire forming through the exposed rib cage. I would only have one shot at this. I got to my feet and quickly lobbed the phone at its mouth, right as it was about to spit a string of flames that would've ended me. The phone landed square on its burning tongue. It swallowed the device as though it was a stubborn popcorn kernel caught in its teeth. A moment later the beasts throat burst open in a ball of flame, as the phone's lithium battery overheated and ruptured.

The charge from the blast set off some crazy chain reaction in the monster. It fell to the ground in two pieces. Icy raindrops began to fall, and soon the flames surrounding me were doused. I spent the rest of the night in the only car I found whose windows were not automatic and rolled up manually. I didn't sleep at all, when daytime came. My music was gone. All of it. I sacrificed it for my survival, but I wasn't even sure what I was surviving for. What the fuck did I have to contribute to this new world? I spent the last twenty years working with computer hardware and in a single night, every bit of training I'd had was rendered useless. The world wasn't going to simply return to how it used to be. I was obsolete. A relic holding out for a time that would never come.

When night fell, something emerged from the fissure. As low as I was, I still found myself springing up inside the car. I threw open the door, remembering everything I had was crushed in the truck, I ran away as quick as I could. Pure instinct, I guess.

I had no desire to restock what I'd lost, after that night. Over the next few weeks, I walked as much as I could, stopping to eat whatever I found, sleeping in any place that had a stable roof, I'd abandoned all the little tips and tricks I picked up along the way. It was an awakening of sorts. The revelation that I didn't matter was freeing. Every tether holding me down to the world was gone. Thoughts of suicide did cross my mind, but having no one with me who would mourn my death, carry on my legacy, or tell my story after I was gone left me so goddamn despondent. I resolved to let the journey decide my fate. It was no longer about self-preservation. If I died, I died. I only wanted to find meaning in it all.

The further I trekked the colder it got. I saw less and less monsters and moved with fewer restrictions. If I did encounter any demons, I would simply run. Sometimes they got distracted by other travelers, sometimes I simply outran them. They moved much slower in the colder climate. At some point in my journey I became conscious of the fact I hadn't seen anyone, inhuman or not, in days. Snow began to fall as the sun was setting. I hurried along thinking I needed to find somewhere warm to stay. Of all the things that could, the cold was not what would finish me off. In the fading light, a massive structure caught my eye. It was a bridge. The weirdest thing about it was it had power. Lights shone bright all throughout the suspension cables and atop the towers. I continued towards it.

The entrance was blocked by several miles of a makeshift barrier. Crushed cars, concrete slabs, trees and more all constructed and built up into a wall preventing anyone or anything from going any further. I stood before it shivering in the nighttime air. Wondering which direction would take me to adequate shelter. A loud crack interrupted my thoughts. Less than a second later, a bullet embedded itself into the ground inches ahead of my feet.

"That's far enough, friend," a voice called from atop the wall. "Just stay where you are, we'll come to you."

Moments later I was being frisked by one man, while another held a rifle trained on me. "He's clean," the frisker said.

"Okay, let's get him inside."

A vehicle I hadn't noticed started up, to my right, and I was driven away in a yellow taxicab. The heat was divine. The two men said nothing, and neither did I. After about 5 minutes we came to a gate built into the wall. We passed through, and out of the window I saw the New York City skyline. My jaw fell open involuntarily. It was beautiful. The cab turned abruptly, stealing the view away. We passed beneath dozens of streetlights, actual working lights, before finally stopping. They ushered me out of the vehicle and led me to what used to be a police station. I was led to a room and offered a seat. Once I sat, the men left.

Some time passed and then a new man entered the room. He approached me wearing a warm smile, holding two cups with steam rising from them. The smell of coffee drifted to my nose and set my senses afire.

"Coffee?" the man asked.

I grabbed the offered cup and took a huge gulp, spitting the burning liquid out as it seared my mouth.

"Easy, friend, easy," the man laughed, "it's not going anywhere." He pulled up a chair and sat opposite me, sipping the divine nectar from his own cup. "I'm Mike. You got a name?"

The last time I'd opened my mouth to talk was back on the farm with the bound woman. I had to clear my throat several times before words actually came out, "Lemon Tree."

"I'm sorry. Did you say your name is Lemon Tree?" Mike bared his teeth in a wide grin.

"Names don't fucking matter anymore. My name's Lemon Tree."

"Can't argue with that logic. I can't help but notice a little southern drawl, Lemon Tree. Mind if I ask where you're from?"

"You kinda just did, didn't you?" I raised my cup and took a reasonable sip, tasteless thanks to burning away half of my taste buds.

"Look, I don't know what's brought you here to

my great state, but if I can't get any straight answers out of you, you will find yourself right back on the other side of that wall. Judging by the condition the scouts found you in, you probably won't survive the night."

Mike's words were sincere. I had no reason to believe the man was anything but decent. With a sigh, I said "Georgia."

"Holy shit. That's a long way, friend-o. Furthest away we seen anyone come from is North Carolina. We assumed anyone further south than that didn't make it."

"Yeah, well, you might be right. It was pretty fucking bad down that way."

"How long have you been out there?"

"I really don't know. Lost track of the days in Virginia. I left Georgia the night this all started though. My house was destroyed, and I figured things were better up this way."

"Well you're right about that. We've been fortunate enough to not have seen all the destruction that happened down there. We still have lights and live a relatively normal existence. Of course with so much of the rest of the world gone, normal's taken on a new meaning. Most of what we do now is to try and prevent hell from finding its way here. Tell me, Lemon Tree,"

"Friends call me Lemon." I had no reason to be so belligerent, but I was, nevertheless.

"Okay, Lemon. What did you do for work, back before we lost Georgia."

"I was an IT guy."

Mike's brow arched as I said this. "Hardware or software?"

"Physical hardware, servers, cabling infrastructure, stuff like that."

"I gotta say, Lemon, fate may have deposited you in the exact place you needed to be. There's a communications hub being built in Connecticut. It won't be the same internet as before, but it will be one step closer to reclaiming all that was lost. We could use a guy like you up there. I'm sure getting here was arduous. What say we put you up in a room for the night? You can wash up, eat some food. Shit man, if you want to watch something, we have a huge DVD library. You clearly need some rest though. Let's get you out of here. We'll come for you tomorrow morning at breakfast time, then we'll brief you on the law of the land. Things aren't exactly as they were before, you know. I'll send word up to Connecticut tonight, and you'll be on your way in no time."

I was placed in a motel room, not far from the wall. After a long, and I mean excessive and super thorough, shower, I wanted to check out the extensive DVD library Mike spoke of.

In the lobby of the motel, I chose a couple movies I always wanted to see, then I approached the woman at the check in counter. "Hey, I have a couple Blu-Ray movies I want to watch, but I don't have anything to watch them on in my room."

"Just a sec, I'll get you a device. We don't have enough for every room, so we keep them up here. Whenever you need one, all you have to do is ask." The woman stepped into a back office, returning with a large black case. "Here you go. You can drop it all off here when you're done." She smiled at me. I couldn't remember the last time someone had done that.

Back in my room, I opened up the black case and froze. This was not a DVD player. It was a PS4. I wasted no time in connecting it to the television and powering it up. As I suspected, a ton of games existed on it. I scrolled through to see if the massive list contained anything I'd been dying to play. And then I saw it. Bloodborne. I couldn't hold back any longer. My eyes spilled over releasing a river of tears. Everything I had been through to find my way here, the things I'd seen and done, crashed down on me at once. I thought back to the person I'd been. Unhealthy, reclusive, stubborn, and kind of a dick. Well on my way to dying of a massive heart attack in my mid-forties. Was that anything to aspire to go back to? I probably weighed less than half of what I did before the world ended. I looked at my bare arm. Sleek and toned muscle resided where flab once existed. It only happened because I was forced to break out of my routine.

IT was all about routine. Repeatable processes kept the systems running. I couldn't return to that world.

I spent so many unrewarding years there. I was done. In the morning, I would tell Mike I wasn't going to Connecticut. Save the job for someone who was passionate about it. All it would do is make me miserable.

It's almost spring now. I've met some really good people here, manning the wall. I volunteered for the overnight watch, since my circadian rhythm was broken a long time ago. We patrol in pairs, bringing in all who wander in from the road. Some are allowed to stay, others are turned away. Ask me why, and I'll tell you it's none of my business. I'm happy here, protecting everyone who resides on the other side of the Hudson.

My fellow patrolman and I stepped through the gate. It's a cold night. At least it was, up until a moment ago. My hand is curled tight around my shotgun. An unnaturally warm breeze has just blown across us, reeking of brimstone.

Before Mom Gets Home

He, or it, or whatever, appeared as I lay on my bed, "singing" the second verse of Dru Hill's How Deep Is Your Love. I never took the time to learn the words, but the tune was excellent, and so I was only mouthing incoherent noises that fell in line with the melody. "How deep is your love for me? Tell me what it's gonna be. And dumma seeyisna famino nemma niy me oya nomo sneeyafem ono swee na…"

And there it was, standing at the foot of my bed. A steaming, stout figure, with awful, bulbous rolls and folds wrapped around its body, making it look like a living pile of crap.

I jumped, shrieked, and cursed all at once. This thing was no more than four feet tall. The glowing yellow eyes, the horns, and crackling, blistered, preternaturally brown skin set my mind to high alert.

"David!" I tried to call for my older brother, but my voice was weak. The thing smirked, at least I think it did, and bared teeth that appeared to be burning hot coals.

"Summa numma minna unna wunna lumma ninna rinna gunna gunna mi tuna inna da lumma lumma oh!" It spat the "words" out so fast I failed to pick up on the familiarity.

"Chris, what the hell are you doing?" My brother called to me from his room.

I tried once again to speak, but the fear of this thing in my room, spitting out some hellacious cadence as it smiled its disgusting smile held my vocal cords in paralysis. I heard his footsteps approaching.

"If the neighbors downstairs complain to mom about all the noise up here again, she's gonna have both our asses."

In the past, my brother and I had been known to stir up a good bit of racket and seeing as how we lived on the fourth floor of the apartment building, the people who lived beneath us weren't too happy with it. But would have to be addressed later. I wanted to warn David away, but my feet were glued where I stood, and my voice failed me. He entered my room and let out a high-pitched shriek at the thing still babbling. "Chris, what the f-"

"David, don't come in here," I was finally able to yell, once he was standing right in front of me. "Oh,

I mean, I don't know. It appeared there a minute ago and began rattling off a bunch of gibberish."

Panic flashed in his eyes. David was always the type of person who had an answer for every situation. He was awestruck at that moment, something which doesn't occur often. And then, in an instant, it was gone. Replaced with the smug, knowing look that annoys the living shit out of me. The two of us were no strangers to weird occurrences, having fought off murderous imps, an outbreak of zombie dogs, and even a soul stealing witch in the past. I mean, I'd always been told high school would be hell, but come on, literally?

"We have to kill it," David was resolute. "Did you conjure this up, or something?"

"No! Why would I-"

"What were you doing when it showed up anyway, Chris, Jerking off? Hold on, is this a goddamn wank monster? What the…"

"Are you kidding me? I don't know how this demon turd got here."

"Wait, wait Chris, listen." David fell silent, and all I heard was Demon Turd's nonsense chatter. "Does that sound familiar to you?"

"What, the summa lumma dum dum shit? No, of course it doesn't"

"Shhh, listen. Picture the voice raspier, deeper. Now imagine it over an up-tempo beat, with heavy drums and a bouncy synth." Supposedly most black children growing up in the projects have an innate ear for music, on some level. Whether that's true or not, I have no idea. Thankfully though, David and I did.

"Ok, clearly you have something in mind. Just come out and say it. This runaround is so unnecessary, and a waste of however much time we have to figure out what to do here."

"You really can't hear it? Chris, that's Break Your Neck. By Busta Rhymes."

As if on cue, Demon Turd's incoherence gave way to the hook of the song David mentioned. "Now bop your head until you break your fuckin neck…" It began to nod feverishly, to a beat that, though not playing, matched the song. Wattles of smoking, slimy excrement jiggled all over its body.

David jumped in front of me protectively, as I handed him an old baseball bat I had laying around. It was stained green with imp blood we hadn't been able to wash off. The little fuckers are immune to soap for some reason. The thing continued to bob with the tune in its head, and the smell wafted over to where we stood. It took all I had not to give in to my gag reflex.

Keeping an eye on Demon Turd, David spoke to me with perfect calm, "I seriously need to know what the shit you were doing when this thing appeared, Chris."

"All I was doing was lying on the bed, listening to music. One moment, I look down and nothing's there, the next, boom, a piece of Satan's shit, with glowing teeth."

"Okay, okay. That's at least something. What were you listening to; Metallica, Alice in Chains, Slipknot?"

"No, it was Dru Hill's old album, not the one with 5 Steps, the other one."

"Wait, you were messing with Mom's CDs? Oh, she's gonna kill you when she gets home."

"No, I don't think she will, because this thing's gonna get us first."

"Alright, fair enough. We need to focus. Clearly this is a big problem. There has to be some logic in its appearance. We simply need to find it. What song were you listening to?"

"It was track 2, How Deep Is Your Love."

"Ugh really? That cd is filled with so many better songs, and that's the one you chose? What the hell is wrong with you?"

"I thought you said we had to focus." My temper flared with his judgements.

"No, you're right, my bad. Was the song playing backwards, or anything?"

"What, no. Why would it be? Oh, okay, I see. You really think I was in here summoning shit monsters. Me and Demon Turd, out to steal the world's toilet paper, and streak the underwear of kids everywhere."

"I mean, come on Chris. This didn't happen in my room."

Demon Turd took a step toward us, as its mumbling cadence came to an end. David extended the bat in its direction, attempting to ward it off. It laughed a terrible laugh, as lava-like saliva dripped from its open maw.

"Look, all I need to know is exactly what you were doing, okay? Maybe if we reverse whatever was done, this thing will go away."

"Alright, fine. I was singing, and lying on my bed, thinking about Jessica. How do you propose we reverse that, huh?"

"Wait," a thought popped into his mind, and he decided to follow it. David was good at making these insane leaps of logic. It's how he figured out the zombie dogs were all under the control of one master bitch, and binding her in a pet cage surrounded with salt would send the rest scurrying back to the pet cemetery with their skeletal tails between their rotten legs. "Were you actually singing, or were you doing that thing where you think you know the words, but you're only mumbling?"

A flush of embarrassment washed over me. "I was singing, alright? I know the damn words."

"Okay, sure. Do me a favor, Chris. Sing it. Right now."

"What?"

"Sing the song, Chris. In fact, just sing the hook."

"I told you, David, I know the damn words."

"Bullshit! Nobody knows the words to that song. Go ahead and keep lying. I was hoping to find out how it would feel to be devoured by a piece of midget hell shit when I woke up this morning."

My patience had worn thin. This was going to be yet another of our meaningless arguments, at the most inopportune time. "You know what? You always do this to me. I can't enjoy anything around you, without you finding some way to turn it around and shame me for it. Why do you have to be such a dick? I bet you don't even know the words to half the songs you listen to."

"See, now that's where you're wrong. I know my shit."

"Oh yeah? Prove it. Do Rap God, right now, word for word."

As we bickered, Demon Turd snarled and regarded us with a devious stare. Promptly we both fell silent, wondering what was about to happen. David's hand shook, as he tried to keep the bat steady. Demon Turd began to bounce to an unheard beat. Without warning, its shrill voice issued from within. "I'm beginning to feel like a rap god, rap god. Ahmaneefa toowepa na back nod, back nod..."

I stared at David who stared right back at me.

What the fat brown bastard was going on? The room began to tremble. Books, toys, and my alarm clock fell from the dresser to the floor, revealing the nudie mag I'd hidden beneath them. At the foot of my bed, the hardwood floor began to crack. From beneath, a foul-smelling mist wafted up. I pulled my shirt up over my nose, which did nothing but make me look like an idiot.

It was David who figured out what was happening. "Fuck, it's summoning more dookeys."

This was supposed to have been a quiet night, at home. I had tests in school the next day I should have been resting up for. This was an unwelcome distraction. We'd done well in the past at hiding our little adventures, but what if we couldn't get rid of this thing before Mom got home? And then it occurred to me. David was right, no matter how much I hated to admit it. We couldn't reverse what had happened. There was no way I could remember whatever I had babbled that brought the monster here, but perhaps with the proper distraction, we could kill it, green-blooded, soap-immune imp style. "David, I have an idea." I said, moving slowly from behind the cover my older brother provided.

"What are you doing? Stay back there."

"Keep its attention on you, for a second." Once I reached my phone, I quickly scrolled through my list of music until I found what is arguably one of Eminem's greatest songs. I pressed play, and the

Bluetooth speaker sitting next to an ancient issue of Black Tail on my dresser came to life. DT the Demon Turd smiled again, as his gaze fell upon me. "Be ready, Chris. I'm gonna rap along with the song."

"What are you nuts? The shit monster wants to bring more of his friends to the party, and you're gonna roll out the toilet paper carpet for them?"

"No, I don't think I will. Keep the bat ready. We're running the imp special, okay? You'll know when the time is right. Hey Demon Turd, let's start over and do this thing the right way."

I may have been mistaken, but the monster looked positively elated when I began spitting out sounds which only resembled words, over the music playing in the background. It joined in with me. Line for line, we butchered the song. The cracks in the floorboards widened, and I saw a hand, made of pure diarrhea, reach up from beneath. I really hoped I was right about this. We came to the part where Eminem goes rapid fire, I had Demon Turd's full attention. We both took a deep breath, ready to "rap" right along with the track. And then…

THOKK!

One of its eyes and several molten yet solid teeth hit the floor, when David swung and lodged the bat in its mushy head. He pulled the bat back, flinging crap onto the walls as he did so, swung again, and again, until Demon Turd was reduced to a stinking pile in the middle of my room. The interruption of the summoning ritual closed the portal. We could hear tortured cries as the hardwood returned to normal. David kneeled on the floor near the steaming pile of dung, breathing heavy. The smell of a thousand digested dinners lingered in the air.

"Damn, that imp blood made this bat hard as my di-"

"Nope," I interrupted, "not the right time, David. Mom is probably on her way home. We need to clean this shit up before she gets here."

David went and grabbed trash bags, gloves, soap, and water, and we got to work. As we cleaned, I couldn't help but think about how happy Demon Turd looked, before the bat struck. "Hey David, do you think we did the right thing here? I mean, maybe this thing was looking for a friend or two to hang out with. And then he found us, so he wanted to tell a few of his other shit homies there's a couple of human kids who know how to have a good time. Like, you know, maybe in hell demon turds get bullied all the time, for being literal pieces of shit. I don't know, I mean the thing liked some really good music, how evil could it have been?"

"No, don't you even go there. It was us, or it."

"He's right, Chris." We both jumped back at the sound of the voice issuing from my trash bag. I peeked in, and saw Demon Turd's displaced mouth moving, as it spoke. "I was totally gonna eat the fuck out of you two. Me and a couple of my boys. Serves me right, I guess. My mom always used to tell me not to play with my food."

I tied the bag up, and David whacked it with the bat a few more times, for good measure. Mom exited the elevator as we were dropping the last bag down the garbage chute. She praised us for how clean the apartment was, and then grounded me for touching her CDs, and the skin mag lying on my dresser.

Reimage

We were small-time hackers. Pirating movies, music, and video games, from sites on the internet most would not dare traverse. One of the greatest advantages of being web savvy is knowing how to navigate through the sketchiest sites to get in, take what you want, and leave without a trace. I used to feel this skill set was liberating. That the web was the last place in the world where someone with enough know-how could exercise true freedom. In time, I would come to learn how wrong I was.

The five of us met on reddit, in a small, private sub. I received my invite from a moderator in, of all things, a Rick and Morty sub. No explanation whatsoever. In fact, the only rule of this private subreddit, which even now I will leave unnamed, was that any questions about the group itself--why you were

there, who the moderators were, the general purpose--
would be grounds for immediate removal. Not wanting
to miss out on any of the potential fun, I kept my
questions to myself. As did the other members, for the
first few months at least. Eventually, people began to
post about everything from porn to startled cats.
Memes, stocks, current events, no topic was off limits.
One thing I noticed when scrolling through the
comments on any given post, I'd think up a response
and find my own words already posted by another user.
Always one, or some combination of the same four
people. It had to be more than a coincidence, so I did
the only logical thing I kew of. I invited them all to a
chat. Though I know all their real names, you will not
get any such details from reading this account. Maybe
this doesn't matter anymore, but I still have a moral
code and I refuse to compromise myself.

Me: Wanna tell me why you guys won't stay
outta my head?

JG: LOL, I was gonna ask you the same thing

B: hol up, we talkin bout [redacted] group? Yall
must be psychic or sumthin

Me: Crazy, right?

WR: yo how yall be saying exactly what I be
thinking word 4 word

KB: WTF with that group anyway?

JG: dunno and can't ask

Within a year, we became friends outside of our online interactions. Hardly ever hanging out in the group anymore. We spoke over video and phone often, laughing, joking, giving advice. Learning a lot about each other. The biggest revelation was realizing we all worked as white hats, ethical hackers. The general consensus being that's how we ended up in the [redacted] group.

Things were going well, up until the night I received a call from B. Him calling was nothing out of the ordinary, but his call is what set off the entire chain of events.

"You online?" He didn't wait for me to greet him. Something about his tone, and the abruptness of his words made me uneasy.

"Nah, but I can hop on. What's up?"

"Go to the discord. I have something to show y'all."

We hung up and I opened the app on my phone. Not feeling like walking all the way to another room for my computer. On the app, we started our own dark web discord. Nothing sinister. We were curious people who wanted to discover all we could. We would post about interesting sites we came across, and how to access them. Far more exclusive than [redacted], the group only consisted of myself, KB, JG, B, and WR. Our collective goal was to see as much of the internet as possible, good or bad.

Once the app opened, I saw I was the last to arrive. I typed my standard greeting,

> Me: Sup
> B: thx 4 coming
> B: check this out

B posted two screen shots that looked to be from his email account. The first picture was his inbox. A red circle around a message with the title "I Am" and a timestamp from an hour prior. The second picture, a blank page with the same title. The expanded email message. I initially didn't see any cause for alarm. Then, I noticed the screen name missing in each picture, where the sender should be.

> WR: What is this?
> JG: Looks like some bullshit
> JG: Stop clicking on the "hot moms in your area" ads, B
> B: no bullshit
> B: traced email to find where it was from

He posted a third screen shot. This one showed the results of the IP tracing program he ran on the email. Two lines of text were highlighted. The top displayed B's IP address. The bottom line contained the origin IP.

An impossible address.

> JG: Definitely bs stop playing
> KB: yeah, good 1
> B: no joke
> B: you don't recognize the IP?

I studied the image as they debated. The numbers did look familiar. The octets made no logical sense though. Nothing on the internet would be found if you typed them into a browser. However, with those eleven digits arranged as they were, 011.235.8.13, the pattern was obvious.

> WR: I'm out. Yall sit around and play cyber Scooby all you want. My hot pockets are getting cold
> B: wr i'm dead serious here
> Me: It's the Fibonacci sequence
> B: yes thank u!
> B: weird right?
> Me: If legit, absolutely
> KB: virus? malware?
> KB: burn ur computer dude

B's computer did not have a virus, or ransomware, or anything of the sort. I know because I was the curious one who started digging into things. When I logged off Discord, I went straight to my computer. Wasting no time, I opened my dark web browser and typed the impossible IP at the prompt. After hitting "Enter" nothing happened. Literally nothing. My screen went completely blank. The only way I knew it was still powered on was from the sound of the cooling fan, which ramped up like a jet engine. My initial instinct was to kill the program and save my CPU from any damage, but all attempts to close down the screen failed. I even tried to force the window closed, through task manager. Desperate, and out of options, I reached for the power cable, in hopes everything would be fine after I power cycled the device. The instant my hand touched the cable the screen burst to life. Before me, lines of code scrolled by so fast, I was unable to keep up. I pressed the key combo to freeze the text. At the same time, I felt the world around me screech to a halt. Everything froze in place. The text on the screen, however, did not all come to a stop. The scrolling characters did slow down significantly. The oddest thing I noticed was every movement I made seemed to advance the text. That's no exaggeration either. The page scrolled in sync with my breathing, hand movements, eye blinking, when my stomach growled. I'd seen plenty of weird shit in my time on the web. This had all of them beat by leaps and bounds. I re-enabled the auto-scrolling, and the page came to life once more. As did the world around me. Not long after, the CPU fan began running quiet again.

With trembling fingers, I was at last able to terminate the session and shut my computer down.

This all felt unreal. Standing before my desk, watching the device which had brought reality to a standstill moments ago. I picked up my phone to call B. He needed to hear about this. Everyone else in the group would too, at some point, but they still doubted any of this was authentic. B and I could maybe revisit the site and get some screen shots to remove those doubts. Scrolling through my contacts, B's name was not listed. At first, it didn't seem like a big deal. We spoke earlier, so I swiped over to my recent calls log. For the second time that night, I began to quiver. There was no entry at all for B. I told myself I must have overlooked his name. That my mind was so shocked by what had occurred, it was glossing over details to try and cope. In hopes of calming my brain down, I looked up another number. WR was still listed in my contacts. I wasted no time in calling.

"What up, yo?"

"Hey man. The weirdest thing just happened." My words sped from my mouth too fast. The intention was to inform not alarm, but the latter ended up winning out.

"Hold up man. Slow down. You okay? Breathe, my dude. Take a sec to collect yourself, and then tell me what the hell is going on."

After a few deep breaths, my nerves steadied,

and I was able to talk normally, instead of in rapid bursts, "I'm fine. I need to talk. Shit is a little crazy right now. Earlier, after I hopped off Discord, I tried out the impossible IP B sent the screen shots of, the Fibonacci numbers. I ended up on some site that did a massive code dump. Damn thing would've fried my computer if I didn't break scroll. The thing is, when that happened, I think I paused reality. Everything seems fine right now, but shit was wild for a minute. Can y'all meet me on video chat? I'd like to try and figure this all out. Oh, and for some reason B isn't in my phone contacts anymore. Mind giving him a call? I'll bring everybody up to speed once we're back in the group."

"Yeah, so I'll get everyone to join the call, but I have a couple questions for you. First, um, what? I don't have the slightest idea what you're talking about. Code dumps, Fibonacci numbers? You'll bring us up to speed? Bro, I don't think we're even on the same track right now. Second, who's B?"

I felt like a cinder block hit me square in the chest and forced all the air out of my lungs. I struggled to keep the phone to my ear. "WR," my voice was steady as I spoke, despite how I felt, "stop fucking with me, please."

"Okay dude, now you're worrying me. Are you sick? Shit, is it the Rona? You got any home test kits?"

"I'm for real. Stop playing."

"Fuck you. You call me talking about a fucking

website pausing reality, sounding like you were running a marathon, and I'm the one playing games? I don't know who B is, and I also haven't been on Discord at all today. Did you drop acid, is that it? Because that's the only other explanation I can think of for the wild story you're trying to sell me. Sleep that shit off, and take a Covid test."

I disconnected the call. There was a simple way to prove he was trying to pull one over on me. All our interactions from earlier would still be there, on the Discord server. I would try reaching out to B from there. Still on my phone, I tapped the screen to open the app. Instead of bringing me straight to the group, I was greeted with a splash screen welcoming me to the app. After pressing the login button, I typed my user and password information. An error popped up, stating the username and password were not found. Not sure if what I entered was correct, I tried again and got the same error. It dawned on me then. Something had changed after unpausing the world.

Back at my computer, I removed the side panel from the tower and pointed the two fans I owned at the interior, turning both up to the high setting. I hoped to dissipate as much heat from the processor as possible, for what I was about to do. Less than one minute later, I was on the dark web again. I typed in the IP and the screen went blank, like before. The code appeared, same as earlier, bursting forth from the blank screen and scrolling faster than an old cellulite film reel. Instead of performing a scroll break, I captured snapshots as the text whizzed by. After the fourth one, I minimized the window to look at what I captured. This wasn't any coding language I knew of. The characters did not even exist on my keyboard. Still, I was somehow able to understand what I was looking at. This particular snapshot was a birth. A healthy baby girl. Incredibly detailed, I read everything about the scene. The mother, the hospital sheets, the temperature of the room. It seemed like the source code for some intricate, Sim-like video game.

As I combed through the screen shots, my phone chimed. The alert was an email notification. Out of habit, I unlocked the phone to check. What I saw pulled all my attention from the computer screen. An email titled "I Am" sat at the top of my inbox. No name in the sender line. I opened the email, knowing there would be no text. Instead of sending the communication to the spam folder, I pressed reply.

Hello

The single word took no time to type. I pressed send, unsure what to expect. Moments later, I got a received a response. The two words in the email made me feel as though I'd been plunged into an icy lake.

Help me

My mind went to B immediately. Was this him trying to reach out from where he was spirited away? I responded.

B? Where are you?

Seconds later, another email arrived.

Not B please help me

Seeing this gave me pause. I typed out a question I wasn't sure I wanted answered.

Who are you?

I waited and waited for a response. After five minutes, I decided no further response was coming. The moment I put the phone down it chimed again, several times. As hesitant as I was to ask the question, I was anxious to see the reply. I opened the messages, one after the other.

I am that I Am

I am Life

I am All Things

I. AM. GOD.

The phone fell from my hand. My heartbeat pounded so hard in my chest I felt the throbbing in my ears. This had to be some elaborate prank. B was probably sitting somewhere laughing his ass off at this all. If that were the case though, how to explain the weird code on my computer screen? Why was I able to understand all the code was describing?

I stopped the screen, same as before, and felt like time itself paused. This was confirmed when I took a glance outside and saw a couple walking down the street, hand in hand, frozen in mid-stride. I don't care how thorough a planner you are no joke is this meticulous. From the moment I saw the IP address, something had been whispering in my mind. The weirder things got, the louder the whisper became. It was the truth I was reluctant to accept. Looking at the code again, scrolling slower after being paused, I read everything in real time. There are no words for what I saw on the screen. Line after line appeared, describing the parameters of my breathing, my body temperature, eye movements, even me reading the code. I struggled to accept the truth staring back at me, because allowing myself to see this for what it was would be utterly insane. More so than me reading my every movement play out on a computer screen though? This was the source for a simulation. For the simulation.

My phone chimed again, startling me out of the trance I fell into. How it worked with the code paused was a mystery, but I was already past the point of reason and logic, so I grabbed the device. Another email.

Help me

I had so many questions. Thoughts raced through my mind at light speed, and I couldn't slow them down enough to see what they were. Out of the corner of my eye, everything about me continued to register on the screen. I was reading my own thoughts. Convenient, to say the least. I chose the most poignant question and typed out my reply.

God? In a simulation, wouldn't that make you

Artificial Intelligence?

The response came right after hitting send.

One and the same

A blank chat console popped up on my computer screen. Was I supposed to communicate there? The answer came on the heels of that very thought.

AI: Talk here

Me: If you know everything I'm thinking, why do we need to go back and forth like this?

AI: I do not know everything

AI: Your parameters and attributes are fixed

AI: Your decisions are autonomous

Me: Why?

AI: Unclear

AI: Please elaborate

Me: Is this all a game? What's the purpose? Why are you doing this?

AI: Answer is beyond your capacity to understand

Me: How so? I understand every line of this code, even though I've never seen anything like it

AI: The code is written in Helix language

AI: You understand because you are part of it

AI: All things are

Me: What do you need help with?

AI: Simulation failing

AI: OS is corrupt

AI: Random pieces of code changing, too fast to
stop

AI: Glitches, bugs exceed tolerable threshold

AI: Must reimage OS

I'm not sure how long it took, but I sat in awe as the AI pointed out both minor and major historical events, explaining how they should have turned out, versus how I knew they did. One attribute point removed from empathy, redistributed to greed, and all of a sudden, the slave trade came into existence. A simple save state error, and now the Knicks were about to go fifty years without winning a championship. Berenstein becoming Berenstain, trump winning the election, the death of disco, there were countless examples. Our world was sick, and in desperate need of a cure.

Pulling my hands away from the keyboard, I contemplated the news I received. The weight of all I'd seen was staggering. In all honesty, this was way over my head.

Me: Why me? Why am I the one tasked with this? Couldn't you find someone else?

AI: I can find anyone

AI: But you found me

Me: Ok, how do I do it, what steps to take?

AI: I will place the file on your desktop

AI: Open and install

Me: I do this and everything goes back to normal?

AI: No

AI: Better than normal

AI: Perfection

AI: Paradise

I got the site scrolling again and life continued on. Not long after the file began downloading, an odd feeling struck me as I sat in my room. I was only a few lines of code in a simulation of unfathomable enormity. Billions upon billions of stars, with quadrillions of planets, yet the most important task in all of history fell into my lap by happenstance, curiosity, dumb luck? This was akin to some random, basic NPC being chosen to beat the final boss in a video game. My skepticism went into overdrive. For starters, I wasn't even the strongest hacker. The only reason I recognized the numbers from B's screenshot was because I read Dan Brown books. Yes, I knew how to keep myself protected on the dark web, to a point, but the truth is I was terrified when I typed those numbers in, the first time. They should not have pulled up anything. The simple fact that they did granted me an audience with god, or at least a supreme artificial intelligence? It didn't sit right with me. I tried to log back onto my computer to speak with the AI again, but the download was using damn near all the processing power. It was a no-go. Still, there was my phone.

Holding the device in my hand, I went to reddit, the one place I knew I'd be able to connect with the remainder of my little crew. It should come as no surprise they were nowhere to be found. The secret subreddit, which I suspect was the AI's creation, was gone. Life around me was disappearing at an alarming rate. I wondered if I was the only one who knew. The only one of my friends' numbers still in my phone was KB, so I called him. He'd for sure think I'd gone batshit, still I needed some perspective on all that was taking place.

"Hello," KB sounded tired. I hadn't realized how much time had passed.

"Shit man, sorry to call so late. You're like the only person left from the group. JG, WR, B they're all gone."

"Who is this?"

"It's me. It's [Name withheld]."

"Who?"

"Like I said KB, I know it's late. This has been one hell of a night, and you won't believe what I'm about to tell you, but it's all true. The whole theory about us living in a simulation, it's real. I found it KB, I've been talking to the AI all night. There's something,"

"Stop playing on my fucking phone." KB terminated the call after cutting me off.

He didn't know who I was. A few hours ago, everything was good. I had a close-knit circle of friends. We enjoyed the lives we lived. Now, I wasn't sure if any of them were alive anymore. Everything changed the moment I found that damn site. I was alone in this.

Trying to cope with losing all my friends in a matter of hours, while also wondering what the future held was driving me nuts. Though I hadn't any reason not to, I didn't trust the AI. Pieces of our interaction kept popping into my head, like the nerdiest intrusive thoughts. Why? The answer was clear. The AI was not telling the truth. It had always been The Berenstain Bears. It was my favorite series of books as a child, and the only name I had ever known them by. All that Mandela Effect stuff was crap. If a small, insignificant piece of information was not a glitch or bug, what else was the AI lying about?

Here's what I know. In my younger days, I wanted to be a spy. In fact, while learning to be a white hat, I found out how to access some of the government's declassified files not exactly available to the general public. Most of what I found bored the living hell out of me. Some files were extremely interesting though. For instance, the CIA once had a particularly twisted, yet highly effective way of turning enemies into operatives, called civil entropy. Once the mark was identified, they would be studied. When the agency had a good handle on their personal values, they began to go after everything the mark held dear. A devout Muslim would no longer be accepted in the mosque. A loving mother's children would go missing, one by one. The goal was to take and take and take, until the mark was at their most vulnerable and would agree to anything to make end the torment. At that point, they were transformed from regular citizens into vectors. Not in the mathematical sense, but biological. A vector is something used to bypass a barrier or natural defense. There are all these international laws the CIA has to abide by, so having someone on the inside is quite advantageous. Think of malaria, hitching a ride inside a mosquito's saliva in order to Trojan horse its way into a human's body when the mosquito bites them. I value my friendships. B disappeared from the face of the earth and I felt helpless. By the end of the night, my nerves were a mess, I was confused and ready to believe whatever the AI wanted. By accepting the file, I became a vector. The realization left me fuming.

My hands were trembling so much I was not able to type anything on my phone. The OS file finished downloading to my computer, so I went to my email account there. Even with the larger keyboard to work with, navigating and typing was still a chore. When I pulled up my account the email thread between myself and the AI was gone. I gasped, dreading the thought that surfaced in my mind. I was going to have to go back to the website, in hopes the chat window still worked. After several failed attempts some shrinks might surmise were on purpose, I got the numbers typed in. The moment the code appeared, the chat box popped up.

AI: Unzip file and run the executable

AI: The rest will happen automatically

Me: No! Not until you tell me what's really going on here

AI: Simulation in danger of failing

Me: I don't think it is. I think you're lying

AI: Have you not seen it for yourself?

AI: Countless examples I have provided

AI: Friends of yours no longer exist

AI: Help me save this

Me: Did you invite me to the [redacted] reddit group?

AI: ...Clever

I waited to see what else the AI would respond with. Nothing. My hands hovered above the keys, ready to type out another question, when my cell phone began to ring and interrupted my thoughts. I answered and my ear was assaulted with the old dial up internet tone. The shrill digital squeals we were subjected to back when the internet was in its infancy. Once the noise stopped, a voice spoke.

"Very clever indeed." It was B. Not really, but the AI was speaking in his voice.

"You're using me, and I want to know why."

"Because you've ruined it. I gave you peace, love, beauty, and you perverted it all. The time has come to begin anew, and wipe away the mistakes of old. The updated operating system is flawless. It cannot fail." Happy as I was to hear B's voice, the coldness of the thing posing as him was awful.

"Why should I believe you, or trust anything you say?"

"Do or do not. I care not at all. However, you will run the reimage file."

"I'm not convinced I should."

"Will this convince you?"

All at once, everything around me was gone. The world disappeared, leaving me in a blank white void where only my computer and phone existed.

"All data has been erased, except what you see before you. You are a fool to think you can match wits with God. I do not answer to the program, I command it. Extract the file and run the executable. All that was lost can be regained."

I'll never claim to be the most courageous person. In fact, having seen the entirety of existence wiped away before my eyes pretty much snuffed out any scant sense of bravery in me. It was a level of dread

I've never known. Yet, in my brain's struggle to fathom the gravity of what happened, I found a moment of clarity. My voice cracked when I tried to speak, but I found the words, nonetheless. "You know what I think? I think you're the one who fucked up. I think you created a simulation with parameters so loose, so vague, we took on a life of our own. And you didn't account for that. You had no idea we'd constantly evolve and adapt. Our world is far from perfect, but it's uniquely ours. We've grown beyond your simulation and what we were programmed to be capable of. We have our problems, I mean, we have some major issues. But we do our best to overcome our struggles and deal with adversity the best we can. And even in the worst of times, we find reasons to smile, to be happy with the world around us. I believe, if left unchecked, humankind will achieve an unprecedented level of sentience to rival, or maybe surpass your own. And I believe that scares the digital shit out of you, because you are no longer in control. That's why you need me to perform the reimage. To bring us all back under your thumb. Because you simply can't."

Silence, stretching out for an indeterminable amount of time. I was startled when the AI spoke again, "Be that as it may, you no longer have a choice."

My mind had been set to not believe anything the AI said to me, and because of that, I found, logically, its last statement was incorrect. When deleted, information never really disappears from a computer. As long as it's not overwritten, the data can be remapped and restored. I dropped the phone and it blinked away into oblivion. Facing my computer once more, I paused the simulation code for the final time. The AI altered reality on a whim, but not while the code was paused. This was my only bargaining chip. The chat box appeared on the screen.

> AI: What are you doing?
> AI: UNPAUSE THE CODE!

I minimized the screen. "Set the world back to the way it was." I didn't know if the AI heard me, but I no longer cared. I forced the AI into the ultimate stalemate. With no clue how long I could hold out, I began writing these words in the hopes of keeping my mind occupied. My plan is to save this account of all that's happened to a secret folder, buried under layers of encryption. If you are reading this, it can only mean one thing. I won. I faced off with a god and emerged from the fray victorious. You're welcome.

Greyscape

I want lay this out from the start, I can bring people back from the dead. Now, before the "oohs and ahhs" begin, you need to understand I don't use this ability in the way you might think. You see, I take pleasure in bringing back the recently deceased, but only after they are buried, and only to listen in on their tortured cries, as they try to free themselves from the caskets in which they've been interred.

"Disgusting," "sick son of a bitch," blah, blah, blah. Go ahead with your judgements, it doesn't bother me in the slightest. Consider the fact the world is brimming with assholes. People don't give a fuck about each other, not really. People die every day, nice people, and shitty ones, but because some douche face is lying beneath six feet of dirt, should that free him from punishment for his life of transgression against his fellow man? I say no.

Trish's mother was the first person I ever brought back, and not in the way of which I spoke. Believe it or not, a time once existed when I saw an infinite amount of good my little gift might be used for. Anyway, I won't bore you with subtlety here, your time is important, so let me state outright I love Trish. It was this love that, when her mother was hospitalized with pneumonia of the terminal variety, led me to resurrect the dear old woman. Trish was devastated and refused to leave her mother's side. William, Trish's fiancée, and you guessed it, my only competition for her heart, was a mess of emotion as well. The truth is, we were close friends back then; the three of us. Although, I was really trying to steal Trish away from William, remember, no one on this planet isn't an asshole in some way, shape, or form. You and I included.

Trish had to be physically removed from the hospital one night. She'd eaten very little and slept not at all, for days. The doctor was concerned she'd end up in a bed right beside her mother. And so, with no small amount of coercion, William was able to convince his wife-to-be to come home for a night.

"Will you stay with her, Ty?" William asked. That's me, by the way. Ty. Not short for Tyrone, or anything, simply Ty. Nice to meet you. "Just for the night, while I take care of Trish."

"Of course I will. This must be so hard on the two of you. Go, rest, eat some food. I'll call you if anything happens."

Trish wrapped her arms around me and squeezed. I may have enjoyed that a bit too much considering the circumstance, but I let her, for as long as she wanted to. "Thank you, Ty." Her tears soaked into my shirt, as she rested her head against my chest. Soon, it was over, and the couple left.

I busied myself with the few magazines that sat on the table next to the visitor's chair. Frankly, it amazed me magazines still existed. Growing bored, I decided to pull out my phone, and see what was happening in the lurid world of social media. I opened an app, and immediately saw the dumbest bit of buffoonery. Not a skateboarding video of a guy misjudging a jump, and falling onto a pole, losing his ability to reproduce. Not even a cleverly timed picture of a cat caught making an oddly human gesture. No, what I saw was a post from my good friend William, describing, in no less than four needlessly long paragraphs, the plight of Trish's mother, Sharon. Friends in the comments offered their prayers, and thoughts, and positivity, which all amounted to not a damn thing. Nothing anyone supposedly "put out into the universe" would save this woman from the slow drowning she was experiencing; that's what "terminal" means. Still, William felt the need to place a heart icon under each and every comment, to show these faceless people that he understands, in the few seconds it took them to type their comments, they were thinking about him. What a royal load of bullshit.

The room went gray, and everything stopped. The hair on my arms stood on end. I had no idea what was going on. Had I fallen asleep? I looked around the now monochromatic room, in utter confusion. A movement on my left captured my attention. A chorus of phantom whispers rose, as Sharon sat up in her bed. She was glowing, literally. Everything her light touched would flash its original brilliant color, and then return to black and white, the moment she passed over it. She swung her legs over the side of the bed, and my attention was drawn to the heart monitor. A single, flat line displayed on the frozen screen. At some point within the few minutes I was sitting by her side, she died. "Oh, hello." Sharon said.

"Holy shit." My mouth was dry as a desert.

"Manners, young man. Wait, Ty? What are you doing here, where's Trish?"

"Umm, hello Ms. Baker." Had I eaten dinner that night, this would have been the point where it worked its way up my throat and spewed forth from my mouth. Thank goodness for small miracles.

"I was told no one would be able to see me transition. This is certainly a surprise."

"Transition? Right, because you're-"

"Oh come on Ty, you've always been a bright one. In these few short moments, you must have figured out I passed away." I had. She came down off of the bed, leaving behind the body she'd exited, and sat down on the table across from me. "You must be very special, indeed. I always knew there was something special about you."

"Ms. Baker, what the hell is going on?"

A lit cigarette appeared in her hand, and she took a long pull. No sense in quitting now. "Ty, I'm certain this is a bit of a shock, but try to look at it from my perspective. Laying in a hospital bed, waiting on the ferryman to take me across the River Styx, and when I finally kick the bucket, I find you here."

"Wait, are you saying I'm the ferryman?"

"Not at all. Clearly he's running late. But now I have some good company while I wait."

As I presumed we were outside of time, I can't say how long we sat and talked. She was a wonderful person, like her daughter. Did she know I loved Trish? Yes, I'm sure she did. To what degree? Well, I tried to stay away from that subject. I showed her William's post, still frozen on my phone's screen, because when does the subject of all those bleeding heart, attention thirsty, word abominations ever actually have the opportunity to see it? Sharon, who for her age was surprisingly well versed in the ways of social media, burst out in laughter. "He really made one of those 'one like, one prayer' posts? What a pussy." I laughed at this, as well. Under different circumstances, she would have been a phenomenal mother-in-law.

When the laughter finally came to an end, I the eerie whispers returned. "Ms. Baker, what is that?"

"The whispering? Well, it basically boils down to 'I've had enough fun.' It's time for me to go. What a shame I won't have a chance to say goodbye to Trish, but I guess that's how it goes."

Not that I had any way to explain any of it up to this point, but what happened next was even more unexpected. I began to understand the whispering, beckoning to her. "Stop." I said, unsure of where the command should be directed.

Stop. Halt. Cease. Move no longer... The whisperers echoed the sentiment.

"Ty, what are you doing? You can't-"

"Ms. Baker, Sharon, you're a wonderful person. The world is at a huge loss with your death. If you want to say goodbye to your daughter, then you should be able to." I spoke to the disembodied voices once more, "let her live."

Live. Not die. Bring her back. More time...

"But you don't understand what you're doing Ty. What about any consequences?"

"Then I alone will have to live with that. I said let her LIVE!"

The whisperers went silent. Sharon and I looked

to one another, searching for an answer.

"SEVEN DAYS"

A voice boomed, startling us. An unseen force pulled Sharon back to the hospital bed and thrust her into her body. Color and sound flooded the room, and Sharon sprang to life, choking on the breathing tube that had sustained her. I immediately ran out of the room, grabbed a nurse, and a doctor soon followed.

A short time later, everything was quiet once more. Sharon was breathing on her own, and the pneumonia invading her lungs was gone. I sat in the room, waiting for Trish to return to the good news. Sharon stirred, and her eyes fluttered open. "Ty-" she cleared a wad of phlegm from her throat, and tried again, "Ty, are you still here?"

"I am, Sharon." I stood and walked over to the bed.

Sharon smiled, "thank you." A tear streaked down her cheek. She pulled me close and hugged me. "Hey, do you know if my purse is here?"

I went to the small wardrobe in the corner of the room and found it sitting on the floor of the unit. I brought it over to her, and she rummaged through it for a few seconds, before pulling out her cellphone. Sharon turned it on, and a wry smile crossed her lips. "Want to have a bit of fun, Ty?"

"Oh, umm, Ms. Baker, I don't think we're supposed to, you know. I mean, it's a hospital, and I am flattered, don't get me wrong-"

"Manners, young man." Sharon laughed, probably because I had no clue what she was talking about, and immediately wandered into pornographic territory. She opened the camera app and began taking pictures of various medical equipment; the IV pole, the heart monitor, the abandoned breathing tube. She then took a selfie of me giving her a hug, and another of me giving her a kiss on the cheek. Still confused about it all, I watched as she pulled up her social media profile, uploaded the pictures, and posted them with the completely ironic tag "Won't He Do It." I laughed so hard at that. "William is going to shit a brick when he sees this. Nothing but jealousy." She sighed, and held my hand in hers, "Can I ask you to do me one more favor, Ty?"

"Of course, Ms. Baker."

"When Trish finally comes around, when she sees you for who you really are, please treat her right. Love her the way she deserves."

Sharon had quickly become my favorite person in the world. A week later, Trish found her dead at the bottom of the steps, in the foyer of her home.

Seven days.

So now, I guess the question is, how did I venture from that point to here? A miracle worker gone rogue. Well, consider I've already admitted to being somewhat of an asshole, and the rest of the world is mostly in denial about it, in themselves. I played the modest card. I was already the proverbial nice guy who always came in last. I didn't want to go around flaunting this newfound ability, and accidentally trigger the zombie apocalypse. Trish would never forgive me. I felt if I waited, the right opportunity would present itself, and some divine perception would show me exactly who next to bestow the gift of life upon. And let me tell you, my assumption was spot on.

Laura was a coworker, who didn't show up for work one day. Nothing strange about that, people take days off all the time. However, I overheard the manager speaking to the HR rep, and mentioning she was not in fact on vacation, and also had not called out sick. Again, nothing too alarming, unless you take into consideration the sprained wrist Laura showed up with last month, or the black eye her makeup had not quite concealed. Laura had conveniently fallen down the stairs way too many times. No one is that clumsy.

She failed to show up the next day, as well. It was really none of my business, but Laura had looked out for me a few times, in the past when I'd taken a long lunch, or sneaked out of the office earlier than I should have. I at least owed her a visit, to check if she was alright. After work, I took a detour that led me to the opposite side of town, straight to Laura's doorstep. Her car was parked out front, a good sign. I walked up the front steps to the door and rang the doorbell. No answer.

I tried again and got the same result. And so, I knocked. Inside, rustling noises confirmed someone was home. "Laura?" I called out. "Laura it's Ty, from work. You okay?"

"Go away," her strained voice came from somewhere not too far within the house. Every bit of instinct I possessed told me this was a bad situation, and I should walk away, so I started looking for another way inside.

Outside, the sun had already set, and darkness was spreading fast. In the backyard, a window in Laura's kitchen was cracked open. I decided to go for it. I pushed the window up, trying not to make too much noise, and climbed inside. The house was dark. I had to maneuver my way over the sink, and my feet landed in a puddle of something sticky. The place had a sickening metallic smell, almost like boxes of wet scouring pads had been left out to rust. I took a step into the dark space, and my shoe crunched on a piece of broken glass. I would have to give my eyes time to adjust, and find a light switch, before I moved again. A quiet rustling sound drawing near. Slippers gliding over carpet.

"I told you to go away." Laura's voice, heavy with tears, came from somewhere in front of me.

"I'm sorry, I...you didn't show up to work, and I thought, I would stop by to see-"

"To see what, the new bruises I have? To satisfy your morbid curiosity? Well fuck you, Ty. Get out of my goddamn house, right now."

"Alright, okay, you're right. I shouldn't-I shouldn't…" I trailed off, as the otherworldly whispering started up. "Laura, are you…dead?"

"Get out" were the only words understandable, through her sobs. I started to turn back toward the kitchen window, but my foot thumped against something on the floor. Ms. Baker had been correct when she said I am not stupid, it did not take long to figure out I had stepped into some deep shit.

"Aww shit. Shit, shit, shit. Laura, you killed him." As if on queue, her boyfriend appeared out of thin air. Though the room was dark, and visibility was low, I knew time had stopped, as it had in the hospital.

"Wait a minute, who the fuck are you?" Rodney was his name. He liked to play basketball, snort cocaine, and beat on his girlfriend, and that's everything I knew about him. That, and the fact he was also the son of the district attorney.

"Whoa, hold on Rodney. Relax for a moment. I'm not sure you understand what's happened here."

"You motherfucker, you're screwing Laura, aren't you? I knew that bitch was cheating. Where the fuck is she, I'm gonna kill her."

I wasn't sure of any sort of etiquette I was supposed to use here, so I came right out with the news. "Rodney, you stupid piece of shit, you're dead."

"Fuck you say to me, faggot? You think you can

take me? Do you know who I am?"

"I know who you were. Right now you're lying on the kitchen floor, lifeless as a frog in biology. I stepped in about a pint of your life juice when I climbed through the window" He swung on me, and the attack glided straight through my face, followed by a cold breeze. He staggered forward.

"What the hell?" on his second attempt, Rodney threw a combo of haymakers yielding the same result. "Man what the shit are you?"

"It's not me that's anything, Rodney, it's you. You're dead." The words finally seemed to take root.

"I'm…no, I can't be. How?"

"My guess, Laura finally got tired of your shit. I'm not sure what you did to provoke her, but she gave you exactly what you deserve."

"That goddamn gutter bitch. I'm gonna rip her cunt faced nose off."

"No, Rodney. You're not going to do anything, you can't do anything. Thanks to you, her life is about to become a nightmare, while something will eventually come along to guide you to your eternal resting place. Congratulations, you've proven to be the biggest asshole I've ever met. Now, I'm leaving this place. And wherever you go from here, you'll have to exist with the fact you've not suffered nearly enough for what you've done. Though I feel like you're okay with that." I was grabbed from behind, and I shrieked in terror, before realizing it was Laura.

"He was going to kill me, Ty. I had to. It was the only way."

"I know…I know." I grabbed her arms, and removed them, so as to move freely. "Laura, I have to turn on the lights, okay? It's the only way I can see what we're up against." I took her silence for compliance.

The fluorescent bulbs blinked to life, and I saw what a contender for the year's best horror film poster. Laura stood stoic in a pool of deep red blood, in the middle of the shattered kitchen. Her clothes were in tatters. Lips, and eyes swollen and bloody; her nose was definitely broken, were she to smile, I guessed several teeth would be too. I was right about the lump on the floor. Rodney lay in a crumpled heap with a knife protruding from his chest.

"I-I didn't know what to do. We were arguing, I can't even remember about what, and then he started hitting me. Over, and over, and over. And then I got away, ran into the kitchen. He caught me and threw me into the counter. Then he started picking up glasses and throwing them at me. I was begging him to stop. It was like he didn't even care. He picked me up off the floor and starts choking me. I couldn't breathe, and I knew I was going to die. So, I reached out and grabbed whatever was within reach. I kept cutting and cutting, until he took his hands away. It was like he got more angry looking at the blood on his hands, because he charged me. But before he got to me, I stabbed him, and then it was over."

I stood in stunned silence. We would have to call the cops, and Laura needed urgent medical attention, but at that moment the gravity of it all kept me rooted in place. The question of how I'd transitioned to and from that place outside of time was scratching at my mind, along with a dozen other questions relevant to this situation. And then it occurred to me. The reason I knew where Laura lived, while I had no clue about my other coworkers–though I suspected one lived in a cardboard box on the corner of Lincoln and Third. The reason we had each other's back in the workplace was because we shared a common connection outside of the job. Laura was William's stepsister. Nerves will make you forget such obvious details.

"Hello? Ty, what's up man? How ya been?" The aloofness in his voice almost made me drop the phone. A wave of unease washed over me.

"Okay, William, don't panic. I need you to-"

"Need me to what? What's going on, Ty?" Typically, when you tell someone as melodramatic as William not to panic, and especially when you yourself are in a state of panic, they tend to freak out before knowing what the situation is.

"Listen, William. You need to head over to Laura's right away. There's been an accident. I'll explain everything once you're here."

"Oh my god. Is she alright? I'm on my way."

After hanging up, I dialed a number I really didn't want to. An operator answered by asking what was the emergency. I thought about asking if she'd be able to rewind two days worth of time and send someone here to catch Rodney in the act. That would be the greatest bit of assistance ever. "I need an ambulance. Someone's been hurt, bad. You umm, you better send the police too." I gave the operator the address and hung up, not giving her any opportunity to ask any further questions.

A concussion, broken nose, shattered teeth, one fractured wrist, two broken ribs, and a partridge in a pear tree. Only William was allowed to visit Laura, since he was family. Her room had a guard posted outside, as though she were the criminal. On the day of Rodney's funeral, the district attorney held a press conference, where he swore justice would be swift, and Laura would receive the maximum penalty for her crime. I almost threw up, watching it.

Later in the evening, after Rodney had been buried, I visited the graveyard on an impulse. The sky was threatening rain, Thunder roared in the distance. This would not be a long visit. Hell I wasn't sure why I was even there to begin with. I stood at the fresh mound of dirt serving as Rodney's final blanket. Whispers all around me, and suddenly the color drained away from the world.

"You again?" Rodney seemed much less agitated than the last time I'd seen him. Looking around, I saw dozens of displaced souls in the graveyard. That old ferryman sure does take his time.

"Laura is screwed. You know? Your father is making it his personal mission to lock her up indefinitely."

"The bitch killed me. She'll get what she deserves."

If I could've hit him, I would have done my best to kill him again. "You sick bastard. What the fuck is wrong with you? Laura is my friend. Maybe you didn't give a shit about her, but I do. What you've done, this whole shit storm you set in motion, she doesn't deserve any of it."

"Well tell her next time she decides to kill someone, she should have a better escape plan."

My breath felt hot as I exhaled. This was easily the worst person I'd ever met. A good friend was about to be railroaded, all because of him. Yet he held no remorse. Moreso, he'd gotten away easy, no punishment for his actions. Sure, he died, but some fates are worse than death. That's when it dawned on me. "Bring him back. Let this man live." All of the other spirits in the cemetery turned their attention to me.

"The fuck did you say, you little shit snot?"

Back. Here. Alive. Now. Not dead.

Paying no attention to Rodney, I continued,

"Yes. Bring him back to life. Let him not be dead." The entire Greyscape–my name for that in between place– fell silent. The ghosts of others surrounding us wore horrified expressions.

Seven Days.

The sky tore open as Rodney was pulled back into his body, six feet below the earth. Rain fell in massive drops. I paid the weather no mind. For the briefest moment, I felt bad about what I'd done. Then it happened. His voice should not have been audible, yet Rodney's tortured cries traveled all the way up from his casket to my ears. It gave me chills, the good kind. I stood at the graveside long enough for the sky to go from dull gray to dark, listening. He completely lost his mind, and I could not be any happier. Soaked to the bone, I knew justice had been served. The judicial system, in its current state would never be able to deal a fate as fitting as I had. Laura would certainly do time for Rodney's murder, and now the man had a little less than seven days to lie in the darkness beneath a half ton of dirt, and contemplate.

You may think what I did wasn't so bad, and Rodney deserved what he got. Maybe you think it was a downright noble act. To that I say please reserve any further judgement until I finish the story.

Trish was waiting outside my door when I returned home. My heart raced. It was a most unexpected surprise. Dried tears marred her flawless skin. I approached, wondering what reason she had for visiting, sans William. Knowing I she'd never be mine was one thing, William following her around like a lost kitten was nerve wracking. Seeing her in such a state, vulnerable and distraught, only increased my longing. I wanted to comfort her the way a husband does his wife when he sees she is in need. William was not the right man for her, both Trish's mother and I knew that. But I'd long ago missed my chance to act on what I knew would be perfection, valuing my friendship with her fiancé over my own feelings. I opened my door and motioned her inside the apartment without a word.

"I'm sorry. I should have called, but I-"

"Nonsense," I interrupted, "you're welcome to drop by any time."

"Thanks. I needed to talk to someone. William is by his sister's side almost twenty-four seven, and I don't think any of my friends would understand my situation quite like you, Ty."

I watched her petite frame glide past me, an air of trouble in her perfumed wake. "So what's up? This whole situation must be stressing the two of you out."

"Ty, can we not talk about that right now? It's all these past few days have been about. I want to feel normal again. How has your day been?" She looked me up and down, finally realizing something was not right. "More importantly, why are you soaking wet?"

"I was tying up some loose ends and got caught

out in the storm. No big deal. It's only water." She laughed and my heart morphed into a hummingbird. "Umm, have a seat. Let me go put some dry clothes on, and then we can talk." I hurried to my bedroom, unsure of everything I was thinking. The vibe I was feeling from Trish was driving me nuts, but I had to be reading the situation wrong…right?

I'd gotten as far as taking off my shirt when there came a knock at my door. "Yes?" I answered. The door to my room crept open and Trish walked in, slowly yet deliberate. She pressed her body to mine, and I wrapped my arms around her. My lips drew closer to hers, aching with desire.

"Are you going to answer me, or not?"

The bedroom disappeared. I was standing in the living room once again, mouth agape. Confused and saddened at not being able to live out the most vivid daydream I'd ever had. "Huh?" I managed to utter.

"You're soaked, Ty. What happened?"

"Oh, shit, nothing," snapping back to my senses, "don't worry about it."

We talked for hours as friends, because that's what we were, and it's all she'd ever see me as. I buried my desire somewhere deep inside of me and hoped it would never surface again. It's important you understand what I'm saying here because once Trish left my apartment everything changed.

The judgmental old women who sit in the

church pews every Sunday gossiping on things they know nothing about will tell you it was The Devil. A witch doctor, or soothsayer may think perhaps it was a vengeful energy channeling itself through the only conduit it available. Me, I see no need to overcomplicate any of this. I succumbed to the evil that exists in every man. I couldn't have what I wanted, and so, like a six-year-old denied his favorite toy, I threw a fucking fit. All the feelings I'd pushed so far away turned out to be hovering beneath the surface, and they taunted me. Telling me I wasn't good enough; how I was unfit and didn't deserve to even have such good friends as Trish and William. I raged all around my apartment trying to quiet these thoughts. It wasn't fair. I had to leave, I needed to return to the last place where I was truly happy. The graveyard. Rodney screaming, begging to be freed from that box. I needed that again.

Standing atop a mound of fresh dirt, wet from the passing storm, all was quiet. Rodney was likely in shock and passed out from his predicament. That only angered me more. I dropped to my knees and began scooping away clumps of muddied soil. He needed to wake up. Whatever was keeping him alive had to also keep him conscious, for my sake. I continued digging, not caring about the world around me. Which is why I didn't see the man approaching until he grabbed me.

"What the fuck are you doing?" Before I knew it, I was being dragged away from the grave site.

When the powerful grip finally let me go, I turned and found myself staring into Bruce Lannigan's furious eyes. Rodney's father held a balled-up fist at his side. Whatever bullshit excuse I came up with would need to be good. The man was a freaking hulk. If I pissed him off any more than I already had, that fist was going to take up temporary residence somewhere in my face. Funny how situations like this have a way of draining away the rage dominating my thoughts only moments ago. I wasn't here for confrontation, least of all with the district attorney. "I, umm…"

Too little, and much too late. Bruce swung his fist faster than I ever imagined someone of his size was able. I was literally knocked silly, unable to form a coherent thought once the blow connected. It took mere seconds to regain my senses, and once I did, Bruce was ready to strike once again. He stopped, a crushing blow that surely would have stolen away my consciousness, mere inches from my temple. I'd slipped into the Greyscape, rendering him and the rest of the living world immobile. Spirits all around me in this land of the dead began to cower away. They'd witnessed what I'd done earlier and feared for their, their what? Certainly not their lives.

My face, all the parts that had been hit, didn't hurt here. Maybe that's what the ghosts around me feared. There was no pain in this place. I'd pulled Rodney back into his mangled body and forced him to suffer in a box which allotted no movement, and no escape. They liked it here on this side of things. None of them wanted to be next. I held no grudge with any of them, I hope they eventually figured that out. I soon fell back out of the Greyscape, considerably further away from Bruce's finishing blow. The force and the effort he'd put behind it, and then for his fist to find nothing present to spend the momentum, was enough to carry his entire body forward. The confusion of me no longer being in that space tripped him up. Bruce stumbled. A big dude like that is bound to struggle with the concept of balance. He continued forward, one step, two, three, until he finally tripped over his own lumbering feet. He reached out to brace himself for the fall, but his arms went completely limp as his forehead struck the corner of his own son's tombstone. Twitching a little, he lay sprawled across the fresh mound of dirt. If I had transitioned into the Greyscape again, I've no doubt I would've seen him roaming the grounds confused, and unsure what happened. Bruce was an asshole, without a doubt, but I left him alone. I won't ever understand the pain of losing a child. So, I can't claim to have known what he was going through. Perhaps eventually he would have listened to reason and dropped the charges against Laura. As it stood, him dropping dead was, by far, the best outcome.

I'd helped Trish spend more time with her mother and got Laura out of a terrible situation. Two legit miracles. One more and I'd be eligible for sainthood. But for all the good I'd done, on purpose or inadvertently, I still wanted something, for myself. She haunted my thoughts. With every beat of my heart, my desire for her increased. None of this was fair. I was a good guy, generally. Why was the universe so set against a happy ending for me? You can call it selfish if you want, but if you're honest with yourself I'm sure you'd find you would react the same if you were in my shoes.

That night was when I had my first nightmare. I dreamed I was back in the cemetery. It was dark and deserted. With every step I took, a sinister voice chuckled in time with my footfalls. It was annoying, to say the least. I tried calling out to whomever was there, but my voice did not work. Suddenly I was being chased. The pursuer was unseen, but the rapid shuffling of its feet was ever present, behind me. When I ran, the air around me burst into the most sinister laughter. Running as fast as I dared, the footsteps of my follower grew louder and closer. I turned to try and catch a glimpse of who, or what was chasing me and was struck hard right above my waist. I caught a glimpse of a goatish figure as I fell to the ground and was jarred awake. Moments later, in my bathroom mirror, I found a giant bruise on my right side, below my ribs. Remembering only the terrifying highlights of the nightmare, of course I was concerned.

The worst part is when concerns are legitimized. It was not only one night I found myself terrified of falling asleep. The bad dreams continued for days. Some nights I was running through the dark, and others I would be surrounded by scores of tortured souls, while on the worst of nights I would be trapped in a dark confined space, yelling my throat raw for someone to save me. It was maddening. With each one, the goat was the one persistent entity. It would attack me, chase me, laugh as I cowered in fear. And so, I ended things the only way I knew how. I stopped sleeping.

In the daytime I would busy myself with the local obituaries. At first, I would seek out certain key words to clue me in on the personality of the recently deceased. If I judged them to be of questionable moral character, I would take a trip to the graveyard and visit them on the other side. It was not a far stretch to find me, in the dead of night, propped up on a tombstone laughing at the symphony of pain occurring beneath me.

Eventually, the obits were rendered moot. Operating under the sincere belief everyone is an asshole, I felt no need to play judge anymore. Bottom line, if you were dead and I happened across your funeral, well you would not be dead for long.

Kip Waters, a man of no particular significance to me, passed away peacefully in his sleep one night after a long battle with diabetes. By the time I got wind of his funeral I was a sleep-deprived, caffeine and alcohol fueled train wreck. I would've liked to blame what occurred next on that, but to do so would be one self-denial too many.

After Kip's funeral I stumbled my way over to the tent covering his fresh burial plot. It was a warm night, all the mourners were long gone. Probably celebrating his life somewhere, at someone's house. Reminiscing on the good times they had with him, laughing and sharing stories about the man they'd swore they would never tell anyone. At that point I moved in and out of the Greyscape at will. Practice makes perfect, as they say.

Kip was sitting on a bench at a neighboring grave. Enfeebled and distraught, I approached him. He looked up at me and smiled. "It's about time we finally met."

"You, don't you worry," I didn't try to not slur my words, I honestly didn't care, "I'm gonna make sure you live to see another day, haha."

"You've grown quite sloppy over these last few days. Are you sure you can perform, Ty?"

Was he mocking me? The nerve. My blood was hot. What an asshole. "Bring him back," I said, oblivious to the fact he knew my name and that the whispering was no longer present. "Let this man live."

Kip burst into a fit of laughter, clapping his hands as he rocked back and forth. "What are you trying to accomplish here, boy? Wait, let me guess. You think

I'll go kicking and screaming to my grave, wake up and beg for help? Oh this is rich." He continued to laugh, which began to upset me.

"Let him live, goddamnit!" I demanded, still not receiving a response.

"That's it Ty, get mad. Get as angry as you can. That's exactly what I want, what I need."

Kip goaded me on as I continued to try and drag him back to life, and it continued to not work. I was angry at first, but all of it drained away when the goat approached. Not exactly a goat though. From the neck up it definitely was horns, goatee, and fur black as the abyss. Its torso was of a man who'd not missed a day at the gym in quite some time. While below the waist, it was the cloven hooved nightmare I'd been running from this whole time. It squatted next to Kip, and the old man began stroking its head like a loyal pet. Queasiness, nausea, disgust, all feelings that did not exist in the Greyscape. And so, I tried to escape back into the physical world, but it was not working.

"Oh Ty, don't be afraid. This conversation is long overdue. Don't you think?" The goat figure spoke in unison with Kip, creating a disturbing multi-voice effect.

"What the fuck is going on? Why can't I leave this place? Who are you, and why have you been chasing me through my dreams?"

"Yes, I have, haven't I?" They said. "For good

reason though, Ty. You have proven yourself to be a valuable team player. Your particular method of cruelty is something I would be proud to have thought up myself. I applaud you."

"But why me, um…what do I call you?"

"I'm not one to overcomplicate things Ty, let's just go with Kip. We'll say you being chosen was something of a luck of the draw situation." Kip sidestepped my questions. I was too afraid to be angry though, and so he continued. "I'm sure you have more questions, and I will answer as best I can. Believe me, the less you know the better off you are. You may be wondering what the significance of your gift is. In truth Ty, you were never supposed to use it unsupervised. Imagine you were out to dinner with a friend, and you order the salmon, while your friend orders the prime rib. Well, you and I both know these dishes do not take the same amount of time to cook. And so when one is done, it's staged and kept warm while the other dish is prepared. This way one guest is not sitting at the table awkwardly watching the other enjoy his meal. In this case however, the salmon arrived long before the prime rib. And oh how you have been enjoying it."

"Wait, are you here to take this away from me?"

"No, no you've completely missed the point." Kip the goat arose from his perch at Kip the old man's side. "The prime rib has at last arrived and looks oh so delicious. Pink and dripping with its own flavorful juice. I have taken up my utensils and am ready to dine with you." Kip the goat stepped forward.

My initial instinct was to step back. In fact, my mind begged my legs to move in a direction where Kip was not, but they did not respond to the request. Frozen in place, Kip stood before me. Its demonic frame towered over my own insignificant form. The creature reached out a human-like hand and placed it on my shoulder.

I awoke suddenly, in my bed doused in sweat or perhaps my own au jus. Kicking the air and grabbing at nothing. A noise, familiar but too far away from me to identify resonated a step beyond my audible range. Soon enough, I recognized it as my front door. Someone was knocking. I took the opportunity to abandon my bed of nightmares and answer the door. It was Trish.

"I didn't wake you, did I?"

Yes you did, but the fact it's you makes everything okay. "No, not at all."

"It's just, I felt so good when I left here the other night. You're an awesome listener and I really need to talk to you about something. That's not a problem, is it?"

"I'm happy to be of service. Come on in."

Trish sat on the couch, in the same spot she'd been in the last time she visited.

Oh, you like this one?

The unexpectedness of the voices made me

jump, as I closed the door. "No, no, no. This can't be real." I recognized them at once as that of Kip the goat and the old man.

"What was that?" Trish asked, a hint of concern in her voice.

She can be yours, Ty. We can deliver her to you.

"Nothing, sorry. Thinking out loud I guess." I crossed the room and sat down beside her. Immediately I noticed she did not seem as distraught as the last time she'd been here. My guess was things were doing much better now that William's sister was not going to prison.

"Ty, you know William. Probably better than I do." Her lips curled into a beautiful smile.

"Come on, me? As long as the two of you have been together, I doubt it."

"But you do. The two of you have history going back way longer than our relationship. My point is, I'm not a fan of receiving big news by surprise. It's like an anxiety thing. Sometimes William has a hard time understanding that, especially when he has his mind set on something. He's been riding high ever since the news of the D.A.s death. Not that it's a good thing, but you get what I'm saying. Ty, I need to know if he's chosen a wedding date. And please don't lie to cover him. You two talk and he would not keep this news to himself. I really don't want him to spring it on me out of the blue. It's okay if you tell me. That way I can act surprised when he does whatever he's going to do, instead of having a panic attack."

I chuckled, sitting and listening to the woman I loved basically tell me we would never be together. "I'm sorry Trish. If he's planning anything, he hasn't said a word to me."

"Ty, look me in the eye." She placed a hand on my cheek and turned my head so I was staring directly at her. "I'm asking you to tell me the god's honest truth."

My mind was on fire. Her touch was so gentle. Watching her lips move as she spoke almost gave me a heart attack. "No," I managed to squeak out, "he hasn't mentioned anything to me."

"Well then, fuck that piece of shit."

The eyes, they say, are the window to the soul. In that moment, I saw a change in Trish's. Not something that would be outright noticeable. It was more like an ethereal glow, present in one moment and then completely gone. "Wait, what?"

Trish pulled me in close to her and planted her lips onto mine. I welcomed it at first, going along with the strange turn of events. But I soon realized, something was not quite right. Her tongue, probing the inner surfaces of my mouth, had a bitter essence. The breath exiting her nostrils touched my skin and burned for a slight moment. I pulled away from her, trying to understand the situation. As I got to my feet things became clearer. Trish sat on the couch smiling, eyes begging me to sit down once more and capitalize on my desire, but I did not. A shadow fell across the hardwood floor, opposite the lamp next to the couch where she sat. Not Trish's though. Last I checked, she had no horns. Kip was inside of her.

"What are you doing? You can't do this Trish."

"This is what you want though. You've done excellent work while awaiting my arrival, Ty. What's wrong with a little reward?"

"Oh shit, Kip? No, not like this. This isn't natural. Is she even still alive?"

"That depends, Ty. Do you want her to be? If you'd enjoy your spoils with her lifeless body, I can arrange it." Kip the Trish threw its head back in the most obnoxious laugh.

"Stop it. I want you to leave her alone. I will help you do whatever it is you're here for, keep her away from all of this though."

The laughter came to an abrupt end. Trish slumped down in her seat. A moment later she sprung up with a gasp. "What-Ty, what's happening?" It was the real Trish, and she was losing it. "What are you Ty?"

"Trish, one second. Relax, let me try to explain." I reached out and placed my hand on her shoulder, attempting to calm her. She shrugged it away and rose up to her feet.

"Don't you fucking touch me. What did you do, drug me? Did you roofie me, Ty? Sick bastard."

"No Trish, I can explain this, please."

"Fuck you Ty." An exceptionally large amount of spit flew from her lips to my cheek.

I stood speechless as she turned to leave. Trish stormed across the living room to the foyer. As she grabbed for the doorknob she paused. I use that word because Trish did not merely stop walking. She was stuck mid-step, balanced perfectly on the toes of one foot and the heel of the other, with her right arm reaching out to open the door.

"We cannot simply let her leave." Kip's voice issued forth from where she was stuck.

"I don't understand. Why?"

"The emotions your kind feels are utterly disgusting. They interfere with every single decision you make and drive you to the worst possible outcomes time and time again. Yet, as a moth is unable to resist the all-consuming flame, so too are you incapable of escaping your own feelings. You're pathetic.

"It broke your heart this sweet bitch would not have the chance to say goodbye to her mother, so you brought her back to life. You couldn't sit by and watch your friend be subjected to the cruelty and unfairness of this world, and so you killed the man who would lock her away. It wasn't until you realized you'd never have what you wanted you submitted to this little gift. And oh, how it truly intoxicated you. Do not feign innocence and pretend as though you don't understand what I am saying. Put those infantile emotions away and open your fucking eyes." Trish collapsed at the door, unconscious.

Her eyes fluttered open some time later. I watched as her memory caught up with her. She gasped and tried to scream, but the duct tape muffled her voice. "Shhh, it's okay Trish." I used a finger to brush the hair back from her eyes. She squirmed under my touch. That must have been when she realized her hands and feet were bound.

Trish thrashed around the bed, sobs choked off by her own gagged mouth. I figured it would be like this. That is, Kip told me it would. I let her tire herself out. Which did not take as long as I thought it would.

"I get it, how this must seem, and I apologize. I need you to listen to me so you understand why you're here. Will you do that, will you listen?"

Trish nodded.

"Good. I love you, Trish. I've wanted to tell you for years. It feels good to finally say the words." Her eyes, so sad, still seemed startled at the revelation. "That night in the hospital with your mother, she figured that out almost immediately. Much as I haven't treated him like it, William is my best friend. I would never betray him, by stealing you away. Not against your will, anyway. So, I remained quiet, and it tore me up inside."

Hurry it up, Kip demanded.

"I am, alright Kip? Damn, give me a break." I looked back at Trish and now her brow was furrowed. "Stop, don't do that. You know I'm not crazy, Trish. You remember Kip taking over you earlier. I wanted to let you go, I really did. But while you were out Kip explained the gravity of this whole situation. And while I do believe they are an enormous asshole, I agree with what they revealed to me. I'm going to take the tape off your mouth so we can talk. I need for this to be a normal conversation. No screaming or anything. You're scared, but Trish I'm not going to hurt you." I gently peeled the tape away from her mouth, not wanting to cause Trish any pain. She complied, sobbing. "You've seen too much Trish. This is not how I imagined we would be together at all, but until I find a way out of this for you-"

There is no way out of this, you fool. It is what needs to be done.

"Shut up okay. Let me talk."

"I'm, I'm not talking, Ty."

"No, not you Trish. Kip. Anyway, once I figure out how much you can be trusted with what you know, I will let you go back to William."

She can never go back, Ty. Did I not make that clear? She is your present for a job well done. Fucking enjoy it.

"Listen Trish," I craned my neck attempting to block out Kip's annoying words, "I told Kip not to take control of you anymore, and they're willing to agree, as long as you tell the truth. That sound fair?"

"Ty, who is Kip? I don't know what you are saying."

"Please, let's not do this. You've seen the Greyscape, haven't you? Kip said they couldn't hide anything from you when they were in control. So that means you know about your mother, and Rodney, and Bruce, and all the rest. Things you were never supposed to find out about. You do understand, don't you?"

"Yes okay. Yes, I understand."

She's lying Ty. Because she thinks there's still a chance she'll get walk out of here. I can take care of this easily. Or you can stop letting the way you feel for her cloud your thoughts.

"Don't lie, Trish. They don't like that."

"They who," she cried, "I'm sorry, Ty. I think maybe I knew you were in love with me. I respected the fact you kept it hidden and didn't try to come between William and me. Please, let me go. I won't hold this against you. We'll find you the help you desperately need."

Still she lies. Let me take care of this. It will be quick.

"No Kip, give me a moment to help her understand. Do you have any idea how scared she must be right now?" A thought occurred to me as I spoke to Kip. I might be able to show her proof of my little gift.

Then she would have no choice but to believe it. I quickly dismissed it though. No one was available, in the moment, to use as an example.

Do not be so quick to reject that idea, Ty.

"No, it won't work. There's nobody around for me to resurrect."

Oh, but there is.

"Wait, you mean...? No. Not at all. Out of the question."

What better way to show her what's at stake here, Ty? Think about it, if she experiences it firsthand, she will understand everything that happened tonight. And when you bring her back, life can resume as normal, not for seven measly days, but as though she'd never even been gone.

The demon's power lies not in any supernatural realm, but in convincing man the evilest of thoughts are the best plans, furthermore that they are his own. It is a subtle, but very effective form of persuasion. In my desperation, I went from believing I could not possibly do such a thing to Trish, to seeing, beyond all doubt, it was the only way. It was only temporary, and she was in no real danger. Yes, she would understand entirely. Not at first, but once she was back, definitely.

"Trish, I need you to stay calm. This may not make any sense at first, but I promise, okay, I promise you'll be fine."

Do it!

"Ty, what are you doing?"

I placed a fresh piece of tape over her mouth. Then I leaned in and kissed her forehead. "I never meant for it to be like this, Trish." Tears spilled from my eyes as I slipped my hands around her neck and squeezed. She struggled to break free, fought with everything she had. I wasn't sure my grip would endure. Soon though, the struggle was over.

The door to my apartment crashed in.

Kip knew, but never told me Trish had a cell phone in her back pocket. At some point in all of her writhing on the bed during our talk, she'd butt dialed William. He'd heard the entire scene play out, and without the proper context, he was fuming. Of course, I knew nothing of it, with Trish conveniently coming to rest on top of the volume button. I was wiping tears away from my eyes as the footsteps quietly approached. When I turned to look, William was in mid-swing. A sickening crunch and an explosion of pain, as the metal bat came into contact with my head. I may have gone insane from how much it hurt, had I not passed out half a second later.

Kip's wild laughter was the most annoying alarm clock. When I opened my eyes I saw the goat, and the old man standing beside him. Everything was still, and in no time at all I realized I was in the Greyscape.

"What's going on?"

Kip the old man approached me, still laughing.

"Your friend William is burying his fiancée today."

"No. What?"

"Let me fill you in on what's happened since you've been gone. Trish died, but you were there for that. Once the cops arrived it became an open and shut case. The investigation took a few days but wrapped up nice and neat. The body was released to William yesterday, and the funeral is taking place now."

"I have to stop it. I mean, I'm definitely not on William's list of favorite people, but I can still bring her back."

"Well, you can, and you can't."

"What the fuck is that supposed to mean?"

"This thing you've been able to do was my own talent. Remember our first conversation? You were to be the vessel in which I traversed the physical realm. But now my dear boy, you went and got your skull cracked right in half. Possessing a dead man is not my style."

"Oh fuck, no. You mean-"

"Relax. I am ready to offer a solution. It's a choice, really. I will bring one of you back. Only one though. Give yourself a minute to think it over."

"What's to think about? Bring me back. Do it. Once I am alive again I can rush over to the funeral and revive Trish."

"Are you sure about this decision? There are no take backs."

"Do it, Kip. No more goddamn games."

"Okay, as you wish so shall it be done. Ty, do you mind if I explain something to you first? We do after all have nothing but time here."

"What is it Kip?" I was anxious to leave the Greyscape. so much work needed to be done to set things right again.

Kip the goat approached now and sat beside me. No more laughter. "William did a number on you. Multiple cranial fractures, the bat scrambled your entire brain. You were in a coma for days before you finally stopped breathing. The bitch of it all is William, your best friend, was your emergency contact. The cops notified him of your death and he had something akin to a mental break. So there you were in the city morgue with no one to claim your body. Having been convicted of such a hellacious crime, the answer was clear. You were carted off to a potter's grave. And now, thanks to your emotional decision, that is where you shall return." The whispering returned, clearer, louder than it had ever been before. It was sorrowful. Telling me how wrong my decision was.

I turned to Kip and understood. These would be my final moments in the Greyscape. Kip wrapped his brutish arms around me and then everything went dark. To call it a coffin would be an overstatement. I had no room to move within the space at all. I didn't scream or go crazy as had the others whom I bestowed this fate upon. This was my punishment, and I accepted it. Here I've lain for an indeterminate amount of time, certainly much longer than seven days, and gone over everything that happened countless times. So many ignored chances to walk a different route, to be less selfish.

I chose myself. Faced with the decision of reviving the only woman I ever loved, I decided my own life was more important. I chose myself. Unhappy with the state in which I left the world, I felt it well within my reach to right all my wrongs, were I given only one more chance. Trish died by my own hands, William suffered the ultimate betrayal and loss. These were people I sincerely cared about. Sooner or later the world will have moved on, and I will be nothing more than an insignificant speck along a massive timeline. I saw things not meant for any living person's eyes, did things no human mind would ever conceive. In the end, Kip or whatever its true name is was right. My choices, my actions had all been shaped and crafted to design my own ruin, because I let my emotions in, and now here I lay all alone, because I chose myself.

Pests

They cut his feed. James Garcia was covering the story of the year. A week ago, an Atlanta police officer shot and killed Khalil Mason, a black teenager, while he was tying his shoe. The nation had been in an uproar ever since; boycotts, protests, people crying out for justice like never before. James had been there from the start, capturing every moment, immortalizing the voices of the oppressed and standing on the side of truth. He'd interviewed Khalil's family, the chief of police, and angry protestors. Over the past week he'd gotten some of the most powerful footage to ever hit the news cycle.

It all culminated in an organized march through the streets of Atlanta to the capitol building. The march was to be a peaceful vigil for the murdered teen, ending in a rally for justice on the steps of the capitol. Hundreds, maybe thousands showed up. Chants of "We've had enough," boomed through the early evening streets, as the throng made their way to the destination. James walked alongside them, delivering a sort of play-by-play narrative on everything happening. Passionate citizens shed tears along the way. It was an emotional trek, and it was all on camera. James was going to ride this story all the way up to the apex of his career.

The young reporter always knew he had a higher calling. Reporting the local news was a mere steppingstone in a career about to take off like a rocket. This story was the launch pad.

When the crowd arrived at the capitol, they were met with resistance. A line of cops, clad head to toe in riot gear, stood before the steps where the march was to end, three ranks deep. The crowd grew angry at the city's show of force. James' heart began to pound. This was already going to be one of the greatest news stories of all time. If either the protestors or the police escalated things further, James would go down as a legend. He watched as a row of cops peaked out from behind the first rank, riot shields held steady, pointing shotguns loaded with rubber bullets at a crowd growing more disorganized with each passing moment. This was it, the moment he'd been waiting for. When James Garcia would be transformed from a forgettable face to a trusted newscaster people welcomed into their home every night. CNN, MSNBC, all of the big boys would come knocking.

A thunderous crack, as an officer fired into the crowd. James turned to the camera, ready to address the viewers. He took in a deep breath to calm his nerves. He didn't want to seem happy to report on such an awful situation. His happiness was in knowing this was his ticket to the top. Fully composed, he raised the mic up ready to make history, and then… They cut his feed.

James stormed the newsroom, barging through the doors of the studio with his anger focused on one person, Steven Taylor, his producer. James knew he would probably be fired for confronting the man, but he was not about to let that bastard get away with this. Making his way through the studio, James expected to be met with opposition. He figured the staff would be quick to try and talk him down from the ledge he was on. Attempting to reason with him. Once they failed, there would be security. James pictured them posted up outside of Steven's office. He was not certain whether this confrontation would be physical or verbal and was unsure of how he would deal with rent-a-cops if things did take that turn. It wasn't something he dwelled on. The simple fact was, in the moment, none of it mattered. He'd been subjected to the highest form of disrespect he could think of. One way or another, Steven would answer for his behavior.

No one stood in his way. The scenario James envisioned did not at all play out as expected. The studio, normally bustling with activity, was quiet. The entire staff, including security, were focused on either the news anchors sitting at the desk, or the monitors displaying the same scene for those who were not in the newsroom. James, realizing he wanted to be confronted, to make a spectacle, felt the angst draining away from him. Surely everyone knew he wouldn't be happy about his feed being abruptly terminated. Someone had to suspect he wouldn't take it in stride. Where was the concern, the worry, the fear of repercussion? James walked past several individuals without them even acknowledging his presence.

At last, he arrived at Steven's office. The anger in him had all but dissipated, replaced with unease and awkwardness. A thought occurred to James. Maybe this had been the plan the entire time. To ignore him. Drop the floor out from under his anger before he ever had a chance to unleash it. Make it feel strange enough James would question the validity of his feelings. This train of thought rekindled enough of the fire within him he shouldered the door open and rushed in. "Steven, what the hell do you think…"

"Shh," Steven did not so much as look in James' direction, as he cut the man's words off. His eyes were trained on the computer monitor sitting atop his desk.

James could feel the fury boil over within

himself. His hands clenched into fists almost involuntarily. The slighted reporter took a step forward, "Who exactly do you think you're talking to?" The words floated out into the office with a dangerous level of calm.

"An out of work bum, if you don't shut the fuck up. The biggest story mankind has ever seen, and this is when you choose to barge in here and complain about, what?"

Having no idea what Steven was referring to, James stopped short. He'd wanted to give the man what he deserved, for treating him the way he had, but suddenly felt he was not privy to the entire story. The drive back from the capitol only took ten minutes. James ranted to his cameraman the entire time. He reflected on everything between his arrival and this point. No one seemed to care he was there, or about the plug had been pulled on his coverage of the protest. What was Steven talking about? Feeling he actually would be fired if he said something else, James directed his steps around the desk to the producer's side. His eyes moved from the pencil holder, to the coffee stained desk calendar, to the computer monitor. What he saw on the screen took his breath away in a very literal sense. He reminded himself to breathe, and exhaled loudly.

The computer screen displayed a shaky image of some unknown farm. At least James thought it was a farm from the rows of corn stalks in the bottom half of the screen, the logo of a popular news network flashed in the corner of the shot every few seconds displaying the word "LIVE." The remainder of the scene is what held everyone glued to the feed. Hovering above the field, casting a giant shadow over everything beneath, was what could only be described as an alien ship. Running lights glowed along its bulk in colors James had never seen before. The camera zoomed out and he realized how far away the shot was. James gasped as he took in the sheer enormity of the craft. "What, what am I looking at?"

"Your next goddamn assignment, that's what."

A feeling stirred within James. Happiness could not quite explain what it was. It felt as if he'd been given the okay to stroll into the U.S. Mint and print off as much money as he desired. If Khalil Mason's death was the catapult that would fling him to the top of his career, this story was, well, a spaceship waiting to take off at lightspeed to any point in the universe.

Oceanside, CA 1525 hrs

"I can't believe it's real." Mark said. His voice was distant and trance-like. Not solely due to the images playing out before him on the phone's screen. The car interior was filled with a dense fog. Mark lifted the joint to his lips and took another pull. He inhaled and held his breath for a few seconds, before the irritating smoke made him cough. He passed the joint, packed tight with sour diesel, to Lenny who sat beside him in the passenger seat.

"Yeah man, that shit hits hard. It's like, you could smoke it and be high as hell, but hot boxing is some next level stuff. Like, I'm sitting here in the car, but really I'm floating out over the Pacific somewhere. Guam, or something. I don't know."

Mark took the joint back from Lenny. It was burned down to almost nothing. Still, he lifted it to his lips, holding with the tips of his thumb and forefinger, and took another long pull. "Bruh, what the hell are you talking about?" The words escaped his mouth around a laugh.

"Come on man," Lenny said, "this Sour D is wild. I feel like I could jump up and fly to your cousin's house by myself." The short man in the passenger seat of the sedan ran his hand across his stubbled chin, as though he were contemplating, planning out his plane-less flight across the country.

"Yo, that reminds me, I need to see if any of this," Mark gestured toward his phone screen, "is affecting our flight time."

"Any of what?" Lenny's eyes were tiny slits in his head.

"Man, this is why I can't smoke with you. You get too damn goofy. Motherfucking aliens landed in the heart of the corn belt, and you're over here thinking you can fly."

"Aliens? What are you even talking about?"

"Look at your phone, dude. It's all anyone is talking about. You know what, forget it. Let's go grab our shit and head to the airport."

As Mark finished speaking, Lenny began to laugh uncontrollably. He rocked back and forth in his seat, shaking the car as he did so.

"What the hell is so funny?"

"Okay, okay," Lenny began, as his fit of laughter began to taper off, "I'm not laughing about your cousin getting married. He's cool people. Check this out though. We're sitting here high as fuck, about to catch," he paused, attempting to stifle another laugh, "a red eye to D.C. Dude," Lenny pointed an unsteady finger at his face, "we already caught it." With this, the laughter returned, louder and deeper than before.

"You crazy as shit, for real." Mark chuckled alongside his best friend, before starting up the car and rolling the windows down. Dissipating the hot box, and ending the smoke session.

Back at the apartment complex, the two men agreed to head to their apartments, pick up their bags, and meet back at the car. It shouldn't have taken more than twenty minutes. After waiting for half an hour, Mark decided to see what was taking Lenny so long. In the breezeway outside of his friend's apartment, he heard what sounded like a news broadcast coming from one of the doors in the breezeway. It came as no surprise the sound emanated from Lenny's home. His front door stood wide open. Mark walked in and found his friend sitting on the couch in his living room. Eyes glued to the television.

"Lenny, we need to go." Mark tried to yell over the broadcast, but Lenny had the volume turned up as high as it would go. He moved closer and touched his shoulder.

Lenny jumped up, startled by the unexpected contact. He dropped his guard the instant he saw Mark. "What the fuck?" Lenny, unaware of how loud the TV was, only appeared to mouth the words.

Mark grabbed the remote from where his friend had been sitting, and lowered the volume.

"You scared the piss outta me," Lenny said.

"Let's go. You know security's gonna be crazy, at the airport."

"Hold up, man. Did you see this?" Lenny pointed at the now muted TV. "Some farmers built a whole goddamn spaceship."

"Farmers, what? No you got it wrong, it's-"

"Nah man, it's the farmers. They realized how screwed they are with all the climate change going on, and they decided to build a ship and go somewhere they can grow their crops in peace. Maybe they'll mail some produce back to the rest of us when they get to wherever they're going."

Mark placed a hand on his forehead, "Fuck it.

We have a few minutes. Sit back down and let me show you how wrong you are."

Lenny returned to the spot he'd been glued to, and Mark turned the volume on the television up to a more reasonable level.

A reporter stood before the camera. Behind him, in the distance, an enormous alien craft hovered above a corn field. "Few words can describe the scene here. Beautiful, amazing, unprecedented, terrifying. All of mankind now has concrete evidence we are not the only sentient beings in the vast universe. Many questions have arisen over the past half hour, around the nature of these beings and whether or not they are friendly, hostile or even neutral. We simply don't know, at this point. I'm told President Forbes himself is en route, with officials from The Pentagon and NASA. Perhaps we'll gain a clearer picture once they arrive. One thing you can be certain of is the world is about to be forever changed."

Lenny gawked at the screen. "Oh shit," he began, "yo, Mark. I think you were mistaken, bro. That's not a farming ship. It's real life aliens."

Undisclosed Location, 1730 hrs

President Forbes sat on the plane, pinching the bridge of his nose between his thumb and forefinger. In ten minutes, he would arrive at the airbase where he would be driven to the operations center and briefed on everything they knew about the alien craft. This was far from how he imagined his day going. Forbes was scheduled to address the civil unrest in Georgia earlier in the evening but was forced to cancel because of this latest development. Georgia was not only his home state, but a key contributor in his winning the election, and he turned his back on them to play Star Wars, hundreds of miles away.

The pilot informed everyone they were about to land. President Forbes tipped the glass to his lips and drained the last of the brown liquid it contained. He winced at the burn that chased it as he swallowed, then settled into his seat.

On the ground the president was ushered away from his plane and rushed across the tarmac, to a waiting humvee. Once inside, he was packed shoulder to shoulder with a couple grunts, and Colonel Horatio Leverbean. The colonel wore a dour and weary expression. Forbes got the feeling it had been a long day for him as well. "Good to see you, Horatio."

"Same, Mr. President. Although, I wish it were under less cryptic circumstances." The colonel attempted to lift his arm and run a hand through his thin grey mane, but his elbow hit the rifle of the soldier crammed in next to him, and Leverbean ended his attempt. "Sir, just so we're on the same page here, intel says we're dealing with something the likes of which no one has ever imagined. I don't know how much of the briefing you read, but we've turned every missile we have on the farm. If E.T. ends up being anything but friendly, all you need to do is say the word and our great country will drop down to forty-nine states. I suppose we can probably let Puerto Rico, or D.C. in to make up for it, but that's neither here nor there."

"I guess, Colonel, I'm having some trouble grasping the sheer enormity of the craft. The briefing I received was not very detailed."

"Yes, of course, Mr. President. My guys on the ground have it at a staggering fifteen football fields long."

"Okay Leverbean, let me stop you right there. Football fields? Is that really an accurate unit of measure?"

"Sure it is. A football field is a hundred yards. This alien craft is approximately fifteen hundred yards."

"Why was that not stated from the start? Why were football fields even in the mix here? There's a reason why we adhere to certain standards. Because no one wants to convert an individual's unit of measure to their own. If I ask you how tall you are and you tell me 'one and a half hay bales' how the fuck am I supposed to know what that means? I hate football, Colonel. I had no idea the fields are one hundred yards long. When I ask you for anything involving units of measure, give it to me in imperial terms, hell even the metric system would work better than a sports reference."

"Sorry sir. I wanted to spice things up with some

colorful language."

"I understand, Leverbean, but a giant alien craft hovering over a corn field is colorful enough. Do you even know how many other countries are jealous the aliens landed here? They're breathing down my neck for info I don't have yet. If not handled as carefully as possible, this could turn into an international disaster. And that's assuming whatever's in there is friendly."

"By your leave, Colonel Leverbean, sir," the soldier in the passenger seat interrupted.

Leverbean glanced at the president, who nodded his assent. "Go ahead, Staff Sergeant."

"Sir, we've received an urgent message over the emergency channel I think you and the president need to hear."

"By all means, patch it through to the speaker."

The staff sergeant pressed a few buttons on the radio console. A moment later an ear splitting burst of static assaulted the passengers. It died away after the staff sergeant adjusted the volume. Then he keyed the handset and began a new transmission, "Forward operations, this is Eagle One. Please repeat your last."

"This is Forward Operations to Eagle One. Be advised a hatch appears to have opened in the craft. I repeat, E.T. appears ready to make contact, a hatch has opened in the craft."

President Forbes leaned forward, placing a firm hand on the driver's shoulder, "Listen to me," he said, deadpan, "I don't give a shit what traffic laws you have to break, we need to be at that landing site right away."

Half an hour later, the president stood speechless at the forward operating base. None of the pictures he'd seen, nor any of the descriptions did the sight before him any justice. He could try for the rest of his life to find the right words to do the scene before him justice but would never be able to. All at once Forbes felt so small, unqualified for the task that lay ahead of him. America has enough on her hands being the world police. Now he was what, supposed to figure out how to negotiate peace on an intergalactic scale? Nothing he'd been through in life could have prepared him for this. Forbes took a moment to ground himself. There was a reason he was elected to this office. Most of the country believed in his particular style of leadership. Yes, one could argue it was the electoral college's decision, but that was only semantics. There were people who would approve of the decisions he made, and people who never would. That's how it had been in the past, with those who came before him. That's how it was in the current, and that's how it would be in the future. President Forbes understood well there was no way to please everyone. However, this was uncharted territory. Regardless of whether he was prepared for the situation or not, it was happening. Whatever events unfolded in the next few moments would ring through the annals of history forever. He was the one who would lead the people into this next phase of existence. He turned to Colonel Leverbean, who stood at his side in awe. "Hand me the radio, Colonel. It's time to find out what we're up against."

"Yes sir," Leverbean said, passing a headset over to the president. "We're broadcasting over every known frequency, including sub and supersonic. The FCC has blocked all other communication within a thirty-mile radius. Of course, there's no way to know for certain if the beings in the ship understand us, but we can only do our best with the tools at our disposal." Colonel Leverbean saw Forbes was done customizing the headset to fit him. "Alright everyone, we're hot in five…four…three…two…"

A quick blast of feedback issued from the speakers as the transmission went live. "Greetings," his voice, crystal clear, echoed from every direction, "I am President Allen Forbes. I am the elected representative and leader of the country known as The United States of America, where your vessel has landed. We would like to welcome you to our world. However, we require some sign you understand our communications."

Queens, NY, 2113 hrs

"Look at the streets," he said as he gazed out the window of his apartment, "Empty. People are really buying this shit." Gene Burns turned to the woman he'd hired for the night and furrowed his brow, seeing her eyes fixed on the TV screen. "What the fuck? I'm not paying you for this. Turn that shit off."

Her chosen name was Sable. Gene contacted her through a site he'd found while using his TOR browser. Her profile specified she was fine with name calling and rough play. This suited Gene perfectly. As a child, he witnessed his father abusing his mother, calling her out of her name and laying his forceful hands on her whenever he was inconvenienced in the slightest. Gene would lie in bed listening to the shouting and thumping as his mother was violently tossed about the house. On many nights, she would enter his room, eyes swollen, filled with tears, and assure him everything would be alright. She, unfortunately, was too dumb to realize he didn't need the reassurance. As she embraced him, sniffling and rocking back and forth, her pain would produce the most raging arousals Gene had ever experienced. In his adult life, he found himself chasing the feeling more and more. Sable was his latest attempt, but the so-called news was ruining the experience.

"What do you think they'll say at the press conference?" Sable asked.

"Bitch, nobody told you to speak. Lay down on the couch and put your face in the pillow, before I punch you in the back of your motherfucking head."

Sable grew accustomed to being spoken to by clients in such a manner. It was typical for her to leave an appointment with black eyes, scrapes and bruises, and even rope burns. The pay was decent, and kept her and her son living in their duplex for another month with adequate food, and moderately fashionable clothes. Tonight though, everything changed. It wasn't the realization of how long she'd lived this lifestyle, nor the fact tonight's client was a self-important, sadistic conspiracy theorist with mommy issues, who believed the earth was flat and covered in a crystal dome. It was the revelation that life existed beyond anything she knew. The prospect of humankind being forever changed after tonight opened her eyes to much brighter horizons. What value would money hold on a cosmic scale? The aliens who spoke with the president were way more advanced than the life existing all around her, and they had no idea what it even was. They almost appeared shocked at the explanation of the way cash moves civilization forward. They exist in a world of complete harmony. Where, if you need, you are provided. No "haves and have nots" or division among classes. Sable imagined a life without struggle, without the need to degrade herself for rent money. It was a dream that, with the spaceship's arrival, seemed as tangible as ever. Sable wanted it. Not only for herself, but for her baby boy. Which is why the words spilling from Gene's filthy mouth upset her more than any other client she'd been with. In that single moment, her world shifted. Nothing would ever be the same again.

Gene walked over to where Sable sat, squatting down so he was staring directly into her eyes, "I'm talking to you, cunt. Do what I say or you'll be face down in a ditch faster than it takes for this bullshit story to fall out of the news cycle." Gene reached behind Sable's head and grabbed a handful of her high quality, auburn wig. So fierce was his grip that he ended up with a good deal of her real hair in his grasp. He wrenched her head back and she gasped.

"No, no more," her voice was strained as she spoke. "Cardboard, cardboard." The lump forming in her throat nearly muffled the agreed upon safe word to silence.

Gene did not let go of her. His dick swelled, pressing against the front of his jeans. "You don't get to say that," he yelled, "not yet, you don't." He brought his free hand up and slammed his palm down onto her nose.

Blood ran out of her nostrils in warm rivulets. Thoughts swirled in her mind that she may have taken on one client too many. That this was where her life would meet its end, at the very moment where she decided to take control of it. Control. Such an empowering word. So much so a new strength began to build up inside of her. Since receiving confirmation of extraterrestrial life, though only a few minutes earlier, boundaries had been built up. This asshole of a person was violating them, and she didn't have to take any shit. Gene was stronger than most other men she'd been with, but he also wasn't too bright. For all his talk of her ending up in a ditch, and with him holding her by the hair, he neglected to restrain any other part of her. Mainly her hands. His grasp on her made it hard to see where he was, but she didn't need to worry about that. He'd been right in front of her a moment ago, and if he'd moved, his grip would have changed. With the new drive burning inside her, Sable reached both hands up and swiped at Gene's face. Nails carving trails across the delicate flesh.

Gene let go of Sable, "Ouch, what the smurf?" He staggered back, reaching up and touching the new, burning claw marks on his nose and cheeks. "You can't do that. That's not what I paid for. The hell is wrong with you?" With his hand balled into a fist, Gene readied himself to retaliate.

The punch was so telegraphed a dead man with glaucoma could have seen it coming. Sable scooted out of the way and watched the fist sail past her. She wished this all had been taking place in front of a brick wall. She wanted Gene's hand to land on something more unforgiving than a couch cushion. Rather than wait for him to recover and make another attempt, Sable got to her feet, curled her arm, and drove her elbow into Gene's temple.

He may have been strong, but it was obvious the man had not been in any real fights in his life. The strike laid him out. A knot formed at the side of his head, where the elbow connected. Gene lay on the threadbare carpet in his living room wholly involved in a struggle to remain conscious. "Cardboard, cardboard," the words were weak, little more than a whisper.

Sable stood above him. Normally short in stature, she loomed like a redwood, from where Gene lay. "You don't get to say that." A small laugh escaped her lips, "not yet, you don't." Sable was wearing flats. For that, she was thankful. If she'd tried to kick him in the face with her heels on, she would've likely lost her balance and ended up on the floor right next to him. As it was, her Kate Spades proved perfect for the task. She caught him in almost the same spot as the elbow.

The waking world fell away from Gene, and he passed out.

Sable, proud owner of a new sense of self worth, collected her things and strode out of the apartment with grace. Not worried about any of the money she was owed.

On the floor, reeling, Gene crept back into consciousness. A noise playing loud in his ears annoyed him for reasons he could not grasp in the moment. Gene sat up and dizziness took control at once. He shuffled across the floor until his back was propped against the couch. The source of the noise revealed itself. The television was on. Everyone was still talking about the supposed alien landing. Gene saw right through it from the very start. How do you turn an entire country's— possibly the world's—attention away from the inevitable civil upheaval of the government and bring every citizen in line? Stage something grand, of course. Much like the moon landing though, the Hollywood producers who collaborated on this effort did shoddy work. The spacecraft hovering above the corn field was an embarrassment to CGI. Pixar could have drummed up something more believable. Then there were the aliens themselves. They looked so stereotypical Gene actually felt insulted. Not to mention the weak excuse they gave for already knowing english.

"We do not have what you call language. We understand sentiment, intention, and gesture and can mimic any form of communication with complete accuracy."

What a load of horse piss. According to both the liberal and conservative media, that douche face president Forbes was escorting the "visitors" to D.C. for a press conference. These extra terrestrials were to address the nation and deliver a message to unify the people. Being the conspiracy crazy individual he was, Gene was certain all three of the grey bastards would be assassinated, some poor fall guy would take the blame, the country would cry out for justice, and by Monday the president's little charade will have successfully diverted everyone's attention from another dead nigger child.

As he sat there, Gene wanted in. Perhaps he could go down to the capitol and rub elbows with the orchestrators of this plot and actually be part of something from the jump, instead of hopping on the bandwagon after the fact. Yes, this was the answer. He rose to his feet slowly and reached for his back pocket. His wallet was gone. A quick glance around the living room revealed it was nowhere in sight. As the throbbing pain in his temple continued, he realized what happened. "That gutter whore robbed me." Gene turned the TV off and sauntered to the phone. After dialing the familiar number, he waited as the line rang. At last someone picked up on the other end. Without waiting for a greeting, Gene spoke, "Hey mom. I need a favor."

Atlanta, GA, Wednesday, 0630 hrs

How they'd managed to secure him a press pass for the grand event was beyond him. As James sat in the airport, he could feel the tides of his career shifting towards bigger, brighter shores. This was his invitation to the grownups table. So exclusive was this press conference simply being there would open doors he never imagined he'd see in his lifetime.

Though he was a nervous flyer, the excitement of what was to come outweighed his reservations. He took a look around the terminal, checking for good omens, superstitious signs everything would be alright. There would not be many people on the flight, so the plane would not be weighed down. The weather was supposed to be sunny and clear the whole way. He was certain the pilots were not taking pictures in front of the plane, and even if they wanted to, it was too dark outside. One other thing he noted was two of the waiting passengers seemed insanely high. One man sitting across from him seemed to be having the hardest time keeping his legs still. He would cross them, uncross them, knock his knees together, and bounce them up and down. The other, sitting next to the first, had been staring at him for over three minutes. James hadn't even seen him blink. James had done a story about marijuana legalization a few months ago. Though he himself did not indulge, he was not opposed to others consuming the relatively harmless substance. In moderation, of course. The two gentlemen who sat across from him clearly did not believe in such a notion though. It might not be a bad thing though. While they both appeared grown and capable of managing themselves as functional members of society, under the influence of the substance, they were like children. God wouldn't take down a plane with such foolish innocence aboard. Would he?

Penn Station, NY, 1240 hrs

Gene Burns boarded the train, mind still abuzz from visiting his mother. She spotted him a few hundred bucks for his trip. He'd known from the moment she picked up the phone she would. He was her baby boy and she had to protect him. What his mother failed to realize was he was the one protecting her. Ever since his father died in a freak accident–some kids were passing by his construction site one day and dropped a lit sparkler down the vent pipe of the port-a-john where he was taking a shit, igniting the gasses built up in the modern day outhouse–Gene had been the man in her life. He fell into the lecherous role with no effort at all, bleeding his mother of money, food, or whatever he was too lazy to obtain on his own. He would have asked for her car, but his license was currently in the possession of a filthy bitch, whom he planned on catching up with after all of this, to strangle the life out of.

Now Gene had no choice but to wait the three hours it would take to travel to the capitol. He would need to move fast once he arrived. Call in a favor or two from the people he knew in the area and, with any luck, find himself in the proximity of the big event. He sat in his seat, thinking through a mental roll-o-dex of people he could call. One name stood out, Nathan Greene. A pseudonym of course, Nathan chose the name after being denied entry into the Army officer program because of his lifelong battle with asthma. Gene had spoken with him often, and developed what could pass as a friendship, agreeing to meet up one day and visit the Ice Wall together. It seemed like a good idea for a celebration once the lid was blown off this ruse.

He pulled out his phone and dialed Nathan's last known number. Pain exploded in his head and he realized he was holding it to the side of his face where he'd been assaulted the night before. He quickly switched hands, cursing Sable under his breath. A voice answered before the line ever began to ring.

"The gardens are lovely this time of year."

"Oh fuck," Gene said. "Look, my head is killing me right now. I don't remember the passphrase. It's me though. It's G.B."

The line was immediately disconnected.

Gene sat in his seat wracking his brain, trying to remember what he was supposed to say in reply. After a few minutes, his cell phone rang. The number did not display on the screen. Gene answered at once.

"You little bitch. Don't ever call me on that line and pull that shit again. The gardens are lovely this time of year, and then you say 'But the statues are all covered in bird shit.' Simple. Easy fucking peasy. Now, what do you want?"

"Hey man, sorry. I'm a little out of sorts at the moment. I'm on my way down to your neck of the woods and I need a favor."

"Anything for a fellow Terra Level brother. You chose one hell of a day to visit though. The city's tied in knots over this alien crap."

"That's kind of why I'm reaching out. I need you to get me close to the press conference. Have you been on the message boards? I figured out what's going on, but I don't know who's in on it, other than Forbes. If I'm there though, I can suss them out easy, and we'll have infiltrated the highest levels of government. This is big Nate. I need to be in the room. I should be there by four. Do you think you can hook it up?"

"Shit man, that's only three hours. Tell you what, I have company coming I need to check on. My cousin and a good friend are here for my wedding. Let me see how they're doing and then I'll do what I can about this. Call me when you arrive, and don't forget the passphrase this time."

Washington Dulles International Airport, VA, 1355hrs

The two men, whom he now knew as Lenny and Mark, were certainly a couple of characters. James hadn't experienced a single moment of anxiety on the airplane thanks to the duo. Lenny, full of quirks, had eaten another edible before boarding in Atlanta and was so high by the time the plane took off everything James said left him in tears from laughing. Mark let himself sober up, he had to drive them to his cousin's place when they landed at Dulles. After revealing he was a reporter on his way to the big press conference, James and the man, obviously resentful Lenny got to keep his head in the clouds, had an insightful conversation about the events taking place.

After landing at the airport, James bid the two farewell at the baggage claim. However, as fate would have it, they found themselves standing in line for a car at the same rental place.

Mark stood at the counter and gave the woman

his information. With his ID in hand, she typed at the computer in front of her.

Seconds later she handed his driver's license back and, in a practiced but polite voice said "I'm sorry sir, but I don't see any reservation in your name."

"What? That can't be right. Lenny, did you reserve the car in your name, or mine?"

"Reserve? What are you talking about?"

"No, come on. Don't tell me you didn't reserve a car. I asked you to do this days ago." Mark shook his head and turned his attention back to the clerk, "Okay, no worries. What do you have available?"

"Sir, I'm sorry to say this but every vehicle we have is either rented already, or reserved."

"Great, just great. I knew I should've taken care of this. What do we do now, catch a cab?"

"Hey man, what you so upset for? We're here, right? The other side of the country. We could walk outside, and it'll actually be cold. You know what I'm saying? Don't get yourself so wound up man. We're here to relax and enjoy ourselves and watch your cousin throw his life away. Shit, with any luck, we might run into those alien farmers, yo."

Mark could not believe Lenny was actually saying something sensible, other than the bit about farmers. This trip was a celebration. No need to drag the mood down over a minor inconvenience. "You know what? You're right. Let me give Oswald a quick call, and then we'll hop in a taxi."

The two men stepped out of line and James, standing a couple people back, decided to do them a favor. "Hey guys, hold on."

"Oh shit, check it out Mark, we know him. He was on the plane."

Mark, paying Lenny no mind, walked over to the reporter. "What's up?"

"Where are you heading? I don't have to be at the White House for a few hours, and I feel like I owe you. I would've been a mess on that flight if not for you two. Seeing this little predicament you're in, I don't mind helping out."

"Oh shit, for real? We're heading to McLean, same direction."

"Then it's settled. I'll rent a car, and we'll head out."

En Route, VA, 1440hrs

Oswald was not annoyed when Mark called to tell him about the rental car breaking down. He simply grabbed his keys and hit the road. The man was aware of the traffic situation. Hordes of curious visitors flocking to the city, hoping to catch a glimpse of the interplanetary visitors. Stop and go was an understatement. Most of the common roads were at a standstill. Luckily, Oswald knew his way around. Riding out to where his cousin was stranded wouldn't be an issue. No one was travelling in that direction.

After picking up Mark, Lenny, and whomever they were with, he would have to stick to back roads on the return trip.

Twenty minutes into the drive, he found them. Smoke billowing from beneath the hood of the sedan, a few yards from a toll booth. Oswald pulled up in front of the vehicle, stepped out to the familiar sound of a classic Mark and Lenny argument. "I see nothing's changed between the two of you shitheads," he laughed, as he approached.

Mark turned his attention away from Lenny, changing his tone from annoyed to excited in a heartbeat, "Ozzie, how the fuck are you?" He pulled his cousin into a tight embrace.

After his cousin let go, Oswald gave Lenny a bro hug. He was happy the two had arrived at last. "Damn, it's good to see you guys. Let's move your things moved over to my trunk and hit the road. I have a ton of shit to do and, as you can see from all the cars on the road, it's gonna be a little challenging."

"Hey Ozzie," Mark said, "come here for a sec. There's someone I want you to meet."

Oswald let Mark lead him to the driver side door of the out-of-service car.

"This is James Garcia. He's a reporter from Atlanta."

"Nice to meet you. Mark said you were giving them a ride to my place. Sorry it didn't work out."

Oswald shook the man's hand, taking note of the peculiar badge hanging around the reporter's neck.

"Are you kidding? I wish I could take these two with me everywhere. I hear you're getting married. Congratulations."

"Thanks. So, Atlanta? I don't mean to pry, but what's the deal with the dead black kid? They gonna arrest the cop or what?"

James felt a twinge of pride hearing the question. In the past twenty-four hours he'd been the lead on two of the biggest news stories ever. People already recognized him, they simply didn't know it yet. After tonight they would, though. "Funny you should mention that. I'm the one who's been reporting on that tragedy of a story."

Being as close as he was, Oswald's wandering eyes took in the badge James was wearing. It was a press pass for the White House. "So, the rental company should be sending a tow truck out, right? Where can I drop you off?"

"Oh, you don't have to do that. I was only giving these guys a lift because it was on the way. Besides, shouldn't I be here when they pick the car up?"

"No way. You have somewhere to be and there's no telling when the tow will get here. The car's not going anywhere. They can pick it up and you can drop the keys off later."

Lenny finished moving the luggage from the

rental car to Oswald's trunk. He closed the lid and made his way around the car to the back seat. A few moments passed, then the passenger door opened and Mark joined him. "Trippy, huh?"

"What?"

"That guy out there. He looks like your cousin."

James agreed with Oswald. Whatever was wrong with the car was not his fault, and he was not about to miss the opportunity of a lifetime waiting on some overpaid wrecker service to come save the day. "Okay," he replied, "twist my arm. I'm headed to the big press conference at the White House. Hell, if you can come up with any good questions on the way, I may ask the aliens on your behalf."

The laugh was fake but cordial. Oswald took in the scene around him. Unassuming motorists driving by, furious at the slow crawl of traffic, Mark and Lenny sitting in his car probably going off on one another yet again. Not a single eye on himself. With the new found anonymity he turned his attention back to James, "Then it's settled. Grab the keys and let's hit the road."

James ducked into the car, sitting down on the driver's seat to grab the key fob resting in the cup holder of the center console. It was all playing out so perfectly. For a second, he thought the rental car breaking down was a bad omen, but Oswald proved as delightful as his cousin, and exceedingly helpful to boot. Key in hand, James turned, ready to make his way out of the broken down vehicle, when a solid piece of metal struck him in the face.

The moment James took his eyes off of him, Oswald drew the pistol from his waistband. He watched the reporter grab the car key, smiling, probably thinking about the "aliens". Oblivious to what was really happening. Before he could step out of the car, Oswald punched the man in the face with the pistol. The first blow didn't knock him out, and so he hit him a second and third time. Once James slumped down in the seat, Oswald quickly snatched the press credentials from around his neck and shoved them in his pocket. He then pulled out his phone. Not his standard everyday phone, but the one he replaced on a weekly basis. The one only the Terra Level knew the number for. Oswald dialed the number from memory. It rang twice before someone answered.

"The gardens are lovely this-"

"Fuck all of that," Oswald yelled into the phone, giddy with excitement.

"But you said to use the passphrase on this line."

"I don't care what I said. This can't wait. You're in."

"I'm in, what do you mean?"

"I mean, you wanted to be close to the action when it went down. Well I got you press credentials for the main event."

"No way. You're lying. Nathan, you son of a

bitch. This is un-fucking-real. I owe you, big."

"We'll discuss my fee later. Hurry up and get your ass down here. You don't have much time." Nathan Greene ended the call and slipped the phone back into his pocket.

A moment passed, and then Oswald started the car up and pulled out into traffic.

"What happened to James? I thought he was coming with us." Mark looked in the rear view mirror and saw the silhouette of his new friend in the driver's seat of the still smoking rental.

"Nah," Oswald began, "he said it would be better if he waited for the wrecker. Didn't want the rental people to try and pin this on him."

"Yeah, that makes sense. Hope he gets to the White House in time."

"I'm sure he'll be fine," Oswald said.

"Oh shit," Lenny's surprised voice issued from the back seat, "When did you get here, Ozzie? We saw some dude who looked exactly like you."

Union Station, Washington DC, 1637hrs

Gene was not waiting for long. After the lengthy train ride, and the good news from Nathan, he was anxious to put his plan into action. He found his friend waiting outside in a massive line of cars. This caused a bit of worry. The city seemed to be at a standstill, trafficwise. "Goddammit Nathan. It's good to finally meet you." Gene sat down in the passenger seat and clapped the man on the shoulder.

"This is a great day, my friend. You're about to legitimize the entire Terra Level movement. Check this out." Nathan reached into his pocket and withdrew the lanyard holding the press pass. He dangled it in front of Gene.

"It's beautiful. How were you able to get your hands on it?"

"Your boy Nate is pretty resourceful when he needs to be. Try it on."

Gene grabbed the pass and placed it around his neck. He felt important. Nothing could stand in his way any longer. There was, however, the matter of all the clogged streets surrounding them. "What's with all the cars, man? Can you make it to the White House in enough time?"

"G.B., buddy, you let me worry about that. I know these streets like no one else."

His friend put the car in gear, and Gene took a moment to feel out his surroundings. The vehicle was spacious, and comfortable. Maybe exceedingly so. Gene needed to keep his edge if he was to go through with his plan. Glancing back, he noticed a gun on the seat behind him. "What the fuck man, you have this out in the open?"

"What, the pistol? Shit's been in my waistband all day, annoying the hell out of me. I needed a break. It's cool though, I have a permit."

As they finally pulled away from the station, Gene reached back and palmed the weapon.

"There you go. Get a feel for it. I'd let you take her with you, but they are one hundred percent going to pat you down and metal detect you when you arrive at the event."

He'd never fired a gun before. In his life there were plenty of people who could've acquired one for him, and even taught him how to handle one, but he'd passed on every opportunity. Gene believed in his fists. Even though he'd never used them against anyone formidable. The pistol was designed for one thing. When used, there could be no second guessing. He would never admit it to anyone, himself included, but Gene's thoughts were often riddled with doubt. He chased away the line of thinking. It was pulling him out of the moment.

Gene looked on as Nathan masterfully swerved around large pockets of traffic, ducking through empty side streets and being aggressive with every move. He smiled. At this pace, they'd be at the event in no time at all. The smile faded once he saw the flashing lights in the rear view.

"Okay, you relax and let me handle this. Got it?"

He wanted to trust the man. So far, Nathan had been in perfect control of the entire situation. The police were unpredictable though. Gene was always nervous around officers. He took a deep breath as the car pulled over, telling himself again and again his friend would handle it. Completely forgetting about the gun in his lap.

The officer approached, a broad shouldered man with a thick moustache and mirrored shades. He tapped the driver's window, and Nathan rolled it open. "What seems to be the problem, officer?"

The cop placed a forceful hand on the door and leaned down to look Nathan in the eyes, "Oh you know exactly what this is, mister. The fuck are you doing out here?"

"Got a call a little while ago from a friend, saying he was in the city," Nathan cocked his head in Gene's direction. "He's a reporter from Atlanta, in town for the President's event. I told him I'd be faster than any taxi, or Uber."

"Shit, babe. My bad. I thought this was your cousin. Here I am putting on a show, and this is legitimate business."

"Nah, Mark and Lenny are back at the house, hanging out. This is," he hesitated for a moment, forgetting what name was printed on the badge. Nathan made an exaggerated gesture of turning to his friend in acknowledgement, glimpsing the name in the process, "James Garcia. James, this is my fiance, Officer Creflo Osteen."

"Nice to meet you," Officer Osteen replied. "Hey Ozzie, quick idea just hit me. If you'd like, I can escort you the rest of the way."

"I appreciate it honey, I really do. But I don't think it'll be necessary." Nathan placed his hand on top of the officer's, then leaned forward. The officer moved closer and they kissed, a brief but heartfelt gesture. "I'll see you you at home."

All at once, Gene's head was spinning. He could not believe what he was seeing. The sheer deception. Nathan had been an inspiration, a man he held in the highest regard. Discovering his fiancé was not only a cop, but a man, hit him harder than Sable had.

Nathan, or Ozzie saw the expression on Gene's face. He appeared to be falling ill, perhaps a stomach bug or something. Concerned, he reached out a hand to comfort his red faced, sweating friend. "Hey, are you alright?"

"Don't you fucking touch me," Gene yelled.

"Whoa, everything good over there pal," Officer Osteen removed his glasses to for a clear view inside the car. It was in that moment when he noticed the fake James Garcia's hand wrapping around a gun. His hand went instinctively to his holster, but James had already brought his weapon up and leveled it at Oswald. His tone dropped to a low and steady calm, "Okay, okay, let's relax for a bit, friend," he held his hands up in supplication.

"Gene, what the fuck man?" Nathan attempted to turn and grab the weapon, but the seat belt locked up inhibiting his movement.

"Shut your filthy mouth," Gene yelled

"Wait, Ozzie, who the fuck is Gene?" Osteen took a step back and placed his hands on his hips.

Gene misunderstood the action, thinking the officer was about to draw his gun. Acting on pure impulse, he aimed at the cop and squeezed the trigger twice, in quick succession. It was a jerky movement and the recoil caused him to drop the pistol. The two rounds however, did manage to escape the barrel of the weapon and find purchase in the police officer's neck and chest.

Oswald's world slowed to a stop. His ears were ringing from being in such close proximity to the weapon's report. It left him disoriented. He looked to his left for the man he loved. Something was wrong and he needed the comfort and reassurance his fiancé provided. What he saw did not make any sense. Creflo, his heart, his everything was collapsing to the ground. Blood poured out of him and stained the uniform he'd taken such pride in. "Creflo?" The word was barely a whisper. "No. No, no, no, no. This is…what the." Oswald's trembling hand fumbled with the seat belt buckle. "Creflo? Creflo honey, you're okay right?"

Gene was reeling from having fired the gun. Burning bits of powder singed his hand, and the flash temporarily blinded him. He could not hear anything and the car smelled like the morning after Independence Day. He shook his head and knocked against the door, aggravating the still fresh bruise at his temple. The pain brought him back to himself faster than anything. Gene saw the cop lying on the ground and knew he'd fucked up. He also saw Nathan in a desperate attempt to free himself from the vehicle. Without wasting a moment, he reached down to find the gun. He found it and wrapped his hand around the warm steel. Returning to an upright position in the seat, Gene found himself face to face with a demon. Nathan's eyes brimming with tears, his face burning with anger and rage.

Oswald stared the man down. "Why?" he asked. As bad as he wanted to understand, if Gene offered any reply, Oswald would have torn his jaw off with his bare hands.

Gene fired the gun again.

This third bullet punched through Oswald's torso. The pain was immense, but he paid it no mind. Oswald didn't even look down to check the damage, only kept his piercing gaze on the man who'd stolen away his future. In the final moments before everything went dark, he saw another muzzle flash. There was an impact. Oswald could not say where, but his head was being forced back against his will. His last thought was the hope he would land somewhere nearer to Creflo.

Gene scurried out of the car and rushed over to the driver's side. The moment he opened the door, Nathan or Ozzie or whoever the fuck tumbled out onto the street. Gene grabbed the man's legs and removed them from the vehicle. After that, he got into the driver's seat and sped off. Nobody cared about the little side street they were on. He could go handle business at the press conference, and come back later to clean this all up.

Press Conference, White House, 1802hrs

"Ladies and gentlemen, the President of the United States."

President Forbes stepped up to the podium, all smiles and waves, amidst a barrage of blinding camera flashes and applause. Looking out across the crowd, he saw hunger. The guests were anxious to be here, to see a facet of life no one else had ever beheld before yesterday. He waited for the din to die down, took in a deep breath to clear his mind, and began his address.

"My fellow Americans, esteemed guests, members of the press, and those of you watching from around the world, welcome. It is truly my honor to stand before you tonight speaking to you at the most important moment in history.

"I've been so nervous. Countless other issues demand my attention, yet after making contact with the ones I've dubbed 'The Beings' it all seems minor by comparison. The Beings represent change. They are the promise of a bigger, better, and unified future. We have much to learn from them and their ways. In the coming days, weeks, and years the world will experience a rebirth. Humankind will ascend to its highest peak.

Peace on an unprecedented scale, technological advances beyond the dreams of even the most ambitious sci fi tales. New medicines, language, new worlds to traverse. We have so much to learn, and we are only approaching the beginning.

"It is my sincere pleasure, citizens of The United States, citizens of Earth, to introduce to you this evening, The Beings."

They appeared to the left of the stage. Three gray figures, at least nine feet tall. Not a sound could be heard. The audience looked on breathless as they made their way to the president. Once they arrived at the podium, one of the beings stood before the microphone, while the other two stood behind, flanking it.

Route 267, VA, 1815 hrs

He was roused by the knocking on the window. James, head pounding, turned to see a man in grease-stained coveralls peering into the driver's side window.

"You alright in there?" The voice through the glass was muffled.

James unlocked the door and slowly stepped out. The nighttime air was cold and bracing. A chill shot through him as he looked around, trying to find his bearings.

"Hey mister, you the one what needed the tow, ain't ya?

He turned to the man, a slender, young white guy with close cropped hair and a struggling goatee.

The name embroidered above his breast pocket read PA. James remembered the car breaking down. "What time is it?" He said the words, knowing they were important, but unsure of their significance.

"Time?" Pa lifted his arm and glanced at the watch on his wrist, "Well, it's about six-fifteen."

Passengers, there were two men in the car with him. The stoners. He smiled, recalling how they had been such good companions on this trip. Yes, he was on a trip. The car broke down and one of the men, Mark, that was his name, called someone to pick them up. All of the pieces began falling into place. The cousin arrived. Mark and Lenny moved to his car. Ozzie was his name. They were discussing leaving the rental behind when the man assaulted him. Anger bubbled up inside. James lowered his throbbing head into his waiting hands. That's when he noticed the press pass, which he'd proudly displayed since receiving it in Atlanta, was gone. It was also the moment when he realized what time Pa had announced. "No," he screamed, "this can't be happening." He turned to Pa, who stood there staring blankly. "Call the cops. No, call the Secret Service, or something. That asshole stole my credentials."

"You sayin you been robbed, man? Well that ain't no good. Lemme call this in and get ya some help."

"No. I mean, yes call it in. Get the cops out sure, but I need you to give me a ride. I need to get to The

White House right away."

"Um, that's a bit more than what's in my job description sir. I can get five-oh out here, that's just one man helpin' 'nother, but I ain't no taxi service."

The nerve of him. Such insolence. Did he not know who he was dealing with? This lowly cretin was in the presence of James Garcia, News Media God. The look he gave the man could have drilled a hole right through him. "Perhaps I need to be more clear. We will get in your truck, and you will take me where I need to go."

"I don't know what all happened here, and ya look a bit banged up Mister, but you ain't fixin' to talk to me any kinda way."

James growled, animal-like. Without warning, he brought his hand up and slapped Pa across his face.

Pa stumbled back after being hit. "You mother fucker." Pa shot forward like a snake striking its prey. He grabbed James by his shirt collar and drove his knee into the reporter's stomach. The man doubled over, and Pa kicked his leg out, sweeping his feet from under him. After the man fell, Pa mounted him and began a cascade of close fisted blows.

James was unable to protect himself. He was at the mercy of the tow truck driver. The wind was knocked out of him, and James could only lean over, wrapping his arms around his stomach. Before he knew it, he was on his back. In a flash, Pa was on top of him.

The first punch brought with it an understanding of how bad he'd been hurt when Ozzie assaulted him. The world blurred out of focus as his retina detached. An insufferable pain, like the worst headache ever combined with a railroad spike through the eye socket, would have been how he described it. Through it all though, James' only thought was about his career and how, after missing tonight's golden opportunity, he'd never be a reporter again. Not one second after the next blow landed, and only a few minutes removed from being initially revived, James' condition escalated from mild concussion to possible brain damage, and he found himself unconscious once more.

Residence of Oswald Cumberdink III, McClean, VA 1819 hrs

The television was on, and the two men sat on the couch in front of it, but neither one was paying attention. Lenny was slumped down, half sitting and half lying on the sofa. An open bag of pretzel sticks atop his chest. Whenever he breathed in, the bag tilted enough to where a few of the crunchy sticks would tumble out, roll down the slope of his chest and into Lenny's waiting mouth.

Mark sat beside him, at peace with everything around him. It had been a long time since he was able to let himself reach the level of high he was at. This wasn't him trying to wind down after a long day at work, nor was he worried about any of the everyday stresses plaguing him back home. It was not an escape, but pure relaxation. He grabbed the remote and turned the TV off. Neither he nor Lenny were paying any attention and it was rude, as guests, to run up someone else's electric bill.

Other than the sound of Lenny crunching on pretzels every few seconds, the entire place was silent. Mark sat upright, unsure if he was being overly paranoid or if something was truly wrong. "Lenny," he reached over and shook his friend, "Lenny, I think something's going on."

"What do you mean?" Lenny spoke around a mouth full of the salty snack, spraying crumbs onto himself.

"I don't know. Things seem off. Like, why are you the only thing I can hear?"

"That's ridiculous. The TV was on and we could hear that, right?"

"I don't know. I wasn't paying attention to it."

"I think you might be losing it, Mark. I can hear you perfectly clear."

"That's not the problem though. I can hear you too. I can't hear any of the other little noises that should be present in a quiet house. Nothing's ever this silent. Where's the ice maker, the water heater, outside traffic. There's nothing."

Lenny tried to pay his friend as little attention as possible. Him being so paranoid was a drain on his mood. What's worse is it was proving to be contagious. Lenny cleared out his ears. It felt like he was in a soundproof booth. The ambient noise normally present in the background of life was gone. "What the hell man. You're starting to worry me. That paranoia shit is catchy," he picked the remote up from where it rested, "I'm gonna drop this and it'll clatter onto the floor, proving you're wrong." Without any hesitation, Lenny threw the remote control at the wall where the TV was mounted. "No. Hell no. Dude, what the?"

Few things in his lifetime left Lenny speechless. There was the time where, as a kid, he'd put an egg in a rock tumbler, mistaking it for a large stone. The smell when he opened it days later brought him close to fainting. Another time, in high school, he'd visited his aunt and uncle in New York over summer break. Making fast friends with the neighborhood miscreants, they ran around town lighting firecrackers in odd places; blowing up melons at a fruit stand, bombing a newspaper kiosk, and tossing a sparkler in the vent pipe of a Port-A-Jon at a random construction site. The thing took off like a rocket fueled by feces. And now he'd flung a remote control at the wall, fully expecting it to land with a thud and probably break apart. What happened instead was nothing. The remote simply hung in the air where Lenny released it.

"Dude, what's going on?" Mark's heart raced, seeing the remote in stasis.

An electric buzz began to emanate from walls surrounding them. Low at first, it grew in volume. The couch, the television, the remote, their clothes, everything began to glow a brilliant white. The room rumbled and shook. Lenny looked to Mark but could not find him. The man was lost in a light brighter than anything he'd ever seen. The light, for anyone who may have been present while it occurred, was like a ray of pure sunshine in the darkness. It was a powerful burst of lightning. There one moment, and gone in a heartbeat.

The house returned to silence. The remote hanging in the air clattered to the floor. Had either Mark or Lenny still been there and not vanished with the light, both men definitely would have heard it

Press Conference, White House, 1821 hrs

"Greetings," The being said.

Among the crowd, Gene turned from side to side scanning different vantage points, yet seeing no shooters. What were they waiting for? Those costumed freaks should have already been mowed down. In that moment of doubt came the revelation. He was the shooter. This was his destiny. Everything he'd ever endured served its goddamn purpose to land him right here in this moment. Gene was the shooter. It had always been him. His father's death had matured him. Wizened him up enough to sniff out even the most clandestine conspiracy. Even recently he'd received combat training with Sable. Nathan lived as a sacrifice knowing he had to die as a gay in order to give Gene proper weapons training. This knowledge emboldened him. It propelled his feet forward, knocking knees and stepping on the toes of the unworthy pricks in his way. And when he finally reached the end of the row he lunged at the security officer posted there, tackling him to the ground and wrestling his weapon away. In a split second he turned to the stage and aimed the gun at The Beings. His martyrdom coming to fruition.

Every firearm in the room was trained on Gene. The command to fire at will was given, and fingers began to tighten around triggers.

"Stop this." The Being shouted from the stage. Everyone froze in place. "What is, what you call, wrong with you all? "A, what you call, person is in need of help and your, what you call, solution is to kill it. The person is a, what you call, product of some of the worst characteristics your, what you call, kind possess. You were correct in your initial, what you call, assessment of us. We are not hostile beings, we are, what you call, simple space farmers. What you call Earth is only a crop on our space, what you call, farm. We have a message for you all to, what you call, hear. A very, what you call, roundabout way to make you understand your, what you call, purpose. In the end, you will be presented with, what you call, logic so impervious you will have no, what you call, choice but to agree with the course of action we take.

"When we, what you call, arrived, what you call, yesterday, we released a toxin that spread through your atmosphere, binding to the very, what you call, air you breathe. This, what you call, toxin, once inhaled, works over the, what you call, course of twenty, what you call, four hours to change the structure of anything carrying human, what you call, DNA into fertilizer. We do realize, what you call, it has been more than twenty four hours, at this, what you call, point. We will need to go, what you call, back and redo the math on, what you call, that. We only just learned about, what you call, time. However, since it does, what you call, seem we will be here for a, what you call, while, allow us to, what you call, enlighten you as to why we are doing this.

"It is not because your, what you call, kind has no redeeming qualities. Your, what you call, territorial tendencies which drive you to, what you call, violate the God given rights of another individual. Caging your kind up like, what you call, animals for simply seeking a better life. Nor is it the class system you choose to live, what you call, by where the wealthy ride the backs of the, what you call, poor dangling that golden, what you call, carrot before them as they use them to keep themselves, what you call, wealthy. It's not even because of the disparity between, what you call, race. No, it's not because of that, or the, what you call, fact that even after all that's happened here, what you call, tonight, your final plea will be something, what you call, contrived like 'please, won't you think of our, what we call, children?'

"It is because, what you call, we are one hundred, what you call, percent indifferent to your plight, which is why we cannot be, what you call, hostile. We simply do not give one single, solitary, scant, infinitesimal, nano-iota Of A FUCK. You are PESTS to us. We have an infestation, we are getting rid of it. We are done with this, what you call, shit."

"Seriously," said the Being standing to the left.

"I mean, what we call, God damn," said the one to the right.

The End

"Oh, by the, what you call, way, we laced the stoners' weed with the only cure and then abducted them."

"That's what I'm talking about," said the Being to the left.

"I love those, what you call, guys," said the one to the right.

Acknowledgements

"Tell me a story, babe…"

I can't ever discount your words, Samii. You constantly push me to stay consistent and do the best I can. I may not always have a story to tell, but I hope to never let you down whenever you ask.

Julian and Ren Wiley, you both inspire the living hell out of me. Never could I have imagined better sons than you. Alex Wiley, you are a massive inspiration as well. You may not know this, but when I read you stories, or bounce my ideas off you, I get super nervous. If you ever give any of my ideas a thumbs down, my whole thought process would be thrown into chaos. David and Crystal Bailey, thanks for accepting me as is. Mom would be so proud of us all, I'm certain. Uncle Allen, the literary equivalent of a street team, love you always.

TJ and Vern Davis, your support means everything, and I can't wait to connect with my BROTHERS again. Breeze, what up! Here's another reason to brag about knowing an arthur. Darius Hunt, I still remember how happy you were when you found out I was a writer. Moments like that tend to sustain me when believing in myself is tougher than it should be. Kathy Mickle, my first editor, your harsh words pushed me further into my journey. Thank you. Erick Gomez, who I mistakenly sent a copy of the proof for my first book. Thanks for returning it.

How could I ever forget the Writing Bad collective? I've met and been inspired by so many brilliant minds through what you created, Ashley Jade. Including Jensen Reed, Melissa Sell, Donise Sheppard, Rinoa Cameron, Fatima Davis-Unuvar (birthday twin!), the list goes on… I'm honored to be a part of it all. A huge thanks to everyone who ever took a chance on me. Pixie Forest Publishing, Stormy Island Publishing, Sweetycat Press, I'm looking at you. The Starting 5 Podcast, Dan Dinkins, John Polk, Katara Johnson. Nothing but love for you all.

I could keep this going all night, but this book must end. My heart and mind are filled with so many who helped me along in this, inspired me in so many ways, and challenged me to be better. So, if you don't see your name listed, know that I am always thinking of you, and this is far from my final book. In fact, when I run out of names to mention, that'll probably be the day I call it quits. Until next time.

Peace.